PORTIA MACINTOSH has been 'making stuff up' for as long as she can remember – or so she says. Whether it was blaming her siblings for that broken vase when she was growing up, blagging her way backstage during her rock chick phase or, most recently, whatever justification she can fabricate to explain away those lunchtime cocktails, Portia just loves telling tales.

After years working as a music journalist, Portia decided it was time to use her powers for good and started writing novels instead.

Bestseller Portia writes hilarious romcoms, drawing on her real life experiences to show what it's really like being a woman today – especially one who doesn't quite have her life together yet.

PORTIA MACINTOSH has been 'making stuff up' for as long as she can remember – or so she says. Whether it was blaming her siblings for that broken vase when she was growing up, blagging her way backstage during her rock chick phase or, most recently, whatever it is she can think of to explain away those lunchtime cocktails, Portia just loves telling tales.

After years working as a music journalist, Portia decided it was time to use her powers for good and started writing novels instead.

Bestseller Portia writes hilarious romcoms, drawing on her real life experiences to show what it's really like being a woman today – especially one who doesn't quite have her life together yet.

The Time of Our Lives

PORTIA MACINTOSH

ONE PLACE. MANY STORIES

This novel is entirely a work of fiction. The names, characters and incidents portrayed in it are the work of the author's imagination. Any resemblance to actual persons, living or dead, events or localities is entirely coincidental.

HQ
An imprint of HarperCollins*Publishers* Ltd
1 London Bridge Street
London SE1 9GF

This edition 2019

1
First published in Great Britain by
HQ, an imprint of HarperCollins*Publishers* Ltd 2019

Portia MacIntosh asserts the moral right to be identified as the author of this work.
A catalogue record for this book is available from the British Library.

ISBN 9780008330903

MIX
Paper from responsible sources
FSC C007454

This book is produced from independently certified FSC™ paper to ensure responsible forest management.

For more information visit: www.harpercollins.co.uk/green

Printed and bound in Great Britain by
CPI Group (UK) Ltd, Melksham, SN12 6TR

For Joe & Joey

Prologue

New Year's Day, 2009

I've always had bad timing.

I never budget for long enough in the bathroom. I've missed more buses than I've made. I was even born late – seventeen days late, to be exact – which took me from being the creative, passionate, stubborn Leo that I think I am, to being the organised, practical, shy Virgo that I absolutely am not.

Last night though … last night was something else. Last night it felt like time was actually against me.

Missed connections, a case of mistaken identity – what does it matter? As the clock struck midnight, dragging me from 2008 to 2009, I realised exactly what can happen when you're in the right place at the right time, or the wrong place at the wrong time.

Yep, I've always had bad timing. But last night, it ruined everything.

Chapter 1

Now

I've never been one for inspirational quotes. You know the ones, they constantly pop up on your Facebook news feed; white text on a colourful or scenic background, usually shared by some distant cousin, old school friend, or random acquaintance you don't remember befriending – shared because it's just so damn profound and relatable.

'Don't be a woman that needs a man, be a woman that a man needs' emblazoned across a sunset, as though the two are somehow related, or the famous 'Marilyn Monroe' one: 'If you can't handle me at my worst, you don't deserve me at my best' which I really don't think anyone should subscribe too, because it basically translates to: 'If you don't put up with me when I'm being a bitch, you don't deserve me when I'm being nice.'

As much as I hate these quotes, I saw one today that felt very apt (not that I felt the need to hit the share button though). It said: 'The friends you make at university are your friends for life' and that one must be true because if it weren't, I wouldn't be driving down a dark country lane in Norfolk, on my way to my old uni friend's wedding.

I alternate concentrating on the road with scanning the darkness for signs of life. One of my colleagues told me there was a lot to see in Norfolk, but not here, not tonight. There is absolutely nothing to see here.

It did cross my mind, to make an excuse – I have to work, I'm having dental surgery, I'm on holiday – but these days people book their weddings so far in advance, they don't even give you the chance to come up with an excuse that is both polite *and* gets you off the hook. I had to RSVP to this thing almost two years ago. Can you imagine being engaged for two years? I can't even imagine having a boyfriend for two years. That's probably why I'm so anxious about this wedding tomorrow.

Matt, the groom, is one of five people I shared a house with in Manchester during my third year at uni. It's been ten years since we all graduated and five years since we all saw each other last.

For the most part, we've always been the worst kind of millennials. With the exception of Ed, who is more than making up for our collective shortfall with his four children so far, we all stumbled into our thirties unwed and childless. The rest of us are contributing to a country with an aging population and a declining birth rate, because we're all way too busy with our jobs and our lives, and it's just so easy to think we can put off these things until later. But as my mum keeps reminding me, I'm losing daylight, eggs, and the figure to bag myself a decent man – all of which sound like something from a bygone era, or a sci-fi movie with a dystopian future for women. But when my mum was my age – 31 – she'd already had me *and* my sister, so I guess you can't blame her for thinking I'm wasting my life.

The problem now is that it's so easy to compare myself to my uni friends. We all had the same start in adult life, we all got degrees and then we went off into the world (well, I didn't go off anywhere, I stayed in Manchester) and we all got jobs in our fields. Relationship-wise, we're all at very different stages. But while Ed is married, Matt is getting married tomorrow, Zach and Fiona are engaged (yes, to each other), and Mark (or Clarky, as he's more commonly known to those who tolerate him) has a girlfriend, I am still single. I'm not sure that counts as a stage. I don't really feel like I've left the starting line yet.

I glance at the digital clock in my car. The red glowing numbers tell me that it's nearly 10.30 p.m. So much for saying I'd arrive early and have a drink with my old friends. I'm sure everyone will be in bed by now, so that they can be up early for the wedding tomorrow.

I notice car headlights in my rear-view mirror – the first sign of life I've seen on this road and I'm not sure if it puts me at ease or makes me feel nervous. I've seen too many horror movies, I think.

The lights grow bigger, brighter, and they appear to be heading straight for me. As the car gets too close to mine, I speed up a little to try and put some space between us, but the car behind only goes faster.

As my speed increases, so does my heartbeat and my breathing. I feel my hands begin to sweat, but I daren't adjust the grip on the steering wheel that I'm holding so tightly, I can see my knuckles turning white.

It all happens so quickly. Suddenly the car behind – a red sports car with a private plate – pulls out from behind me, moving onto the other side of the narrow country road to overtake me, before speeding off ahead.

I loosen my grip as I watch its lights grow smaller and smaller until they disappear.

Finally alone again, I puff air from my cheeks. What an arsehole, driving like that on a lonely country road at this time of night. I don't care where he has to be, no one is in that much of a hurry that they have to drive so recklessly. I suppose I ruined his fun, sticking to the speed limit in my Polo that's seen better days.

The thumping in my chest slows down around the time I spot the Willows Lodge Hotel floodlit in the distance. Thank God. At least when I leave in a couple of days, I'll be driving in the daylight. Drivers like that are almost always nocturnal, aren't they? No sign of them during the day and then, under the cloak of darkness, they come out in their ridiculous cars to drive like maniacs. I could just about tell that it was a man in the car – a man with too little in his pants and too much in his bank, if you ask me.

I pull into the hotel car park, turn off my engine and breathe a sigh of relief. I'd say thank God I'm here, but I'd rather be anywhere else. Well, apart from car wrapped around a tree courtesy of someone who is overcompensating for something.

I give myself a brief internal pep talk to try and psych myself up (*You can do this, Luca. You're a strong, independent woman, Luca* etc). I'm not sure it works, but I get out of my car, grab my hold-all from the boot, and make my way across the floodlit gravel car park.

As I walk between the parked cars, I can't help but look over my shoulder every now and then. It feels so lonely out here, with no sign of life anywhere. The only sound I can hear is from the stones crunching under my feet as I walk – at least I'd be able to hear footsteps, if someone were to try and creep up behind me.

I remind myself to keep my imagination in check, but it doesn't matter. Something distracts me. I'm almost at the hotel entrance when something catches my eye: a red sports car. It's not the same one that sped past me, is it? I hover a hand over the car and feel heat radiating from its hot body. And then there's that number plate, that tosser private plate that makes me hate this guy already.

Maybe it's because I'm all frazzled over this wedding business or maybe it is because he genuinely scared me, but I do something completely out of character from me. I take a pen and a piece of paper from my bag, and I write a note.

I'm not usually the kind of girl to write: 'no one is impressed by your driving or your car' on the back of a receipt before placing it under the windscreen wiper. In fact, it's so unlike me to do something like this that I quickly grab my bags and retreat to the safety of the hotel, before anyone sees me.

As I check in, I notice a little sign on the counter advertising homemade red velvet cake. That's exactly what I need to take the edge of a rubbish evening.

'Is it too late to get some cake?' I ask the receptionist.

'There might be some left,' she replies. 'If you ask in the bar.'

The receptionist points to a small, empty looking bar in an adjoining room.

Another thing that is out of character for me is hanging out in bars on my own, but I can't really face going to my room just yet, and some cake would be lovely. I might even have a drink too. A quick nightcap, just to relax me little. Then I'll go to my room, climb into my bed, and get a nice early night in preparation for the big day tomorrow. I do have a tendency to be late, but I absolutely cannot do that tomorrow – I want my friends to think at least one thing changed since the last time they saw me.

Chapter 2

I pitch up at the empty bar, like some kind of downbeat film noir detective.

When a barman appears, I order a slice of red velvet cake and a Disaronno and coke, with all the enthusiasm and cheer of a death row inmate ordering their last meal.

'Cheer up,' he says brightly. 'It might never happen.'

Half the problem is that it never happened – nothing has ever happened, and it feels like nothing will ever happen. I'm not the sort of girl things happen to, and, at 31 years of age, I'm not even sure I qualify as a girl anymore.

I mentally pinch myself, and tick myself off for being so melodramatic. My life is not that bad, it just seems it when I compare it to my friends' lives. Well, it's not that it seems bad … it's just … uneventful.

'This might put a smile on your face,' the barman says, setting down an extra-large slice of cake in front of me. 'This is all that was left. It wasn't enough to cut into two slices, and we only would've thrown the smaller bit away.'

'Wow,' I blurt. It *is* huge. 'Thanks.'

I laugh to myself as I rotate the plate, viewing the giant slice from all angles. There's no way I'll eat this – I'd be ashamed of myself if I could – but I'll certainly give it my best shot.

'Jack and coke please,' I hear a man say next to me. The fact that someone else is in the bar gifts me a little comfort. Drinking here alone, I was dangerously close to becoming a cliché. 'And a slice of red velvet cake, please. Just saw the ad for it at reception.'

'Sorry, sir. This lady just bought the last piece,' the bar man replies, pointing towards me.

I look up, to see whose day I've ruined.

The man looks down at my giant slice of cake, and back up at me. Suddenly, I feel like a pig. Not just because he's a handsome guy, but because I look like I'm about to take down this huge slice all on my own.

'Do you want to share it?' I ask him. 'This is way more than I can eat.'

'Really?' he replies with a smile.

'Sure,' I reply.

'Can I get you another drink, to say thanks?' he asks me.

'That would be great, thanks.'

'Top my new friend up too,' the man replies, handing over his card. 'And another fork please.'

'Thanks,' I say again, quickly straightening my back, smoothing out my outfit, and subtly tszujing my hair.

'You're welcome,' he replies. 'I'm Pete.'

'I'm Luca,' I say, shaking the hand he's offering me. 'It's nice to have some company.'

'You here alone?' he asks, eagerly plunging his fork into the cake.

'I am,' I reply. 'My friends are getting married tomorrow.'

'Same.'

'You're here alone or you're here for a wedding?' I ask.

'Both,' he says. 'Matt and Kat?'

'Yes,' I squeak excitedly. 'You know them?'

'I do, I lived with Kat at uni, actually. We shared a house.'

I laugh at the unbelievable coincidence.

'Same. I lived with Matt during third year.'

He laughs. 'That's weird.'

For a moment, I can't help but examine my new friend. He must be about my age, if he went to uni with Kat.

Pete is not a bad-looking man. He has blond hair that I don't think is too long, but he has it pulled into a man bun on the back of his head. It's a man bun and not a topknot – the two are most definitely very different looks. On a topknot's Instagram he'll be posing for photos with sedated tigers on holiday, and capturing his latest Nando's acquisition before he wolfs it down. A man bun though, he's the kind of guy to have pictures of him wearing cardigans, snuggled up to golden retriever puppies.

Pete has chiselled good looks, like maybe Michelangelo carved him after he practised on David. But while his features may be almost razor sharp, he's got this warmth about him. A real kindness in his cool blue eyes.

'It will be nice to have an ally here,' he says, rubbing his stubbly chin sheepishly. 'Everyone I know here has come as a couple.'

'Same,' I reply, baffled by yet another coincidence.

Starting to relax a little, I take my first bite of cake. Rich, chocolatey sponge smothered in sweet, cream cheese frosting. It's everything I hoped it would be and more – I still don't think I could've eaten the entire slice though.

'So, what do you do?' Pete asks.

'Me?' Though I'm not sure who else he could be talking to, we're the only ones here.

'Yes, you,' he laughs.

It's been so long since a good-looking, charming guy showed a genuine interest in me, I thought I'd better make sure it was actually me he was interested in.

'I work in the PR department at ABO – Anything But Ordinary,' I reply.

'The clothing company,' Pete says.

I nod.

'I bet that keeps you busy,' he says, with a knowing look.

'You heard about that,' I needlessly point out. 'Yep, still reeling from that one.'

Pete is referring to events a few months ago, when the company CEO was recorded saying she didn't want 'fat girls' modelling her clothes in ad campaigns.

'I'm actively looking for a new job,' I tell him. 'Something more worthwhile, something that makes me feel like I'm doing something important. What do you do?'

'I am a global programme manager for an environmental charity.'

'Now that's a worthwhile job,' I reply, feeling slightly jealous.

'Sometimes we have PR crises,' he says.

'Oh really?'

'The pinta tortoise became extinct in 2012 – on *our* watch. Where were we?!'

'Are you allowed to make jokes about extinct animals?' I ask, before I dare laugh at his comment that I'm sure was solely intended just to put me at ease about my crap job.

'They never kick off about it,' he replies. 'Not like angry anti-fur activists.'

Oh, that's what he was referring to a moment ago. The fact that, last year, ABO was caught up in the big scandal where it was revealed many high-street and online retailers were selling items made from real fur, that were labelled faux fur.

'Where are you from?' he asks.

'I grew up outside Manchester,' I tell him. 'But I live in Manchester now. You?'

'London. Lived there all my life too.'

'You just don't see that kind of loyalty to hometowns anymore, do you?' I joke.

'You don't,' he replies. 'It's almost everything that's wrong with the world. Well, that and your company selling mittens made of racoon dog fur.'

'We hate fat people too, don't forget that,' I joke.

'And yet you probably love fat animals,' he replies. 'Because they have the most fur.'

'I'll be sure to tell our CEO. Her inexplicable, blind dislike of anyone bigger than a size ten might have prevented her from realising that.'

It's so nice, sitting here with Pete, having a drink, eating cake, and making jokes with one another. If there is any way tomorrow can just be more of the same, it might not be so bad after all. Before I know it, nearly an hour has gone by.

'We made short work of the cake,' he says, nodding towards our empty plate.

'We did,' I reply. 'Teamwork makes the dream work.'

'It does,' he laughs. 'Just think what damage we can do to the wedding cake tomorrow.'

We smile at each other for a second, until we're interrupted by the bar man.

'Bar's closing,' he says. As soon as he realises he's interrupting something, he quickly adds, 'In five minutes.'

'Well, I'd better get to bed,' I say. 'Don't want to be late in the morning.'

'Same,' he says. 'But … I'd love to spend more time with you tomorrow.'

'I'd like that a lot.' I feel a big, dumb smile spread across my face.

Pete's gaze quickly moves from my eyes to my lips.

'Is that cake frosting?' he asks with a laugh.

Mortified, I quickly raise my hand to wipe my face.

'I'll get it,' he says, leaning forward to lightly plant his lips on mine.

I don't know if there actually was any frosting on my face, or if this was just a smooth move to kiss me – you never know, he might have just really loved the cake – but I feel like I'm floating on air right now. I cannot stress enough that this sort of thing just does not happen to me. Maybe it wouldn't be happening to me at all, if we weren't a little tipsy.

But then it hits me, all at once, the grave mistake I think I've made. The red car, the one that overtook me, the one that arrived just before me – didn't Pete say he'd just arrived too? Now, this type of stuff absolutely does happen to me – scaring off potential love interests by leaving them passive aggressive notes.

I quickly pull away.

'Sorry,' he blurts. 'I shouldn't have …'

'No, it's not that,' I say. 'Did you drive here?'

'I did,' he replies, confused as to why this is at all relevant to why I wouldn't want to kiss him.

Crap.

'What do you drive?' I ask.

'A Nissan Leaf – a blue one. It's an electric car … why?' he laughs.

Double crap. It wasn't even him. Now I just seem like I really care about cars.

'Sorry. It's just that, when I arrived, I nearly had an accident with another car, and when I saw it in the car park, I left an angry note. I was worried it might have been your car.'

Pete laughs.

'It sounds like you have a very eventful life, Luca.'

'I really don't.'

'Well, maybe we can try this again tomorrow?' he suggests.

'That would be great.'

'It will be nice to have someone to spend the day with, seeing as though we're the sad, single friends.'

I playfully wince.

'Too soon to make jokes like that?' he asks.

'Too real,' I reply with a smile.

'Sweet dreams, Luca,' he says, leaving me alone in the bar.

I sigh. Wow. When I repeatedly turned down Matt and Kat's offer of a plus one (not because I didn't want one, but because

I had no one to ask) I felt certain I'd be alone at this wedding and, look at me now, I've got a date.

I knock back the last of my drink before heading to my room.

They've given me a twin room – which I suspect is because they knew I'd be coming alone – but it's a lovely big room with a stunning view of the hotel gardens. Even though it's dark, I can see the marquee across the lawn, where I imagine the wedding reception will be held tomorrow.

Suddenly I don't care about anything. I don't care that I'm here alone, I don't care that I've got a twin room because I'm oh-so very single, I don't even care that I am single, or that I have a morally iffy job. All I can think about is Pete, and that kiss … and now I can't wait until morning.

Chapter 3

Then – 9th September 2008

'What … the fuck … is this?' Matt asks, staring down at his plate.

We're all staring down at our plates. Clarky isn't though, he's gleefully slapping the bottom of a bottle of salad cream, dropping large blobs all over his dinner.

When he placed … whatever this is in front of me, I didn't think it could get any worse, but the addition of salad cream makes it so, so much worse. I'm so relieved it is an optional extra.

'What's wrong with it?' Clarky asks.

'What's right with it?' Zach chimes in. His Glaswegian accent always sounds stronger when he's confused or when he's drunk. Today, I think he's just confused.

Clarky looks genuinely baffled by our reaction. He stabs a little sausage meaningfully and pops it in his mouth.

'Mmm, it's great,' he insists theatrically.

'It's weird,' Fiona corrects him.

Clarky's face falls at her remark.

'It's …' I take stock of the contents of my plate. 'It's salad, baked beans with sausages, and fish fingers?'

'Yeah,' Clarky confirms. 'Dig in.'

For our third year of uni, we decided that it would make more sense for our friendship group to rent one big house together, and not only has it worked out cheaper, but we've got this massive house, with loads of space for hanging out together and throwing parties. We only finished moving in four days ago, and thought it might be fun to take it in turns cooking for the house.

'Just try it,' Clarky insists.

Mark 'Clarky' Clarkson has been on the same course as me for two years now, and while I might have lots in common with the others, Clarky isn't really someone I'm overly taken with. He's one of those 'lad lad lad' types, always ogling girls, making sexist comments, thinking he's way smarter than everyone else when really, he's only getting through his BA by the skin of his teeth. Clarky is from Liverpool, and has a strong Scouse accent that can almost always be heard yelling at some video game or other. He isn't very tall, but what he lacks in height, he more than makes up for in self-confidence.

'Just because you say it's a dish, doesn't mean it is,' Matt points out.

Before Clarky has a chance to reply, Ed arrives home.

Ed is the only housemate who isn't studying media; he's studying to be a doctor, and while we might all be around the same age, Ed feels like a real adult. He's old beyond his years – he even looks older, but I think that's because he dresses like a middle-aged man in addition to acting like one.

'How's the grind at the board game shop?' Matt asks Ed the second he walks through the door.

'Boring?' Clarky suggests, cracking up at his own joke.

Ed works tirelessly to pay his way through uni. One day, when he's a rich doctor, it will all have been worth it, and no one will be making fun of him because he spent a summer selling board games.

'I'm starving,' he says, sitting down. 'You guys didn't have to wait for me.'

'We weren't waiting for you,' Matt laughs. 'We were waiting for Clarky to explain what it is.'

Ed, who thinks he's somewhat of a culinary expert, finally looks down at what we're having. He just laughs.

'Oh, I'm sorry we didn't all bring cookbooks to uni with us,' Clarky claps back.

I have to admit, I did find it a little bizarre that Ed moved in with no less than four cookbooks, but that's just Ed.

'I made a leg of lamb with all the trimmings,' Ed reminds him.

He did, the night after I cooked, and it made my efforts seem as amateur as they were.

'So … is it a salad?' Fiona asks.

Fiona 'Fifi' Rees is our resident Welsh lady, and the only other girl living here. We made friends on the first day of uni and we've stayed friends ever since. We shared a flat together last year, before we decided to get somewhere bigger with the boys this year. I love Fifi because she's just this bubbly, blonde, bright light that's a real pleasure to be around. She's the optimist that I need in my life, to stop me acting like everything is all doom and gloom. She's got a will-they-won't-they thing going on with Zach. I think we all wish they'd hurry up and get together, but Fifi isn't convinced he's all that into her, and Zach seems to have an aversion to girlfriends for some reason.

'It's a sort of salad,' Clarky replies.

'I was going to make salad,' Fifi says, sounding a little annoyed that Clarky has beaten her to it.

'Your salad will be better than this,' Zach assures her.

Her salad might actually be salad, this is not a salad.

'Ergh, get a room,' Clarky says. He doesn't have much patience when it comes to Fifi and Zach's flirting. 'It's surf and turf.'

Everyone burst out laughing.

'Bollocks,' Ed replies.

'Why is it so spicy?' Matt asks, coughing and spluttering after bravely taking a bite.

'I put chilli in it,' Clarky explains.

'Amazing, that it's killing my taste buds and yet still tastes awful,' Ed muses.

Clarky repeats his words back to him, mocking his Cambridgeshire accent.

'I'm not good with spicy stuff,' I say politely. 'Sorry.'

'Well, Luca, you have blue hair,' he tells me. 'So I don't trust your taste anyway.'

I push my plate away a little, to emphasise that I'm not eating it. What on earth is he thinking, serving us fish fingers and beans with sausages, laced with copious amounts of chilli, on a bed of salad. Baked beans on salad!

'My mum used to make it for me,' Clarky tells us.

'Well, you should have been taken into care,' Zach tells him.

With the general consensus being that we're absolutely not eating it, it isn't long before we decide to order pizzas. Clarky, adamant that he is a cordon bleu chef, eats not only his own plate of food, but makes a start on someone else's too.

We abandon the formality of the kitchen table to eat pizza and watch *Anchorman* in our massive living room. After initially refusing to watch it with us because we wouldn't eat his mum's recipe, Clarky has had a change of heart and sat down with us after all.

'That's your culinary career down the pan,' Matt tells him, persisting with the teasing after most of us have let it go.

Clarky bats his hand.

'As if that's what I'd want to do,' he insists. 'I want a job that impresses women.'

'Like?' Matt asks him.

'I dunno, like a pilot or an astronaut or something.'

'You won't meet many chicks in space,' Ed points out.

'You shouldn't be studying media then, that's not gonna get you far,' Zach tells him.

'So, Clarky reckons he'll be a pilot, Ed is gonna be a doctor,' Matt says. 'What about the rest of us? Personally, not to set my sights too high, but I'm gonna be the next Steve Jobs.'

'I wanna work in film,' Zach says.

'Me too!' Fifi squeaks. I notice Clarky roll his eyes. 'What about you, Luca?'

'Erm,' I start, wracking my brains. The truth is that I'm not entirely sure yet. 'Maybe advertising.'

'Boring,' Clarky heckles.

'Who do we think will be the first to get married?' Fifi asks.

'Ed,' we all reply, pretty much in unison.

'And the last?' she says.

Everyone says Clarky's name, apart from Clarky who simply points at himself with both fingers.

'It's hard to imagine us as real adults,' Fifi muses. 'Some of us more than others.'

'Stop talking over the film,' Clarky insists.

'Sorry,' she snaps. 'I didn't realise Will Ferrell was so important.'

'Do you really think we'll grow up?' Matt laughs, glancing between this slice of pizza that's sitting on his lap and the dumb movie on the TV. 'Well, I mean the rest of us – Ed is already grown up.'

'We'll know Ed has properly grown up when he has kids,' I point out.

'And we'll know you've grown up when you get over your daft punk phase and stop dying your hair stupid colours,' Clarky tells me.

'I didn't know you were into Daft Punk, Luca,' Matt jokes.

'We'll know you've grown up when you finally learn how to cook,' Zach tells Clarky.

'And we'll know you've grown up when you finally get a girlfriend,' Clarky replies.

'Not everyone wants saddling with a girlfriend,' Zach says defensively. I notice Fifi look visibly disappointed.

'What about me and Fifi?' Matt asks.

'When Fifi starts using her real first name,' Clarky points out.

'And when you stop using headlocks to show affection,' Ed tells Matt. 'Maybe some of us will grow up, maybe some of us won't. I reckon we'll all stay friends though.'

We exchange half-smiles before getting back to the film.

'Unless Clarky kills us with his cooking,' Matt adds, unable to resist one last dig.

Chapter 4

Now

'Fifi,' I call over, spotting my friend hovering outside the hotel's reception room, where the wedding ceremony is about to take place.

'Luca, oh my gosh,' she replies, smiling widely as she pulls me in for a hug. 'Wow, no one has called me Fifi in years. Zach, when was the last time someone called me Fifi?'

'Uni,' he laughs. 'She dropped the nickname when she was applying for jobs.'

'I don't mind one Fi though,' she assures me.

'How's it going?' Zach asks, hugging me.

'All great,' I tell him. 'How are you two? It'll be your wedding soon, right? I got my save the date.'

'Next year,' she replies.

Fiona's grin spreads from one ear to the next. She was always such a bright, positive person, but she seems so happy with Zach, and I'm so happy for them. For a while, we thought the two of the might never get together and look at them now, happily engaged.

'You still have funky hair,' she points out.

I place a hand on my long, blonde and rose gold ombre curls.

'It was never like Luca to look ordinary,' Zach points out.

When I was at uni, I enjoyed a sort of alternative fashion. I had the ridiculous style of a six-year-old, combined with the provocative look of a punk. It was never a lifestyle choice, purely a fashion one. These days, I dress more my age. More my figure too. I'm a curvy size twelve – more like a fourteen if I'm in a shop that favours the thin, or if I've just eaten my own weight in carbs. I did once manage to fit into a size-ten dress after having the stomach flu, but that didn't seem like an ideal long-term solution. Probably just easier to try and make peace with my body as it is.

Today I'm wearing a Bardot skater dress – in rose gold, to match my hair – with a pair of white Louboutin heels covered in cute little spikes, which I thought would serve as a nice nod to my rebellious side that still lingers deep within me.

PR is all about spin. You can make things seem better, you can make them seem worse – if you're good, you can make them seem like something entirely different.

From head-to-toe, I absolutely could not afford this outfit, but in many ways this is going to be a lot like a school reunion, seeing people I haven't seen since I was young, and obviously I want to seem like I'm doing much better than I am. I suppose, if I'm careful with these shoes, I might even be able to get away with returning them, which I know is awful, but it might be a good idea if I want to eat next month. Either way, so long as I present myself as something more impressive than my reality, I'll be happy with my work for the wedding.

I'm not usually the type to rely on designer clothes to make myself pass as presentable, but when I started shopping for a wedding outfit, I felt at a loss. As I moved from changing room to changing room, I'd notice a new hang-up in each mirror. In River Island I felt like I looked every inch my 31 years. In Oasis I noticed the circles under my eyes were growing darker with each night I stayed up late over thinking things. In Zara I was reminded that my bum was big – but not Kardashian big, camper van big.

I have always dwarfed my tiny friend Fiona, who fails to measures up to my 5'7" with her petit 5'2" frame, but today she's obviously teamed her long, flowing blue dress with flat shoes (I suppose no one can tell what's hiding under long dresses, you could disguise anything), which just makes me look all the more like a giant in my heels. Zach is wearing a blue suit in almost exactly the same shade as Fiona's dress, which I doubt was an accident.

'Where are the others?' I ask.

'Matt is in there, looking like a lamb headed for the slaughter,' Zach laughs. 'Ed has just nipped to the toilet. No sign of Clarky and his bird yet.'

'Have you met her?' I ask him.

They both shake their heads.

'I've seen her on Facebook,' Zach says. 'Looks like a bit of a bimbo.'

'Just Clarky's type then,' I reply.

'Luca,' I hear Ed call from behind me.

I spin around on my heels, grabbing him for a hug.

'Ed,' I squeak as he kisses me on both cheeks. 'How are you? Where's Stella? Where're the kids?'

'No kids allowed,' he says, finally releasing me. 'Stella stayed home to look after them.'

'That's a shame,' I reply.

'Is it? I live with five women, this is my first day off in years!'

Ed seems really excited at the thought of having a night off from all his women. It'll probably do him good, having a day off from his responsibilities. As if being a paediatrician isn't a stressful enough job, having four small children of his own can't help.

'Five women,' Zach repeats back to him.

'Well, we had Louisa, then Erin. I wanted a boy so we said

we'd have one last go at it, but then we got Bethany and Sally, our twins.'

'Don't you have a TV in your house?' Zach laughs. 'Stop having kids.'

'It just keeps happening!'

'Ed, you're a doctor,' I point out. 'I know you know how babies are made.'

Ed laughs.

Ed has always seemed grown up – and he's always looked much older than us – but now, more than ever, he you'd struggle to believe we all went to uni together. He's wearing a cream suit with a blue shirt and a black tie, along with the thick black-rimmed glasses he didn't need when we lived together. He's also getting his middle-aged spread a little prematurely, but he's not a bad-looking guy. Being a family guy just seems to suit him in a way that I can't imagine happening with any of the rest of us. I think we're all quite immature and selfish still.

'What about Clarky?' Ed says, changing the subject.

'What about him?' I ask.

'You guys not been checking your phones? He just dropped a message in the group chat, he's coming alone. He and Bella broke up.'

'When?' Fiona says nosily, leaning in a little to get the gossip.

'He didn't say,' Ed laughs. 'We can ask him when we see him. Think he's running a bit late.'

If I hadn't arrived last night, it would've been me running late today, for sure. Were it anyone but Clarky, I might have sympathy for them.

'If you'd all like to make your way inside,' a hotel employee calls out. 'Bride's side on the left, groom's on the right.'

We make our way into the reception room, taking five seats in a row, saving one for Clarky when he finally arrives.

I glance around the room for Pete, the guy I met last night, but I can't spot him. Then I look for Matt, finally spotting him hovering by one of the large pillars dotted throughout the room. He must feel my eyes on him because he notices me too and pops over to see us.

'You look petrified,' I blurt.

'I am!'

Matt is usually so full of confidence, so it's weird to see him looking so scared.

'Where's Clarky and Bella?' he asks, noticing their absence almost immediately.

'Clarky is nearly here, traffic is bad,' Ed says, making excuses for him. 'But he's coming alone, he and Bella broke up.'

'Shit,' Matt says. 'What happened?'

'I don't know, but we're excited to find out,' Fiona laughs. 'Good luck.'

'Yeah, good luck,' I echo. 'You're gonna be great.'

'Cheers,' Matt replies, clenching his jaw as he walks down the aisle, getting himself in position, ready for Kat, his fiancé, to make her grand entrance.

The room falls silent, ready for the ceremony to begin, which just makes it all the more obvious when Clarky comes charging in, running down the aisle, plonking himself on the chair next to me. Luckily we're sat quite near the back, so he doesn't have far to run. I notice the clicking of a few tongues from guests sitting close to us, but Clarky is immune to criticism.

'Sorry I'm late,' he says, panting. 'How's it going?'

'Good,' I reply. 'How are you?'

'Yeah, sound,' he says.

For someone who has supposedly broken up with his girlfriend recently, he seems in pretty good spirits.

As I turn to face forwards, I notice Matt coming down the aisle towards us.

'Can I borrow you?' he says. Surely now isn't the time to be telling Clarky off? It's not like this is especially out of character for him anyway. But then I realise he's talking to *me*.

'Me?' I squeak. 'Why?'

'Just quick,' he insists, holding out a hand to pull me from my seat, before walking me to a door at the side of the room.

'What's wrong?' I ask him once we're still. 'You're not having a second thoughts, are you?'

'What? No, of course not,' he replies. 'One of Kat's bridesmaids has gone into labour.'

'Oh my God,' I reply.

'Thing is, apparently Kat is upset, she says it's going to ruin the day. That it's going to throw off the whole aesthetic, and that there's no one to do the bridesmaid's duties.'

'Doesn't she have other bridesmaids?' I ask.

'Yeah, but they're *all* pregnant. I'm scared to ask what happened on the hen party …'

I laugh. It's so like Matt to make a joke, even in times of crisis.

'Wow, what a weird coincidence – is it to make sure she looks super thin in the pictures?'

An obvious joke, because Kat has a very athletic figure. I wouldn't put such a manoeuvre past some more controlling brides though.

'Please can you step in?' he begs.

'Me?' I reply in disbelief.

'Don't worry, being pregnant isn't a requirement.'

'Kat wants *me*?'

I think Kat and I have been in the same room on maybe two occasions, and I spent the first time accidentally calling her Kate the whole day. She was too polite to point it out, but not polite enough to let it stop her shooting me dirty looks all day.

'Well, sort of,' he says. He pulls out a pair of gloves from his pocket. 'These are the gloves the bridesmaids are wearing – same colour as the dresses. And your dress matches.'

'Oh, God, do I have to do this?' I say nervously.

'Please, please, please,' he begs. 'Apparently Kat's really upset, and this is important. It's nothing, really. You're just a placeholder.'

'Charming,' I laugh. 'OK, fine, if it's that important to you, I'll do it.'

I adjust my dress self-consciously. I've never been a bridesmaid before, and I've never been all that upset about it. I hate having everyone's eyes on me, which makes me wonder how I'd ever get married – should anyone ever ask.

Matt grabs me and squeezes me tightly.

'You're amazing,' he says. 'Just go with Auntie May, she'll tell you what to do.'

Matt knocks on the door before dashing off again.

Auntie May peeps through, looks me up and down, and grabs me by the forearm, pulling me through the door before quickly closing it behind her.

'Thank you for doing this,' she says as she ushers me along the corridor.

Once we're at the entrance to the reception room, she lightly pushes me to the edge of the doorway.

'It's so simple,' she says. 'The music will start, just make your way slowly down the aisle, take nice slow steps, until you get to the end. Just mirror the groomsmen, all the bridesmaids will be standing in line. There are three of you, three groomsmen, you'll be in neat little lines, sound good?'

Ergh, I have to walk down the aisle? How slow is slow? Do you put one foot forward before bringing the other in line with it, or do you just walk normally, but slowed down?

The music starts.

'The others will be here any second,' she says, thrusting flowers into my hand. 'We're already running late, go, go.'

I am out of both my depth and my comfort zone, but I do as Auntie May asks, slowly making my way down the aisle, doing some kind of inconsistent combination of the steps I mentioned before.

I glance at my friends as I pass their seats and they look genuinely baffled to see me walking down the aisle.

'What the …' I hear Clarky quietly start as I pass him.

After what feels like an hour, I finally find myself passing the front row, but that's when I notice him, standing there at the end of the aisle. Not Matt, next to him. Standing dutifully by his friend's side, in a matching black suit, is Tom Hoult, the man who broke my heart.

My jaw drops as he silently mouths a hello in my direction. I take my position, fixing my eyes on the aisle instead of on him. It's almost too painful to look at him.

A pregnant bridesmaid with a dress amazingly similar to mine makes her way down the aisle before taking her spot next to me. I don't allow myself to think about Tom being here, I just focus on the task at hand, but as I watch the third and final bridesmaid approach – another girl in a rose gold dress with a cute little baby bump – I realise that I recognise her too. It's Cleo. What could be worse than the man who broke my heart being here? The woman who helped him do it being here with him.

Chapter 5

Today is not the day I thought it was going to be – not at all. I had no idea Tom was going to be here. I had no idea Cleo would be with him – with him *and* pregnant, no less. I haven't really thought about Tom in a long time. Well, I haven't seen him in ten years, and he isn't on Facebook, so it's not like I see his face everyday, not like I do with the others. When things went bad between us, sure, I moped for a while, but then I picked myself up and I moved on. What else could I have done? Of course, I didn't think I'd ever have to see him again, and yet here he is. Here and looking gorgeous as ever, and Cleo still looks perfect too. She's pregnant and somehow still petite. Her impossibly shiny brown hair is pulled into a ballerina bun on the top of her head, with the exception of a few, small, perfectly formed curls that hang down, framing her cute little face.

I try to push it out of my head, because another thing I didn't anticipate today was that I would have to take over for one of the bridesmaids – and I'm not only having to take her place walking down the aisle, but it turns out I'm taking over her duties too. While the marquee is being prepared for the wedding breakfast, everyone is gathered in the hotel gardens, enjoying drinks from the outdoor bar, sitting in the sunshine, posing for photos.

Except me; I've been given the job of going around with the guestbook, with the impossible task of making everyone sign it. People seem to hate signing guestbook for some reason, I think maybe they panic because they don't know what to write in them, but I need them to write *something* so that I can get this over and done with as soon as possible, so I can go back to being a regular guest.

'Can you write for me, dear?' a little old lady asks. 'If I dictate?'

She's a sweet old dear, with a pink rinse to rival my own hair do. I feel a bit sorry for her, sitting here on her own while everyone else busies themselves socialising, but she seems happy enough taking in view, relaxing in the sunshine.

'Of course I will,' I reply, writing down the lovely – but long – message she dictates. At least it will take up some of the space left by the guests I haven't been able to pin down.

'That's so kind of you,' she says. 'So, how do you know Katherine?'

'I don't really know her that well,' I admit. 'I'm just filling in. One of her bridesmaids went into labour.'

The old woman laughs wildly.

'I did warn her not to have three pregnant bridesmaids,' she insists. 'I'm Joan, Katherine's grandma.'

'Nice to meet you,' I say. 'I'm a friend of Matt's.'

'Oh, Matt is such a lovely young man,' she says. 'And speaking of lovely young men …'

Tom leans forward to kiss Kat's grandma on the cheek.

'Now then,' he says. 'Are you causing trouble? You haven't written anything naughty in that book, have you?'

Ergh, I'd forgotten about Tom's charming way with the ladies.

Joan cackles.

'Let's see,' he insists. 'I need to sign it anyway.'

I know he does, because I'd been doing an excellent job of avoiding him up until now.

I hand Tom the book, unable to resist holding eye contact

with him for a few seconds. I can't help but stare at him. When you think about your past, you always remember things fondly, don't you? You remember things being better than they were. I think, over the years, I'd managed to convince myself that Tom wasn't all that. I'd question what I ever saw in him and tick myself off if I dared to think any different. But seeing him here today, ten years older, but somehow even better looking than when he was 21, makes me remember just how attracted to him I was.

Tom is a big guy. He's tall, broad, and strong to go with it. He has neat, short dark hair, and a neat, short beard to match. He looks like the very definition of the strong silent type, and yet somehow there's this comforting warmth to him that makes you just want to curl up on his big chest like a little kitten and go to sleep, because you just know that no harm can come to you on his watch. Well, physically at least. If we're talking emotional hurt, that's a whole different story.

'Did you write this?' Tom asks her with a faux gasp.

'This young lady wrote it for me,' she insists, sounding a little concerned. 'Why, what does it say?'

'Don't worry, I'm just teasing,' he insists with a smile, squeezing her shoulder. He turns back to me. 'Can I borrow you for a minute, Luc?'

This is the first thing Tom has said to me in ten years, and it sends a shiver through my body, as though it were a ghost standing before me, saying my name.

'Sure,' I say as confidently as I can, trying not to sound too rattled, before walking over to one of the spare wicker tables with him. He pulls out my chair and nods for me to take a seat before sitting down next to me, placing the open guestbook on the table in front of us.

'Did you write this?' he asks pointing at the page, turning the book for me to get a better look.

'I did,' I reply cautiously. I didn't think I'd ever see him again, but I know how this goes. Should we not be politely but awkwardly making small talk, before resolving to politely but pointedly avoiding each other for the rest of the day?

Tom reaches into his pocket, pulls out his wallet and removes a receipt. He hands it to me.

'Why are you showing me that you bought three bags of Haribo?' I ask him, confused.

'I didn't buy three bags of Haribo,' he tells me. 'You did.'

Confusion consumes my face as I think for a moment. Oh my God, he's right, I absolutely did. On the drive down here. Well, it's not that I thought I could eat three bags, but they were on offer in the service station so it seemed dumb not to buy three for the price of two – do you know how ridiculously expensive Haribo is in service stations?! Anyway, how on earth does Tom have this?

All becomes clear when Tom takes the receipt from me, turns it over, and hands it back. That's when I see my angry note scribbled on the back.

'No one is impressed by your driving or your car,' he reads out loud.

Shit, it was Tom's car that I left that note on.

'Hmm?' I say innocently, trying to disguise my guilt.

'You wrote this,' Tom laughs. 'Look, the way you write an "i", with the little flicks, dotting them with a little circle. It's so distinctive.'

I open my mouth to speak, but no words come out. I don't know what to say.

'Hey, I'm not mad,' he laughs reassuringly. 'I'm just surprised. I didn't think you were the note-leaving kind.'

'I'm not,' I insist, laughing awkwardly.

Tom smiles widely at me and those gorgeous brown eyes of his look straight through my thick skin, just like they used to. He's always had this way of looking at me knowingly, making me feel like he's reading my mind. No matter what my mouth would be saying, I always knew he was peering into my head, seeing exactly what I was thinking and feeling, even if I didn't want him to. This doesn't seem to have worn off with time and, today especially, it feels like a huge invasion of my privacy. It annoys me that he still has that effect on me, and even more so that I still find his eyes so mesmerisingly gorgeous.

'Really, I'm not,' I say again, changing my tune. 'But if you're going to drive like an arsehole, on a narrow country road, late at night …'

'OK, calm down, I get it. Wow, when did you become such an adult?'

'When *didn't* you?' I snap back.

'I am genuinely sorry,' he says softly, like a ticked off child who has just been caught with his hand in the biscuit tin just before dinner. It might be cute, if I weren't so annoyed. 'It's an occupational hazard.'

'Why, are you a Formula One driver?' I ask.

'No, an automotive journalist,' he says with a laugh.

'Right,' I reply. Well, that doesn't excuse it, does it? 'Listen, I need to go finish getting people to sign this, so …'

'OK, sure,' he replies. 'Can we have a catch up when you're done then?'

Ergh. Do we really have to? I don't want to hear all about his amazing job, and his pregnant little missus, and his fast, flash car, and how is life is just better than mine in every possible way.

'Luca, there you are,' Pete says as he approaches us.

'Pete, hello,' I reply, delighted to see him – especially at this particular moment in time.

'You didn't tell me you were a bridesmaid,' he laughs, nodding at my dress.

'I didn't actually know I was a bridesmaid when we met last night. It was definitely a last-minute change,' I tell him, before turning back to Tom briefly. 'I'd better go.'

I notice Tom look Pete up and down, his eyes narrowing as he tries to suss him out. He doesn't look impressed, but why would he? Pete is basically Tom's opposite.

'OK then,' he says. 'Well, can catch up later then, I guess.'

'Yep,' I reply, although I am absolutely going to avoid doing this if possible.

As I walk off with Pete, I take his arm and lean in closer so that I can whisper into his ear.

'Thanks for saving me,' I say.

'Not a problem,' he replies. 'That looked a little intense. Can I get you a drink?'

'Please,' I reply. 'Just an orange juice.'

'Are you sure that all you want?' he asks.

I smile and nod.

'Coming right up then,' he replies. 'Find us somewhere nice to sit.'

I make my way over to a wicker sofa, hiding in the shade of a beautiful willow tree. From here, I have a great view of the gardens, the massive lake, and even my hotel room window. I like knowing that, if it all gets too much here, I can escape to my little hotel room and hide, while still technically feeling like I'm at the wedding. I sit and admire the view until Pete sits down next to me.

'So, what's the story?' he asks.

'The story?'

'The story with the guy,' he says. 'There's always a story with a guy when there's a girl with a look on her face like you have.'

'Ah, you don't want to hear all about that,' I tell him with a bat of my hand. 'It's nothing. Ancient history.' I'm trying to play it down as best I can because I really don't want Pete to think I am a dramatic woman with a dramatic life.

'Of course I want to hear all about it,' he replies. 'It sounds like it might be an interesting tale.'

'We went to uni together,' I tell him, getting the ball rolling. Perhaps I'll only tell him as much as I need to, even if it would be nice to tell an outsider all about it.

'Something happen between you?'

'Yes … well, no … sort of.'

'That sounds complicated.'

I smile at him. I can't tell if he's humouring me, just to be kind. I doubt he actually wants to know about something that happened to me ten years ago, does he?

'Are you sure you want to hear this?'

'Every word of it,' he insists.

I'm really not used to getting attention from men, I'm not quite sure what to do with it.

'OK,' I say, taking a deep breath. 'Tom and Matt were best friends when we were at uni. So when I moved in with Matt I started seeing more and more of Tom, and we grew quite close. We finally made plans for a date … but then he met someone better, so …'

'Cleo?' he asks, with an understanding nod.

'Erm, yes,' I reply. It didn't occur to me that Pete might already know her.

'Not that I'm saying she's better than you or anything like that,' he quickly says. 'But I know her through Kat. I knew about her and Tom being together, but I'd never actually met the guy until now.'

'How does Cleo know Kat?' I ask him curiously.

'They're sisters,' he says. 'Didn't you know that?'

'I didn't,' I admit.

'Yeah. Kat met Matt through Cleo and Tom. I suppose if you and he had got together, Tom wouldn't have ended up with Cleo, Kat wouldn't have met Matt, this wedding wouldn't be happening and you wouldn't have met me.'

I think about the chain of events for a few seconds.

'I suppose I wouldn't have,' I say, smiling at him.

'I thought maybe they might've sat us at the same table but I checked and no such luck,' Pete says, changing the subject.

'That's a shame.'

Not just because I would have loved to sit with him and talk more, but because it means I'll be sitting with Fi and the boys. I don't mind sitting with Fi, I could easily talk to her all day, but I remember all too well what the boys are like, especially at mealtimes.

There's this unidentifiable energy between Pete and me. A tension, since the kiss we shared last night. I might be momentarily rattled by Tom being here, but I can't let my past distract me from what is happening right now. Instead, I should let my present distract me from everything that happened back then. Perhaps Pete can distract me with another kiss, if I'm lucky (read: don't ruin things – or allow my old friends to ruin things for me).

'Well, I think we're about to sit down to eat, but after that,' Pete says, 'we can sit together, have a drink, maybe have a bit of a dance …'

'I'd really like that,' I reply sincerely. 'Well, if we're eating soon I'd better get a move on and get around everyone with this book.'

'Yes, don't let me distract you from your newfound bridesmaid duties,' he laughs. 'That's a great dress, by the way.'

'Thanks. If only it were a different colour, I wouldn't be saddled with bridesmaid duties. It was just in the wrong place at the wrong time.'

Which is pretty much the story of my life …

Chapter 6

Then – 20th September 2008

Things that are important when you move into a new house …

Furniture, that's pretty important, right? There are lots of things you need, even in a student house. Beds, tables, chairs, cutlery, lights, drawers – a whole bunch of stuff. You need a room of your own, somewhere you can sleep, somewhere you can get some privacy. Cleaning rotas are important, probably, and bathroom schedules. But the most important thing of all – the one thing that is more important than all the other things – is the housewarming party, and tonight we're throwing an epic one.

There are fairy lights everywhere, the music is booming, and with the tens and tens of guests who walk through the door, each one brings more and more to alcohol to add the healthy supply we bought in anticipation of the big event.

As the familiar drum beat of The Ting Tings 'That's Not My Name' starts, someone turns up the music.

'Tune,' Clarky declares as he, for some bizarre reason (probably alcohol), walks like an Egyptian across the crowded room.

I glance around the living room, looking for my friends. I watch as Fifi and Zach take part in drinking games. They kiss for a dare, but when the game moves on, Zach puts up a wall between the two of them, like he always does. Clarky sits down at the table and spins the bottle, which lands on Fifi. He looks delighted when she's quick to kiss him, but she's obviously only doing it to make Zach jealous. I know better than to try and get her attention right now, she's a woman on a mission.

Matt is in the kitchen, sitting on the worktop, with a captive group of girls forming a crowd in front of him. He's wearing a fedora, because of course he is. I think he thinks that cool guys at parties wear fedoras, but I can't see that one standing the test of time. This is all classic Matt, turning his cheeky charm on for the ladies. I don't know if he does it because he's interested in one of them (or all of them) or if he just flirts for sport, but you'll always find him flirting in the kitchen at parties, that's for sure.

The house is pretty full – full of more people I don't recognise than people I do. For some reason that I can't quite put my finger on, I'm feeling a little bit overwhelmed by all the noise and all the people. I wonder where Ed is. Ed has never been much of a party animal, he's probably hiding in his room. Perhaps I can go and hang out with him for a while, hide from the party chaos, watch him play FIFA until things calm down or Fifi tears herself away from Zach for long enough to spend a little time with me.

I knock on Ed's door once. Then again. He might have his headphones on, so I open the door just a crack, only enough to see whether or not his light is on (because you never know what you'll walk in on when you live with men who weren't teenagers too long ago), but it isn't, so he's either not in there, or he's fast asleep.

I sigh, heading to my own room where I close the door behind me. The booming of the music and the chatter of the rowdy crowd is only slightly muted by my bedroom door, but it's just nice to get away from all the noise. I leave my lights off, only turning on the little fairy lights that hang above my bed. I sit on the edge of my bed for a second before lying back and closing my eyes. I just need a quick breather before I go back out there. It's just the noise and the people and perhaps because I've had a little to drink. I just need a couple of minutes.

In the sanctuary of my bedroom, I feel myself becoming lighter again. That is, until I hear someone open my door. I quickly sit up.

'Hello,' a man standing in my bedroom doorway says casually.

'Erm, hi,' I reply, not sure what else to say to the stranger, hovering right on the edge of my personal space.

'Can I come in?' he asks.

'I'd rather you—' I start, but the man closes the door behind him before he sits down on the bed next to me. Now he really is in my personal space.

I feel so uncomfortable, having this random man sitting next to me, on my bed.

'So this is your room?' he asks me. 'Or are you just looking for somewhere to hide from the crowd?'

'Both,' I reply, scooting over on the bed so that our thighs are no longer touching. 'Which one of my housemates do you know?'

I feel like each one of my friends is so different that I'll be able to get the measure of this man as soon as I know who he fraternises with.

'Oh, none of them, I don't think,' he replies, running a hand through his messy brown hair.

'What are you studying?' I ask, looking for connections.

'I'm not at uni,' he laughs. 'I just came for the party, me and a few of the lads thought it might be a good place to meet fun people.'

Suddenly it becomes apparent that this man looks a few years older than your average third-year uni student, and I don't want to be cynical, but it sounds like he and his mates have only come here to meet younger girls.

'You look like a virgin,' he tells me.

'What?'

'Madonna. "Like a Virgin". You look like she does in the music video, in that little black vest, with all those necklaces.'

I grab my phone from my bedside table, as casually as I can, like I'm just checking my texts, when what I actually want to do is try to call one of my friends, so they can come in a diffuse this awkward, uncomfortable situation.

'Are you?' he asks. 'A virgin?'

The man leans over to me, placing a hand firmly on the back of my neck as he tries to kiss me.

I try to wiggle from his grasp, but he's holding me pretty tightly.

'Don't,' I say quietly.

'Come on, just relax, lighten up,' he demands, taking my phone from me, tossing it to one side. 'It's a party, you should be enjoying yourself.'

The man pushes me back on the bed, pressing his body down on top of mine. He feels so impossibly heavy and my best efforts do nothing to shift him.

'Get off me,' I shout, trying to wiggle free from under him. 'I said get off!'

The man halts his advances, but remains on top of me, pressing down so I feel like I'm trapped under a car.

'Babe, you need to relax,' he tells me. 'Let your hair down a little.'

He might have stopped trying to kiss me, but he's still on top of me, still trying to reason with me, still trying to get me to change my mind. The thing is, I'm not going to change my mind – there's nothing he can say to convince me – and the fact that we both seem unwilling to compromise absolutely terrifies me.

I try to wiggle out from under him again, and this time I feel his weight lifting from on top of me.

'What the hell are you doing?' I hear a different man shout.

I look up to see someone is dragging the man from my bed by his hair.

'Whoa, whoa, what are you doing, bud?' the first man asks as he's dragged across the room, towards the door.

'She said get off her,' the second man insists. 'Are you deaf?'

I quickly sit up and watch as the second man forcefully shoves the first out of my bedroom door.

'Get out of here,' he tells him. 'And if I ever see you again, you'll regret it.'

I exhale for what feels like the first time in minutes, unable to believe my lucky escape.

My hero leaves my bedroom door wide open, which I think is a deliberate action, to make sure that I'm not scared of him. Then he makes his way over to me, squatting down next to my bed, which I also think might be intentional. Not shutting me in a room with him, not sitting on my bed – it's appreciated.

At least I recognise this man – I've seen him in my lectures and I'm pretty sure he's a friend of Matt's. He's tall and broad, with brown, messy hair pointing in all directions. He's got this cool, easy-going look about him, and he almost always has a smile on his face when I see him around campus. He isn't smiling right now though.

'Are you OK?' he asks me. 'Did he hurt you?'

'I'm fine,' I tell him. 'Just shaken up. Thank you for stepping in. If you hadn't turned up when you did ...' I feel my blood run cold.

'But I did,' he says. 'And if I hadn't, someone else would have heard you shouting. You have nothing to worry about, just take deep breaths. Do you want me to leave you alone or do you want me to stay with you for a bit?'

'Please stay,' I say quickly. 'Just in case he comes back.'

'I don't think he'll dare come back,' he reassures me with a smile, playfully brandishing a fist. He does look kind of big and scary when he's angry, but here, now, I don't feel scared at all. I can see his softer side, and it's going a long way to making me feel a bit more relaxed.

'It's OK, you can close the door,' I tell him, noticing we're having to raise our voices to hear each other over the noise of the party. It really is a miracle he heard me; then again, it felt like I was shouting for my life.

He does as I say, pushing my door closed before sitting down next to me, keeping just enough distance not to spook me, which I appreciate.

'I recognise you from my course,' I say, wiping away one of the tears that has managed to escape.

'Yeah, I recognise you too,' he replies. 'Matt and I are working together on our production project – he invited me tonight.'

'Oh, don't worry about it, apparently anyone can get in,' I say, furious about our non-existent door policy.

'He wasn't someone you knew then?'

'No, I've never seen him before in my life. He isn't a student, I think he was older,' I reply, shuddering at the thought of some creepy older guy infiltrating student parties to prey on young women. I change the subject. 'You're Tom, right?'

'That's me,' he says. 'And you're ...'

'Luca.'

You think that when you finish school you put the God-awful hierarchy of the classroom behind you, but unfortunately uni follows a similar model. On our course, Tom is the cool guy, the one everyone wants to work with, the class clown. Of course I know who Tom is, and of course he doesn't know me.

'I've seen you around – I've noticed your colour-changing hair. I appreciate cool hair.'

'I can see that,' I say, nodding towards Tom's dark, spikey, gravity defying hair.

'Yeah, we look like anime characters,' he laughs.

I laugh too, but as I relax, I start to feel relief, and as the relief washes over me, I burst into tears.

'Hey, hey,' he says, reaching out, placing an arm around me, giving me a big, reassuring squeeze. 'Everything is OK, I promise.

I'm not going to let anyone hurt you. I'll attend all your parties from now on, how about that? I'll wear a suit and an ear piece – the works.'

'You're my hero,' I tell him. 'You should wear a cape.'

With Tom here, I feel so safe. Not just because I've seen him on my course for over two years and because I know that Matt can vouch for him ... I just feel like he really is looking out for me, like nothing bad can happen to me on his watch.

'How about we sneak downstairs, grab some food, come back up here and I'll watch whatever movie you want me to. I don't even care if it has Matthew McConaughey in it.'

'I'd rather watch a Scorsese flick, to be honest,' I admit. 'Give me a young Ray Liotta over Matthew McConaughey, any day.'

'Whoa, OK, we didn't agree you could be cool *and* have good taste,' he jokes. 'Smart, stylish and a cinephile. That's a triple threat.'

I smile.

'Right, come on, let's go steal some pizza, and if anyone so much as looks at you in a way you don't like, I'll go full Joe Pesci on them.'

Chapter 7

Now

I feel like to say this wedding has turned into a circus would be grade-A hyperbole … except I just saw an alarmingly muscular man doing press-ups on the lawn with the mother of the groom on his back. So there's that.

I hurry over to Kat, the bride, with a book full of messages from well-wishers. I've done my best to get around everyone – I think I might've accidentally asked one of the waiters too, but he was more than happy to write something so all is well that ends well. It's finished, I can go back to being a regular guest whose only responsibility is having a drink without making a fool of herself.

'That's great,' Kat says, taking the book from me. 'When I need something else, I'll call on you.'

'You'll call on me?' I reply weakly.

'Yeah, I'll call on you.'

I think the words she is looking for are 'thank' and 'you'.

I pull a face to myself as I walk away, leaving her to the circle of guests that has formed around her. How have I landed myself in this mess? I know how – it's this stupid, beautiful dress that I spent far too much money on. If I were still a goth I would've turned up in something black and slutty and, sure everyone would've asked me if I were attending a funeral (perhaps even a funeral for strippers, depending on who was making the joke) but there's no way I would have been asked to fill in for a bridesmaid dressed like that, and there's no way I'd be assuming boring bridesmaid duties right now – I'm not even sure they'd let me in the photos.

Tom collars me halfway across the lawn. Great. Just what I need.

'Hey, are you ready for that catch up?' he asks me.

'I think we're about to eat actually.' I turn on my heels to walk away but Tom stops me.

'Luca, wait,' he starts. 'I just …'

I turn around and glance at Tom as he runs a hand through his thick, dark hair. I notice the bulge of his bicep stretch the inside of his shirtsleeve to capacity, before immediately telling myself off for looking at him that way. He deserves no credit, at all, for anything, ever.

'I haven't seen you in, what, ten years? I can't believe you're standing here. It's made my day seeing you here, but you just seem like …'

I shrug my shoulders casually. I can't see his eyes, just my reflection in his Ray-Ban sunglasses, and seeing myself be so casual with him when he's so pleased to see me makes me feel horrible.

'Luca Wade,' I hear Cleo's *The Only Way Is Essex* accent squeak behind me.

'Cleo, hello,' I reply with faux enthusiasm.

'You look amazing,' she tells me, pulling me down to her level for a hug. Cleo creeps in at just over five feet – another little lady who makes me feel like a giant beast of a woman.

'So do you,' I tell her, kissing the cheek she's offered me.

As she releases me, she lightly knocks me with her bump.

'Oops, watch out for little Sunny,' she says, placing her hands protectively on her stomach.

'Sorry,' I say, not that I have anything to apologise for. I've always been the kind of person who apologises, even if it isn't my fault – even if it's only a lamppost I've walked into. I just can't seem to lose the reflex.

'Gah. Luca, Luca, Luca. Such a cute name but, you know, I always thought it was a boy's name,' she muses.

'Sunny is a type of weather,' I reply through my best fake smile. 'It's all good.'

Cleo laughs wildly, throwing her head back theatrically.

'You're so funny,' she tells me. 'Tom, didn't I always say Luca was a funny girl?'

She playfully digs him in the ribs with her elbow.

'Yep,' he replies. 'Cleo, can you give us a minute please?'

Cleo pouts. 'OK, sure. But it's nearly time for food,' she tells him. 'Hurry back.'

Ergh, that girl needs to loosen her bun or something, I think it's stopping her brain from working properly. And telling me I have a boy's name, pssh. If there's one thing I remember really well about Cleo, it's that she has mastered the skill of dishing out backhanded compliments.

'Why do girls do that?' Tom asks me.

I look at him for an explanation.

'Greet each other with all the love and excitement you'd feel if you were reunited with a dead relative,' he says. 'Cleo gets all that and you haven't even hugged me yet.'

Tom flashes me that cheeky smile of his that I've always had a soft spot for. It's probably the first thing that attracted me to him, the first time I saw him in one of our lectures, playing the class clown with such charm and warmth.

I think about how much I want to feel his arms around me but, at the same time, the thought of touching him terrifies me. The thought of him touching me after all these years makes me feel like a nervous teenager again, but it's all I can think about now.

Before I have a chance to act, I feel my body lifting off the ground, like I'm being beamed up by an alien spaceship which, to be honest, I don't think would completely ruin my day. I glance down to see that, not only am I only a few feet off the floor, but there are a pair of unusually tanned, bizarrely hairless, absolutely massive arms wrapped around my body.

The person who grabbed me from behind puts me down and spins me round roughly, like an excited child with a puppy, who doesn't quite realise his own strength. As he hugs me, I realise he's the almost terrifyingly muscular man I noticed doing press-ups before. This man isn't just buff in the usual, gym-going way, he's like … young Arnold Schwarzenegger buff. Huge!

The man quickly realises that I don't know who he is.

'It's me,' he says, as though that might shed some light on the situation. 'Tom, my bro, you must recognise me?'

'I didn't realise I had a bro.' Tom laughs, scratching his head. He clearly has no idea who this is either. Still, he shakes his hand. The man must grip him tightly because as soon as he releases him, Tom rubs his own palm with his other hand.

'Does the name Alan ring any bells?' he asks.

'Alan? Her ex-boyfriend Alan?' Tom says in disbelief.

'Yeah,' the macho man says, holding his arms out, a big ta-da smile plastered across his face.

'What, did you eat him or something? Is he hiding in one of your legs?' I joke, unable to believe my eyes.

Alan laughs.

'Alan, I … I can't believe it's you,' I say, looking him up and down, admiring him like I would a statue.

Alan was always a fitness buff, and he was always muscular from the endless hours he would spend in the gym, but now he has to be at least four times the size he was at uni. He barely resembles his former self, it's so weird. Now that I know it's him,

I can just about make out my ex, hidden away inside this beast of a man.

'It isn't Alan anymore, it's Al Atlantic. Winner of the international Mr Macho competition, 2017 *and* 2018. Hoping to win this year too, pick up the hat trick.'

Al Atlantic poses in that way bodybuilders often do, standing to one side, lifting a heel and pointing his fist towards the floor to show off his impressive figure. I couldn't tell you which muscle specifically this pose is intended to showcase, but whichever one it is, it's huge. They're all huge. I'd hazard a guess that even his muscles have muscles.

'Wow, well, congratulations,' I tell him.

I don't really know what else to say. He's another person from my past I wasn't expecting to see here. I don't know why this didn't cross my mind, I was probably too busy worrying about finding a designer dress that didn't make my bum look too big (or my bank balance look too small) and my embarrassing single status when all my friends are in serious relationships.

'I was hoping we could have a catch up,' he says, his eyes wide with optimism.

Ergh, why does everyone want to have a catch up? It's been ten years, no one has time to cover ten years in a quick catch up, do they? Or maybe I'm just self-conscious of the fact that, in my ten years, not much has happened that is worth catching up on. I haven't won one Mr Macho competition, let alone two. Plus, Alan and I didn't exactly end things on the best of terms. When I broke up with him, he took it quite badly, and this is the first time we've spoken since.

'OK, sure,' I say. 'But I think we're about to eat so ...'

'Yeah, OK, I'll come and find you later,' he says. 'Good to see you, Tom.'

Al gives Tom a playful slap on the back, nearly knocking him off his feet. I'd say Al doesn't know his own strength, but from the way he's showing off, I know he absolutely does.

'Yeah, you too,' Tom replies as he stumbles forward. He waits for Al to leave before opening his mouth again. 'Well, that was completely emasculating, wasn't it?'

'Damn, I can't believe that's Alan,' I blurt, ignoring Tom's remark. Well, I'm not about to fall over myself to fluff his ego, am I?

'The gym paid off then,' Tom muses, sounding almost annoyed at Alan for daring to put in so much hard work, and getting such great results from it. 'He's still boring though, isn't he?'

'I'd better get to my table,' I say, quickly changing the subject, trying to end the conversation before it can get going again.

'Does bridesmaid duty not get you promoted to the top table?' he asks.

'It doesn't even get me a "thank you",' I reply.

'Hmm, I was hoping we'd be sitting together. Well, I asked for a catch up first,' he calls after me as I head in the direction of the marquee. 'Don't go letting Alan jump the queue just because he looks like he could strangle someone without breaking a sweat.'

He does indeed look like he could kill someone with his thumb, but the Alan I knew was always way too boring to be confrontational enough to get into a fight.

I glance at the seating chart to see roughly where my table is, before looking in that direction and seeing that my friends have already taken their seats.

Our table is right at the back of the marquee, where it meets the building, next to the kitchen door. Not only do we have the heat coming from in there, as well as countless serving staff constantly whizzing past us, but we're being deprived of the same breeze the rest of the guests are enjoying. On a sweltering day like today, a breeze is absolutely needed. I feel like my make-up is melting and slowly slipping down my face – and not even evenly, so I probably look like some bizarre, abstract Picasso portrait at this point.

'I can't believe they've given us the crappiest table here,' Clarky whines. 'We're his oldest friends.'

'We're pretty far down the pecking order today,' Zach says, knocking back the glass of Prosecco on the table in front of him that I'm pretty sure we're supposed to save for the speeches.

'This day is just getting worse and worse,' Clarky says, knocking back his glass too.

'I think the drinks are for the speeches,' I point out.

'It's OK, this one was Bella's,' Clarky replies.

We all fall awkwardly silent at the first mention of Clarky's ex-girlfriend. Up until now, we've all been quietly ignoring the fact she isn't here, but as two other guests take a seat at our big, round table, the fact that Bella's chair remains empty couldn't be more obvious.

'Ah, buddy, things aren't so bad,' Ed says, patting him on the back.

'They bloody are,' Clarky insists. 'I was going to try and shag a bridesmaid, but they're all fat.'

'They're all pregnant,' Fiona corrects him angrily.

I loudly clear my throat.

Clarky looks over and me, looking me up and down before saying, 'Well, you're not a real bridesmaid, are you? And anyway, I wouldn't shag you, it'd be like shagging my weird sister.'

'I don't know how I'm ever going to heal from this broken heart,' I say sarcastically, pretending to wipe away a tear from my eye.

'You know, when I checked in, the receptionist asked where my guest was, and when I told her she wasn't coming, she got really pissed off with me and told me I should've called ahead,' he says, angrily.

'You should've told her she'd died,' Zach laughs. 'Made her feel bad.'

'I should've told her I'd killed her, more like, then she wouldn't have been rude to me.'

Nothing like the threat of murder to keep a woman in check.

All at once, we're all very aware of the couple sitting on our table, attentively but timidly observing our conversation.

'Hello,' I say politely.

'Hi,' the girl says back.

'Bride or groom?' I ask.

'Bride,' she says.

'We went to uni with the groom,' Ed tells them. 'In fact, we all lived together for a year.'

'Oh really?' the girl replies. 'Toby is Kat's dentist.'

The girl places her engagement-ring-clad hand on her fiancé's arm as she explains their connection.

'What the fuck?' Clarky whines. 'We're his oldest friends and we're sat at the crap table with Kat's dentist and his bird? No offence.'

From the looks on their faces, I'd guess they've taken offence.

'Are you not drinking?' Fiona asks me, nodding towards my orange juice.

'No, I'm trying to keep a clear, sober head,' I say.

'Same,' she replies, showing me her lemonade. 'If I start drinking now, I'll be hammered by tonight. I think I'm getting old.'

'I bumped into Pete again,' I tell her quietly. 'He seems great. I don't want to drink too much and start talking rubbish, I want to spend more time with him, so he can get to know the version of me that I have full oral and physical control over.'

My friend gives her eyebrows a playful wiggle at my choice of words.

'Not like that,' I quickly insist, although I know she knows what I mean really.

We had a spare few minutes after the ceremony, so I told Fi about what happened with Pete last night. It was nice, talking to her about boys just like told times. I miss having a female friend in my life – someone to confide in, someone to give me advice. Fi and I never fell out after uni, we just drifted apart. We all had good intentions to stay in touch and keep our friendships alive, but when you're all living all over the country, juggling hectic jobs with relationships, and house moves … you just put off that night out you swore you'd plan so that everyone could catch up. It's especially hard trying to plan reunions for a group of six, which is probably why we only see each other at weddings.

'Ooh, Luca has a crush,' Fi sings quietly.

'That doesn't usually end well for me,' I point out.

'Yeah, I had a quick chat with Tom. My God, he's gorgeous. He might actually be better looking, now that he's older.'

'Thanks, mate,' I say with a laugh.

'Sorry.'

'It's ancient history,' I assure her. 'Speaking of which, have you seen Alan?'

'No?'

I glance around the room for my man mountain of an ex. He's incredibly easy to spot.

'There he is,' I point out. 'He's some kind of Mr Universe type now.'

'Oh my God,' Fiona blurts.

'What's up?' Zach asks.

'Over there, look, it's Anal Alan,' she tells him.

'Anal Alan?' Kat's dentist's fiancée echoes. Once again, she seems horrified by our conversation. I feel like I should tell her that things are probably only going to get worse as this lot have even more to drink.

'We only called him that because he was always very organised,' I assure them.

'Yeah, not because he was an arsehole,' Zach adds with a chuckle. 'He was though. What's he doing here?'

'Probably pulling the weddings cars along by his belt,' I suggest. 'I saw him doing press-ups with Matt's mum on his back earlier.'

'I bet he's still boring,' Ed says.

'You have a shed where you go to escape from your life,' Clarky points out. 'You're boring too.'

'I suspect we're all kind of boring now,' I say. 'Mr Muscle over there is probably more interesting than all of us put together.'

'What do you two do for work?' Clarky asks the couple.

'I'm a dentist,' Toby reminds him.

'I'm a dental nurse,' the girl adds.

'You work together then?' Clarky asks.

'We do,' he says proudly.

'That must suck. If you've got your missus watching you all day, you can't flirt with the customers, can you?'

I'm not sure if he's making an observation or asking a question.

'They're not customers, they're patients,' Toby corrects Clarky, as his brow furrows angrily. 'And I don't flirt with them, it wouldn't be ethical.'

That's a real shame, because I can think of so many dental puns.

'What do you all do?' he asks us all, getting the subject back on track.

'I'm a producer on a soap,' Zach says, not that he seems all that proud of it. I think he'd rather be making stylish action movies with international location shoots, guns, sexy women and even sexier cars. Instead he produces a soap opera, set just outside Glasgow, in which one of the characters just died by accidentally drinking a spiked drink that was intended for his mum, who it turned out was actually his dad. I learned this watching an omnibus one night last week when I couldn't sleep, so I can't even begin to explain it.

'I'm an acting agent,' Fiona adds. 'But we don't work together.'

'I'm a paediatrician,' Ed says.

'Oh wow, that's impressive,' Toby replies.

'I do social media for a protein company,' Clarky says.

'You want to start using it, mate,' Zach jokes. 'You might grow a bit.'

'Piss off,' he snaps back.

'Clarky is so short, *I'm* his doctor,' Ed quips.

'Alright, alright,' he says. 'Enough of the short jokes. I'm 5'8".'

'*I'm* 5'8",' I point out. The only way he's 5'8" is with his arms in the air. 'I work in PR too, for a fashion retailer.'

We're interrupted by the starters being placed down in front of us. Everyone at the table gets two tiny canapés, apart from Toby and his fiancée, who get a couple of cherry tomatoes and a couple of sticks of celery.

'Tight arse,' Clarky muses, throwing one of the small savoury pastries into his mouth whole. 'I hope the main is decent.'

'I hope it's surf and turf,' Zach jokes, putting on a scouse accent.

'Apparently we're getting a little downtime between our starter and our main,' Fiona tells us.

'What?' the boys all whine in unison.

'I'm starving,' Ed says. 'And drinking heavily, but this is my day off so I don't care.'

He dances in his seat a little, to demonstrate just how carefree he is.

'You enjoy it, mate,' Zach tells him, patting him on the back. 'Before it's back to misery.'

Fiona shuffles uncomfortably in her chair.

'Are you OK?' I ask her.

'Yes, I'm fine,' she replies quietly. 'Sometimes he just says the wrong thing and it winds me up.'

'He's just joking. Ed knows that.'

I look down at my canapés. One of them has a sort of creamy mushroom paste in, which I give to Clarky because I don't like mushrooms, and he'll eat pretty much anything. The other is a ham and cheese thing that isn't too bad, I just wish I had twenty of them. It's past lunchtime now, and the lack of food makes me really happy I decided not to drink. I can see Zach, Ed and Clarky getting quite merry already. Hopefully they are different drunks to the ones they were when we were at uni. The last thing we need today is to see these guys regress ten years.

'Tommy boy,' Clarky sings as Tom approaches our table.

'Hey, how's it going?' he asks everyone.

Everyone makes small talk for a few minutes. Everyone but me. I just watch Tom as he chats. He's got this easy way with people. He treats every word uttered to him like it's important, which makes people feel important, and everything he says in response just oozes with charisma. You know how men have a bad reputation for not really listening? Well, Tom isn't like that. Tom has a brain like a hard drive, storing every little detail.

'Luca, can I borrow you?' he says.

'Are we allowed to leave the table?' Clarky asks, worried.

'It's not school,' Tom laughs. 'We're not eating our mains for a while, we're allowed to circulate.'

'I'm not going to chance it,' Clarky says seriously.

'You'll take a risk, right, Luca?'

'Course she will,' Fiona tells Tom.

'Yep,' I reply reluctantly.

What could be better than hearing all about my not-quite ex's perfect life? Literally anything, I'd imagine.

Chapter 8

Then – 20th December 2008

Thinking about how quickly this year has gone really scares me. If you ever need reminding how quickly your life is passing you by, just think of how quickly one Christmas turns into the next. I said this to Fifi earlier today and she told me it was just my black lipstick talking. Maybe it is just the goth in me, making me all doomy and gloomy … either way, I don't think I should be thinking about this at a Christmas party, do you?

It's weird how festive cheer brings out a different side of people. Matt and Clarky, who are usually all about the banging tunes and the fit birds at a party, are dressed head to toe in ugly festive suits. Matt's suit is covered in colourful baubles and Clarky's is covered in penguins – if I were as short as he is, I'm not sure I'd invite the comparison. They're both currently on the coffee table, raising their glasses as they dance to Wham's 'Last Christmas'.

'I love this song,' Tom says, slinking up alongside me, just as the song finishes. Mariah Carey's 'All I Want For Christmas' starts playing. 'And I hate this one.'

'Same,' I laugh.

'Also, hello,' he says, belatedly greeting me, kissing me on the cheek.

'Hello,' I reply.

It's such a bittersweet feeling, when he kisses me on the cheek. We've grown really close since the night he saved me, but as much as I want us to be more than friends, he's taken on a sort of protective big brother role instead. When I look at him, my stomach does somersaults. When he touches me, I feel this rush of something through my body. This surge of energy that makes me dizzy. But when he looks at me, I think he just sees a victim. Someone helpless who he needs to take care of and protect from the big, bad world.

Matt dances over, wrapping a piece of tinsel around Tom's neck, flossing it like a tooth as he attempts to dance with him. Matt is usually the coolest guy in the room, until Tom turns up and dethrones him. They're like apples and oranges though. While Matt is fun-loving and goofy, Tom is laidback and charming. Tom doesn't dance, he's too cool to dance. He'd never try so hard, and that just makes him all the sexier.

'Tom, Luca, Tom and Luca,' Matt sings before his bizarre gyrating grinds to a halt. 'I see a lot of you two.'

'I do live with you,' I point out.

'And I've just finished a long project with you,' Tom laughs.

Matt hooks an arm around each of us, pulling us in for a group hug.

'Together,' he insists with a knowing grin. 'I see a lot of you together. Hey, you know Ed's hammered already, he's had to go to bed.'

I laugh at how quickly Matt's attention flits from one thing to another.

'Poor Ed,' Tom laughs. 'It's the last party of the year and he's out for the count already.'

'Well, it's funny you should say that,' Matt starts, fidgeting on the spot like a child, shifting his weight back and forth between his feet. 'New Year's Eve, we're having a big party, right here, fancy dress, be there,' he tells us. We both get a kiss on the cheek before he dances off.

'You wouldn't think I lived here, would you?' I laugh. 'Apparently we're having a New Year's Eve party. And I'm invited, so that's great.'

'Well, I'm all for it. I was planning on coming back from Kent for New Year's Eve anyway.'

'Hey Tom.'

We're interrupted by a girl I recognise from our course, but I don't know her name. She's wearing those fake leather leggings that are all the rage, teamed with a flowery headband. Both items are in fashion right now (and I hate both of them with a passion) but even I know that you're not supposed to wear them together.

'Hello,' he replies politely.

'We're playing drinking games ... I just ... I wondered if you wanted to come and play with us?'

'Ah, I'm not really one for drinking games,' he says. 'But thanks for the invitation.'

'Ah, but it's fun. Please?' she begs, unwilling to take no for an answer, batting her long, sparkly false eyelashes at him.

'Well, if it's fun,' he laughs.

Jealousy bubbles in my stomach. I sip my drink to try and stop it reaching my mouth.

'What do you reckon, Luca? Shall we go play?'

The girl's face falls. I don't think she was inviting me too.

'Oh, I'd love to,' I reply, even though I'm not one for drinking games either.

'Cool,' she says, but you can tell from her voice that is absolutely isn't cool.

We arrive at the dining room table just in time to see Zach locking lips with some random girl as Fifi watches on, stoically silent, but I bet she's gutted really. You can't fault her poker face though, which might be part of the reason Zach hasn't asked her out yet. The sooner those two realise they're perfect for each other and finally get together, the better.

'Are you two joining in?' Zach asks us, finally coming up for air.

'Why don't we play something else?' the girl who invited us (read: just Tom) suggests. 'I'm sick of spin the bottle.'

I smile at her knowingly.

'I know what we should play,' Zach says with a clap of his hands, hopping to his feet, dashing off before reappearing with a Jenga box. He dumps the bricks out on the table. Each one has been written on and decorated with different coloured felt-tip pens. This is Zach's customised game of Jenga, where he's written a series of commands, dares and prying personal questions on each brick with the idea that, when you pull one out, you have to do exactly as it says.

'Set them up, Katie,' Zach instructs the girl. At least I know her name now.

After playing for a while we are all a little worse for wear. We've got quite the crowd around us now and I'm lucky that I've gotten off quite lightly so far, especially compared to others. I feel like Tom hasn't had it too rough either, with the exception of Katie waxing one of his legs, and the dare that saw him lick the sponge we use in the kitchen. For the most part, we've both been getting drinking commands, but I'm not much of a drinker at all, so I'm really feeling the effects.

'Dare,' Tom says, after carefully extracting a brick.

Zach looks at me, before turning back to Tom.

'I dare you to tell us who you'd most like to get off with at this table,' Zach says.

Tom laughs.

'Mate, that's a truth, not a dare,' he replies. 'But nice try.'

'OK then, I dare you to kiss Luca.'

'Mate,' he says, laughing awkwardly again.

'Go on, do it,' Zach pushes. 'Do it, do it, do it.'

The crowd join in with the chanting as I feel my cheeks flush. I've spent a lot of time thinking about kissing Tom. I didn't think I'd ever know what it felt like to kiss him, and if finally I did, I didn't think it would be under circumstances like these.

'You sure you don't want to wax my other leg?' Tom laughs.

'Nope, I want you to kiss Luca,' Zach insists firmly.

Fifi, who knows exactly how I feel about Tom, tries to talk Zach out of it.

'I kind of want to see him get his other leg waxed,' she says brightly.

'There you go,' Tom says. 'That's what the audience really wants to see.'

Oh my God, he doesn't want to kiss me. He doesn't want to kiss me, not even while he's drunk, to the point where he would rather have his other leg waxed – and after the first leg nearly made him cry too.

'I don't think he wants to kiss her, dude,' Katie laughs.

There's an awkward silence for a few seconds.

'I'm just going to the bathroom,' I say, trying to hide the crackle in my voice as I hurry out of the room.

Of course I don't really need to go to the bathroom, I need to burst into tears, not only because I'm embarrassed, but because I've been harbouring this secret crush on Tom for a while now, and while something happening between us always seemed like a long shot, now I know exactly how he feels about me and it isn't the same way I feel about him.

I close my bedroom door behind me and plonk myself down on my bed. I'm really hoping a pattern isn't forming where I end each party in my room, in tears.

After a couple of minutes, there's a knock at my door. I quickly wipe my tears before heading over to see who it is, cautiously opening it just enough to tell whoever it is to get lost.

'Hi,' Tom says.

'Hi,' I reply.

'Can I come in?'

'Erm … sure, why not?' I say, opening the door for him.

I plonk myself back down on the bed. Tom sits next to me.

'Are you OK?' he asks.

'Oh, I'm fine,' I reply. 'Tiny bit embarrassed, but fine.'

'You really have nothing to feel embarrassed about,' he insists.

'Hmm, I'm not so sure about that,' I reply.

'Luca …'

'I think the crowd would beg to differ too, You'll lick the sponge we use to do the washing up, but you can't bring yourself to kiss me for a dare.'

'Would you really want to kiss someone who just licked a dirty sponge?' he laughs awkwardly.

I sigh deeply.

'Anyway, who cares?' I say, sounding like I care an awful lot. 'Go back to the party, I'll be back down soon.'

For a few seconds there's nothing but uncomfortable, awkward silence.

'Luca …' he starts again, but quickly loses the words he was going to say.

'Tom, really, it's fine,' I insist. 'I'm just embarrassed.'

Embarrassed and heartbroken, but mentioning the latter will only make me even more embarrassed.

'Luca, it's not that I don't want to kiss you. I really, really want to kiss you.'

I quickly turn my head to look at him, convinced I misheard that.

'But …' he starts. Ah, there's always a "but", isn't there? 'That night we met properly for the first time, well, it wasn't a great night, was it? I could see, even then, what a beautiful, funny, smart girl you were, but you were so scared and so upset. Asking you out wasn't exactly at the top of my list that night, I just wanted to make sure you were OK. And then I started to get to know you better, and you were just as amazing as I thought you were, but I didn't want you to think I was taking advantage of you, or that I'd only helped you for some other reason, or … whatever. Sorry, I'm doing a terrible job of explaining myself.'

I smile at him. He's such a good guy, this is exactly why I have such strong feelings for him. I really feel like he's got my back.

'I *do* want to kiss you. Properly though, not when we're drunk, doing it because there's a crowd of people chanting at us to do it, minutes after I've licked a dirty sponge,' he laughs. 'You deserve better than that.'

'So you don't think I'm too repulsive to kiss?' I say, my eyes filling up a little.

'Don't be crazy.' He takes my hands in his, squeezing them tightly, just like he did that night. 'We've had a bit of a weird start and we're going home for Christmas tomorrow so, how about we start afresh with the New Year?'

'I'd really like that,' I say.

'Well, I'll see you at the New Year's Eve party, and then, maybe on New Year's Day, we'll go on a proper date?' he suggests.

'I'd love that.'

Tom leans forward and kisses me on the cheek. He lingers there for a second and I feel his breath tickling my neck, which sends a little shiver through my body that makes me squirm in my seat.

'It's going to be a long Christmas break,' he says, finally pulling away.

It certainly is, but I can't wait for New Year's Eve now.

Chapter 9

Now

It was Tom's idea for us to catch up so, now that we're here, sitting in the cool shade of a willow tree, struggling to get a conversation started, I don't feel much like helping him.

So …' Tom starts, failing to reach a destination.

'So,' I echo.

'How's life?' he asks.

Ergh, what a vague, pointless question. Unless something interesting is going on, it's impossible to give an interesting answer. Otherwise, no one tells the truth, do they? How's life? Oh, well, work is stressing me out, I haven't had sex in a long time and I'm watching so much Netflix it doesn't just ask me if I'm still watching, it asks me if I'm still alive.

'Good,' I reply. 'How's your life?'

There's a real saltiness to my words that I can't hide, as though I begrudge him having a life without me. It's been ten bloody years, it's about time I let it go.

'It's going well,' he says. 'Work is going really well.'

'Ah, yeah, what did you say you did, car journalism?'

'Something like that,' he laughs. 'What did you fall into?'

'I work in PR, for a fashion retailer.'

'You've always loved fashion,' he says, as though he still knows me. 'Although you've toned it down a lot.'

'I've matured,' I point out. 'Do you still wear the clothes you had at uni?'

'Some of them, yes,' he says with an embarrassed chuckle. 'When I was working abroad I bought new clothes, rather than move loads of stuff around with me. Then, when I moved back home, I picked up all my old things from my parents' house and realise there was still a lot of life left in my old T-shirts.'

'You've moved back to the UK?'

The last I'd heard Tom was working abroad, that's why he wasn't at Ed's wedding five years ago. I have always made a real effort not to ask questions or seem at all interested when people mentioned his name over the years. I suppose it was a defence mechanism, but now that I'm in front of him, and know nothing about him, I feel completely disarmed.

'Yeah, I've moved back to Manchester actually.'

I feel a pang of something in my chest. Shock? Hope? I don't know.

'You live in Manchester?'

'I do.'

'So do I.'

'Yeah, I figured. I thought about looking you up but … I don't know, I figured you'd be married with kids by now and wouldn't want anything to do with me.'

'Nope, no husband, no kids,' I say, almost annoyed that he's made me confess the words out loud, even if they are true.

Before anyone can say anything else, we're interrupted by the bride. This doesn't usually end well for me.

'Luca, I need you for another bridesmaid duty,' Kat says casually, as though I signed up for this. 'Grandma Joan has wandered off. She does this all the time now, but I don't want her missing from the photos so … could you find her please?'

Kat hitches up her dress, turns on her heels and walks away.

'She doesn't even wait for a reply,' I point out.

Tom laughs.

'Well, she's a busy bride, and anyway that sounded more like an order, not a request,' he replies.

'Well, I guess I'd better get looking for Grandma Joan then,' I say, slightly glad of an excuse to end this conversation and get as far away from Tom as possible.

'I'll help you look,' he says.

'You really don't have to do that.'

'Joan loves me,' he reminds me. 'It's no trouble at all. Plus, we can continue our catch up. She likes a drink, I'd check the bar first.'

I don't really know what I can say to that, other than thank you.

As Tom and I make our way through the marquee, I make eye contact with Fiona, who wiggles her eyebrows at me. God knows where she must think we're going together.

As we reach the inside bar, we bump into Pete who, at first seems pleased to see me, but then he realises I'm with Tom and he looks concerned.

'Bridesmaid duties,' I tell him, pulling a face. 'Grandma Joan has gone missing apparently.'

Pete laughs.

'Buy you a drink after?'

'Sure,' I reply.

'I'm not sure what I make of that guy,' Tom says, once we're out of Pete's earshot. Not that anyone asked him.

'You don't even know him,' I remind him.

'I know he's got his hair in a flipping bun,' he points out emphatically. 'And a scruffy eco-friendly suit. He looks like a hippy.'

'Oh, so just because he has a bun and cares about the environment, he's a hippy?'

'Oh, does he care about the environment?' Tom asks mockingly. 'What a dream boat.'

I hold my tongue.

'Wait here,' I tell him, ignoring his remark.

I head into the ladies' room, squeezing past a crowd of especially loud, excitable women on their way out. I check the doors of each cubicle, until I get to the last one, which is locked.

'Hello,' I call out.

'Hello,' I hear a panicked voice call back.

'Joan?'

'Yes, please, you have to help me. I've fallen. I can't get back up.'

I dash into the next cubicle, put the lid down on the toilet, kick my shoes off and climb on top so I can peer over. Poor Joan is lying in a heap on the floor.

I examine the size of the gap my head is currently poking through. I consider whether I could climb over but I'm not sure where I'd have space to land and I think I'm imagining myself as way more athletic than I am, as well as having a much smaller arse than I probably do. Poor Joan is already stuck, let's not throw my fat arse getting wedged between two toilet cubicles into the mix.

'It's going to be absolutely fine,' I reassure her. 'I'll go get help, but I'll be right back.'

'I didn't manage to get my tights back on,' she says, sounding a little embarrassed.

'That is not a problem at all.' I try to sound as calm as possible. 'I'll get someone to open the door and I'll fix you up before anyone sees anything, I promise.'

I carefully step down from the loo, lest we have another accident, and go to find Tom. I spot him outside the toilets, currently in a headlock, courtesy of our resident man mountain, Al Atlantic.

'I need help,' I tell them. 'Kat's grandma has fallen in one of the toilet cubicles. She can't get up and she can't open the door to let me in.'

The three of us rush into the thankfully still empty ladies' room.

'I can sort this, no worries,' Al says confidently.

'Listen, when you open the door, can you just give me a minute to fix her clothes. I promised her,' I tell him quietly.

'Of course,' he says. 'Stand back.'

I bite my lip anxiously as I wonder how Al is going to barge the door open without hurting Joan on the other side, only to watch as he pulls the door from it's hinges. It makes a loud noise as the plastic cracks, but Al makes it look effortless. Then he holds the door just in front of the cubicle, to maintain Joan's privacy while I pop in to straighten up her clothes.

'Thank you, dear,' she says, squeezing my hand. I don't think anyone has ever thanked me and sounded quite so grateful before.

'Don't worry about it,' I assure her. 'Are you hurt?'

'I'm fine, really,' she insists. 'I just can't get back on my feet.'

Al places the door to one side.

'Don't worry, I've got you,' he says chirpily, scooping Joan from the floor with a fireman's lift before carrying her out. Tom and I follow close behind as he carries Joan to the bar.

The bride and groom are there now, doing a lap, greeting their guests, thanking them for coming. When they notice Al carrying Joan, their smiles fall as they hurry over.

'We took a tumble, but we're OK,' Al tells them, carefully placing Joan down on one of the sofas in the bar.

'Grandma, what happened?' Kat asks.

'Oh, I just slipped. It was a silly thing really,' she says. 'I'm embarrassed more than anything.'

'Don't worry,' Tom reassures her. 'My gran got absolutely hammered when my dad remarried.'

'Your dad remarried?' I blurt.

'Yeah,' he replies. 'He's really happy now. I've got a couple of little brothers too.'

'No way, that's amazing,' I say.

Tom used to confide in me about the troubles in his parents' marriage. They argued all the time and it would really get Tom down when he would visit home. I think he felt the most sorry for his dad; his mum had a hard time trusting him and they'd argue about it all the time, whether Tom was around or not. Listening to him talk about it taught me quite early on that, without trust, a relationship is doomed to fail. Doubt will slowly but surely rot your relationship from the inside out, leaving you with nothing but crumbled up pieces that are impossible to put back together. It's so nice to hear that his dad is happy now – and so weird for me to be so invested in his family's wellbeing still.

'Al Atlantic saves the day,' Matt says. 'You look like you could be a superhero.'

'I just need the cape,' he says, flexing his biceps.

Kat beams.

'Right, well, we'd better get back to it,' she says, taking Matt's arm as they head back to their newlywed duties. 'Are you sure you're OK, Grandma?'

'I'm fine, honestly,' Joan insists. 'I just need a sit down and a stiff drink.'

'We can sort that bit,' Tom says. 'We were getting one anyway.'

I realise that the 'we' he's referring to includes me.

'I'll go see if I can find any more damsels in distress,' Al says with an arrogance so subtle, it's only just detectable by the most cynical ears. 'Catch up with you later, Luca.'

Not if I can help it, buddy.

'My God, Al is terrifying,' I say to Tom as we stand at the bar, ordering two cokes and a whiskey for Joan. 'The way he ripped that door off, like it was nothing …'

'Shouldn't you be impressed by stuff like that?' Tom laughs.

'I'm kind of repulsed,' I admit. 'Those veins in his neck …

whenever he moves, they look like they're going to burst. And he's just such an odd colour ...'

'They're bronze, right? Bodybuilders, I mean.'

'He looks more like an Oompa Loompa,' I point out. 'An Oompa Loompa on steroids.'

Tom laughs.

Tom insists on paying for the drinks, so I take Joan her medicinal whiskey.

'Here we go,' I say, setting it down in front of her.

'Thank you, love,' she replies. Joan takes me by the arm firmly. 'And thank you for everything you did for me.'

'Oh, Al did all the hard work,' I insist. 'There's no way I could have ripped that door off like that.'

'No, you did way more. Thank you.'

I smile. I just did what anyone would have done in that situation.

'You two make a lovely couple, you know,' she says.

'Me and Al?' I squeak, horrified at the idea of something happening between my ex and me.

Joan laughs.

'No, you and Tom. You could do a lot worse than Tom.'

Somehow, this gets to me even more than the idea of getting together with Alan.

I look up at Tom as he places my drink down in front of me. As he smiles widely his cheeks dimple and the skin crinkles around his eyes – both features I always used to find so attractive about him. He has this animated face that reacts to every word, every look. You always get Tom's full attention and when you have it, you feel amazing. But I know what it's like to lose it.

Sure, maybe I could do a lot worse than Tom. But I could do a lot better too.

Chapter 10

Then – New Year's Eve 2008, 11.40 p.m.

And I'm late. Of course, it isn't my fault this time, not that it matters. No one ever cares why you're late, do they? They only care that you're late in the first place.

I am here though, finally, after one hell of a day and as if I wasn't already excited enough to see Tom for the first time since before Christmas, after the day I've had, I'm craving his touch even more. He's just the tonic I need after a tough day. One hug from him and a few of his easy words, and I'll forget about everything I've been through over the past few hours.

We've been texting nonstop all Christmas, chatting, flirting, sending each other pictures. We've had this running joke, since that night he saved me, that Tom is my hero, so when we were talking about fancy dress costumes for New Year's Eve Tom suggested, in a semi-flirtatious tone, that I might finally get to see him in spandex and a cape. Tom decided he'd go as Batman, so I said I'd go as Catwoman, so we had a sort of cute, matching theme going on, that I previously would've found nauseating but with Tom, I don't care. I want to be cute and matching. I don't care how dorky we'll look, I just can't wait to see him.

I dropped him a message earlier, to let him know that I was going to be a little late, but I can't believe how late I actually am. If this is karma in action, after I did someone a favour, I'd rather opt out from this particular magical points system.

I make my way through our busy house, where the party is already in full swing, but I don't recognise anyone I know. Then again, I'm not likely to, am I? If everyone is in fancy dress ...

I can see Hannah Montana, Indiana Jones, a million Jokers, but no sign of Batman. I dash up to my bedroom – I need to change my clothes anyway – to see what kind of last-minute costume I can bash together, given that I haven't had time to collect my Catwoman costume. What's popular at the moment? All my clothes are dark, all my make-up is dark – it's not like I can just knock together a Hannah Montana costume from what I already have. I think about what I do have – mostly black stuff. I've got it ... Twilight. I'll just stick on one of my usual gothic outfits and cover my skin in body glitter. That's right, isn't it? I know it's a bit half-arsed, but it's all I've got, and it's nearly midnight.

I dash downstairs, carefully pushing my way through the hoards of party-goers to find my hero, to finally get that hug I so desperately need, and the first kiss I've been literally counting down the days for.

Across the large living room, I spy Batman, meaningfully pushing his way through the crowd too. I don't think he's seen me, but I can tell that its Tom from the shape of his body – that tall, broad, sexy, manly frame he has that drives me wild. As everyone counts down the last ten seconds of 2008, I notice Tom walking away from me, so I push harder to get through the crowd. As the clock strikes midnight, I finally get to Tom, just as he grabs a woman in a Catwoman outfit and kisses her passionately. It's the perfect New Year kiss, timed perfectly with the stroke of midnight, but it isn't with me. It's with someone else. Someone dressed as Catwoman. I stand in front of them for a second, staring, my jaw practically on the floor. The girl, whoever she is, kisses Tom back. Well, why wouldn't she? She doesn't know what's going on. She doesn't know that he's supposed to be kissing me, does she?

Devastated and embarrassed, I retreat to my bedroom before Tom spots me. Yet another party I've ended in my bedroom, in tears, crying over a boy. I kick of my shoes and climb into my bed, hugging my pillow as I think about what I should've done, or what I could've done. He's going to realise his mistake at some point, when he comes up for air I imagine, but then what? If I keep out of the way maybe, when he realises, he'll come find me … I wonder if he'll tell me? The thing that's really bugging me is that, as soon as I saw him, costume or not, I knew that it was him. How could he not know that wasn't me he was kissing? How could he not feel it? What the hell happens next?

Chapter 11

Now

My shoes have vanished.

While Tom escorted Joan back to her table, I headed to the toilets to retrieve the heels I had taken off in a panic. They're not where I hurriedly left them, they haven't been considerately placed to one side by a Good Samaritan – they've just disappeared.

After checking every last inch of the ladies' room, I walk out into the bar, scratching my head.

'Are you OK?' Tom asks.

I wonder why he's come back for me, which he sees on my face. That or he's reading my mind just like he used to.

'I thought I'd come back, make sure you got your shoes OK. It was just an excuse to talk more, to be completely honest, but erm …'

He nods towards my bare feet.

'Yeah, they've gone,' I tell him.

'Oh,' he replies.

'Hmm.'

Neither of us knows what to say. Well, why would someone take my shoes?

'Maybe they were handed in at reception,' Tom suggests.

'Maybe.'

'Let's go see.'

Is it strange, that Tom is so invested in my daft problems? You'd think he'd rather be hanging around with Cleo.

'Hello,' I say brightly to the receptionist. 'Has anyone handed in a pair of pink heels?'

The receptionist blinks at me.

'Shoes,' I add, in case that's the bit she's struggling with. 'I left them in the bar toilets and they've gone.'

'You've lost your shoes?' she asks.

What's it to her if I have?! She's looking at me like I'm crazy, for losing the shoes from my feet. I'll bet this is the same receptionist who got sassy with Clarky for turning up without the girlfriend he just dumped.

'No shoes,' she replies without much concern. I suppose to her, they're just shoes. To me they're a huge chunk of my wage for the month and I feel sick. I guess I'm not returning them now. It serves me right, I suppose.

'Thanks anyway,' Tom says as he ushers me away. I think he's worried I'm going to say something about her attitude. I've never been the kind of person who usually says something, but that note I left on his car has probably got him scared.

'Well, I've got some trainers in my room,' I say. 'They'll look a bit daft with my dress but …'

'You'll pull it off,' he says with a smile. 'Where's your room?'

'I'm in one of the cottages that look over the gardens,' I say. 'Just across the car park. Shit!'

'What?'

'I'm going to have to walk across the gravel car park in my bare feet.'

'I'd let you borrow mine but unless you're a twelve …'

'Not even close,' I reply, although I'm probably not all that far away from a size twelve really, not compared to all the little ladies lightly prancing around at the wedding. With above average height comes above average shoe size. Still, that's not a very sexy thing to say out loud.

'OK, hop on.'

'On what?'

'On me. On my back, I'll give you a lift.'

I laugh, but then I realise he's serious.

'What? No. I'm not getting on your back.'

'So you would rather walk across gravel in your bare feet than get on my back?' he asks with a chuckle. 'Is that what you're telling me?'

'No, of course not,' I insist.

'Would you rather I got Al Atla—'

'No,' I say quickly, cutting him off. I do not want to ride my ex-boyfriend.

Tom turns his back to me and squats down a little. I exhale deeply, psyching myself up before wrapping my arms around his neck and my legs around his waist.

'Oh God, I hope I'm not showing my bum,' I say, cringing. I use one hand to try and check my dress hasn't ridden up, but as I slip down Tom's back a little, I quickly grab him tightly again. He secures his grip on my thighs.

For a second, I close my eyes. I take comfort from the warmth of Tom's body, from the secure grip of his hands. I drink up the smell of his aftershave. I feel my grip on his body shift and I can't resist resting my head on him, nuzzling my face into his neck.

'Oi oi,' Clarky bellows.

'You dared to leave the table then,' I reply defensively. Why do I feel like I've been caught out?

'I'm off for a slash,' he says. 'Where are *you two* off?'

'Someone stole my shoes,' I reply, as though it's a perfectly reasonable thing to happen. 'Can you tell everyone I'll be back in five minutes please?'

'Only five minutes?' he replies with a wink. 'Sure.'

I feel my cheeks blushing and I'm so glad that Tom can't see my face right now.

'He hasn't changed much then,' Tom says as he makes his way outside.

'No,' I reply. 'I don't think any of us have.'

'OK, you'll have to give me directions.'

I direct him across the gravel, under the pretty rose archway and around the corner to where you enter the cottages. The gravel is no longer a threat to my bare feet, but Tom carries me up the rickety wooden steps to my room anyway.

Tom takes my keys from me, unlocks the door and carries me inside, placing me down on one of the beds.

'Wow, you have a twin room,' he points out, as though I hadn't noticed. 'I didn't realise they still existed.'

'Yep, let's not waste a double bed on a single girl,' I say, hopping off the bed before searching around the room for the only other pair of shoes I have with me – some sparkly, pink Converse trainers. Well, at least they match my dress and my hair.

'Now those look more like my Luca,' Tom says with a laugh. 'I mean uni Luca … the Luca I know.'

I am briefly taken aback by his use of 'my Luca' – although I suppose he did quickly correct himself, he probably didn't mean for it to come out like that. It's been a long time since I was anything close to being his. Just hearing him talk about those days makes my head spin a little. It feels like I'm being dragged back there.

'They look ridiculous.' I look myself up and down in the mirror. 'But the bare feet looked fractionally weirder, so this will have to do.'

'Speaking of weird,' he starts, glancing around the room. 'This is an odd room. The ones in the hotel are way more modern …'

He isn't wrong. The twin beds and the décor look retro, while the flat-screen TV on the wall and the bathroom are both ultra-modern. The furniture falls somewhere in between, and the dome-shaped light fittings are positively futuristic.

I'd say I would've preferred a room in the hotel to one of the external cottages, but I quite like being here, out of the way of everyone else. It feels like I have an escape.

I adjust my dress, neaten my hair and reapply my lipstick while I'm in front of a mirror.

'We'll have to go for a drink sometime,' Tom suggests, taking a seat on one of the single beds. 'Now that we're living in the same city again.'

'I'm not sure Cleo would like that,' I point out. Her name tastes so sour in my mouth.

'Oh, I'm sure she'd hate it,' he replies. 'But Cleo and I have separated, so ...'

I feel a pang in my chest again. This time it's more of a jolt.

'You're not together anymore?'

'We're not,' he replies. 'Are you really that surprised? Everyone always said we were wrong for each other.'

I nod thoughtfully. They never did seem quite right for each other, which only made it hurt all the more when he chose her over me.

Damn, that must be so awkward, having to spend so much time with your ex at a wedding – much worse than me having to endure Alan popping up, because it has been a literal decade since we broke up. It's even more awkward than all the talk about the empty chair where Clarky's now ex-girlfriend should be sitting.

'I don't think I knew what was good for me when I was younger,' Tom confesses.

'I don't think I know what's good for me now,' I admit, allowing myself to feel just a little bit sorry for him. 'Will you see much of Cleo and the baby?'

I don't know why I'm asking him, it's absolutely none of my business. Anyway, why do I care? What am I doing? The groundwork, to try and figure out if something could happen between us? Would I really want to get involved with someone who had an annoying ex and their child on the scene? It's not that I'm against dating men with kids – I'm possibly getting too old to be that fussy now anyway, in fact, by the time I get married, I'll probably be looking at second-wave bachelors, those who have been married and divorce at least once already – but dating a man who has a child with Cleo is a whole different concept. It isn't the kid that would be the problem, it's the mum. Imagine how much control she'd have over our lives ...

I pinch myself for getting so stupidly and pointlessly ahead of myself. Tom didn't want me back then and I've no reason to think he'd want me now. And even if he did, he had his chance and he blew it.

'Not if I can help it,' he laughs, getting up to look out of the window.

'You don't want to see the baby at all?' I persist, although I suspect I'm starting to make him uncomfortable.

'No?' he replies.

Ergh, that's so like Tom. Just shrugging off his commitments. Making promises he has no intending of keeping is his strong suit. I almost feel sorry for Cleo. *Almost*.

'Wow, you can see almost every inch of the wedding party from up here,' he says, looking out of the window that overlooks the gardens. 'Everyone is back at their tables now.'

'Shit, we'd better hurry,' I say, grabbing my bag and my room key. 'No one is going to notice if I'm not there, but I'm pretty sure they'll notice you missing from the top table.'

And I really don't want anyone to see me walking back in with him. Especially not Pete.

Chapter 12

Now

Back at the table everyone is making small talk. I try to join in, but I can't get Tom off my mind. Tom, my one who got away (or should that be ran away?), who is now not only single again, but living in my hometown. And he wants to meet up. If this had happened years ago, I might've been interested ... but when you've been hurt before, it makes it harder to trust people – especially the people who hurt you in the past. Back when we were at uni, with our whole lives ahead of us, things were so easy. Getting together would've been easy, starting a life together would've been easy. But now Tom comes with so much baggage. A horrible ex, a child with said horrible ex, and then there's the fact that he says he doesn't want anything to do with them. What kind of man admits that, let alone thinks it? Unless he's just telling me what he thinks I want to hear, but in some ways that's even worse. He's let me down before, and now he's going to let Cleo down, and what's to say he won't let me down again in the future? I don't care how charming he is, how helpful he is, how gorgeous he is ... the delicate pieces of my heart are too fragile to go another round in the ring with Tom. And then there's Pete who, granted I have only just met, but he seems like such a wonderful person – and yet I'm wasting my time and my energy on Tom, when really I shouldn't be thinking twice about him, I should be getting to know Pete instead.

'Are you OK Luca?' Ed asks, snapping me from my thoughts.

'Yes,' I say quickly. 'I'm just so hungry.'

'Aren't we all?' Clarky says.

Two stuffed peppers are placed in front of our vegan friends, before the lid is lifted from the large silver pot in the centre of our table.

'What have you guys got then?' Clarky asks the vegans.

'Stuffed peppers,' the girl replies. 'You get served a lot of stuffed peppers when you're a vegan.'

'That must get so boring,' Fi replies.

'It does,' the girl says. 'But it's for a greater cause.'

'Never trust a person who doesn't eat meat,' Clarky says to me under his breath, although I'm pretty sure everyone at the table heard him.

'So, what are *we* having?' I ask, quickly changing the subject. Our vegan friends might not kill animals, but I don't think they'd think twice about murdering Clarky. Then again, I'd probably give them an alibi.

A server comes over and ladles dollops of something onto our plates. It looks like meat and a variety of vegetables, absolutely swimming in gravy.

'It's stew,' Clarky tells us. 'I had a peep earlier. It looked and smelled pretty bland but, don't worry, I took care of it.'

Zach's fork drops, clattering against his plate.

'Mate, what have you done?'

'I just gave it the little kick it needs,' he replies proudly.

'How have you done that?' Zach persists.

No one dares to taste what's on our plates until we find out exactly what he's done – not even the vegans, who are weirdly invested in what's going on.

'I added a little chilli,' he says. 'It needed a kick.'

'Where did you get chilli?' I ask him.

Clarky takes out his wallet to reveal a little plastic tube.

'Oh, mate, come on,' Zach moans. 'What is wrong with you?'

'It needed a kick,' Clarky insists again.

'*You* need a bloody kick,' I tell him.

Ed is the first person brave enough to taste his stew. He stabs a piece of meat and it has barely touched his lips before he's coughing and spluttering, grabbing his pint of beer and chugging it to try and get some relief.

'How much did you put in?' he asks in a voice that is not his own. He sounds like a demon – a demon whose weakness is an inordinate amount of chilli.

'I was trying to do it to our table's pot on the sly,' Clarky says under his breath. 'My hand slipped, but I'm sure it's fine. You've always been a girl.'

I roll my eyes. Because being a girl is such a negative thing to be, right?

Clarky takes a confident mouthful and instantly regrets it. You can tell by the reddening of his cheeks and his bulging, watery eyes. He spits into his napkin before downing his drink too.

'Yeah, it's ruined,' he eventually admits.

'Everyone is far too close to being drunk to be downing their drinks this early in the day,' Fiona says with a sigh.

'It's my day off,' Ed insists. 'And it was medicinal. My teeth were dissolving.'

'Chilli can't dissolve teeth,' our resident dentist unhelpfully points out.

'First of all, I was exaggerating,' Ed says, attempting to snap into serious mode, but not quite pulling it off because he's more than tipsy. 'Second of all, the acid reflux I would get from eating this would be very metridental to my teeth.'

'Detrimental,' I say.

'What did I say?' he asks.

'Metridental.'

Ed cracks up at his drunken babbling. He was always the first one in our house to get drunk back when we were at uni too.

'I can't think of anything more boring than a fight between a doctor and a dentist,' Clarky whines.

'A fight between you and Zach,' Ed reminds him. 'That was like watching a duck fighting a lion.'

'But I won, didn't I?' he says proudly.

'You absolutely didn't,' Zach says with a laugh.

'Yeah, I did.'

'No, you didn't,' Zach snaps back, his light tone quickly disappearing.

I smile at poor Fiona, sitting between them as they bicker. She rubs her temples and exhales deeply.

'Rematch,' Clarky suggests. 'Out there on the lawn.'

'Can you just cause one problem at a time, please,' I beg him. 'We can't eat this food, can we?'

'No, even I can't eat this,' Clarky admits, seemingly forgetting that it was him who got us into this mess.

'I can't even look at it,' Fiona says, lightly covering her mouth with the back of her hand.

I turn to look at the poor couple sharing the table with us. They're staring at us, like they would the monkey enclosure at the zoo, watching with a grim curiosity as we all fling crap at each other.

'Yes,' I say, answering the question they didn't actually ask. 'We're always like this. And, no, it's not going to get better as they drink more.'

The couple smile politely. I definitely don't envy Kat her next dental check-up.

'We have to get rid of it,' Clarky says, straight-faced, with all the seriousness and fear that would be present if you'd suggest getting rid of a body.

'Oh, yeah, Fi and I will just sneak it out in our clutch bags.

It'll only take twelve hours if we work nonstop. What do you think this is, the bloody *Shawshank Redemption*?'

'I wish it was,' he snaps back, although I have no idea what he means by it.

'We just put it back in the pot,' Zach suggests. 'They'll think it's leftovers.'

'This is idiotic,' Fiona says with a sigh. 'I'm going to the loo.'

It is, but I'm not sure what other choice we have. I suppose we could throw Clarky under the bus, but we've always had each other's backs before. I suppose that's one thing we've got going for our weird group – if one of us makes a mistake, the others will fix it.

'I'll come with you,' I say. 'The boys can clean up this mess.'

As we make our way across the marquee, through the bar and into the ladies' room, I feel very self-conscious of my trainers. In any other circumstances, they'd look great, but at a wedding, with a dress, I just look silly. I look like a child who is refusing to dress up – I hope no one thinks this is some kind of feminist, single-girl protest.

'Are you OK?' I ask Fiona the second the door closes behind us.

'I'm … I'm fine,' she says eventually.

I want to say that she doesn't seem herself, but do I really have the right to say that if I haven't seen her in five years? Am I qualified to know what her being herself is anymore?

'Is this giving you ideas for your wedding?' I ask.

'Yes, but not the ones you'd imagine.'

I laugh. 'More what not to do?'

'Something like that,' she replies with a deep sigh, as she disappears into a cubicle.

I sit down on the toilet and stare down at my trainers. I shake my head. Why on earth would someone take my shoes, if not to hand them in? Knowing how expensive they were, I should never have taken them off and left them in the toilets, but I wasn't thinking straight, I was trying to help Joan. The people that bang on about karma have a lot of explaining to do, because my good deeds get me nowhere. That's not why I helped but, come on, Universe, cut me some bloody slack, just for today.

I flush the toilet and begin to straighten up my dress, ready to go back out and face the world.

'… because you're pregnant and you're still slimmer than most of the people here.'

My ears prick up as I catch the tail end of woman's sentence as she walks into the toilets.

'Oh, stop,' another woman replies, and I know instantly, by that faux modest, *TOWIE* tone that it's Cleo.

'You could have any man here.'

'I know,' she replies.

As the toilet flushes in the next cubicle I lean towards the door so I can still hear their conversation. They exchange hello with someone – I think it was Fiona leaving – before continuing their conversation. I wait, and carry on eavesdropping.

'Just between us though,' Cleo starts, lowering her voice. 'Tom wants to get back together.'

'Really?' the other girl squeaks.

'Really,' she replies. 'I knew us breaking up was just a little blip – you know what we're like. But now there's Sunny to think about, and it's just the right thing to do. We both know that.'

As Cleo's friend congratulates her, I let out a deep, involuntary sigh. I was appalled when I thought that Tom wasn't going to stand by her or see his child but – and I hate to admit it, even to myself – I can't help but feel disappointed.

'I'll just have a wee,' Cleo tells her friend.

This is my chance, as soon as Cleo goes into a cubicle I'll make a dash for it, before she comes back out.

'Oh, someone must be in this one,' she says as she tries the door of the cubicle I'm hiding in. 'This is the only one with enough room to close the door properly, with my bump. The others are a tight squeeze. I'll just have to wait.'

Crap.

'Erm, I think they've been in there a while,' her friend says. 'I haven't seen anyone come out while we've been in here.'

'Is everything OK in there?' Cleo calls out sweetly.

Double crap. I'm going to have to come out, or they'll think there's something wrong with me. They're either going to realise I was listening to their conversation, or think I have some kind of stomach issue. I don't know which is more embarrassing.

I quickly give my outfit the once over and check my shoes for rogue loo roll before reluctantly opening the door.

'Hello Cleo,' I say brightly.

'Luca … is everything OK?'

'Oh, fine,' I say with a casual bat of my hand. 'I was just looking for my shoes.'

Cleo looks down at my trainers and stifles a snigger.

'I much preferred the Louboutins you were wearing earlier,' she informs me.

'Yes, well, I left them in here earlier and I guess someone has taken them.'

'I'm not even going to ask why you took your shoes off in the toilets,' she starts, before a huge grin spreads across her face 'Luca Wade, you naughty girl. Have you been up to no good in the toilets?'

'Erm …'

'Well, I don't blame you,' she says. 'We've all seen your boyfriend – Alan is quite the babe now. If I weren't happy and expecting my first child, I'd be shagging in the toilets too, don't worry. God, I'm jealous.'

I bite my tongue as I wash my hands. She doesn't sound jealous, she sounds smug.

'Al is my *ex*-boyfriend,' I remind her. 'And I actually took them off to help Kat's gran.'

'Such a shame,' she continues. 'And I can't believe that someone would just take them. It must have been someone who knows their value.'

'Hmm,' I reply, but then it occurs to me – has Cleo taken my shoes? Not that I think that she's stolen them to sell them or anything, but it's no secret that she doesn't like me, and she did say she noticed them earlier …

Cleo goes into the cubicle, so I head back to my table.

Today is just unbelievable. I am a grown woman. I have a mortgage, I have an apartment – and in that apartment, I have a drawer full of bags for life. If those things don't make for a mature adult, then nothing does. Yet here I am, surrounded by the people from my past, being dragged into the depths of immaturity. Well, I'm not going to let that happen, things have changed – *I* have changed. I'm not going to sit around feeling sorry for myself while Tom choses Cleo over me yet again. I just need to remember that this is only one day. Tomorrow I can go home, back to my life, and while it might be boring sometimes, it definitely beats all this childish drama.

Chapter 13

'There you are,' Fiona says as I sit down next to her. 'I thought you'd left without me.'

'No, I was listening in on Cleo's conversation,' I admit.

'Ooh, did you hear anything interesting?' she asks me quietly, leaning in for an answer that the boys won't be able to hear.

'Well, Tom told me he and Cleo had broken up earlier,' I confess. 'And that he's living in Manchester again.'

'Oh my God, that's amazing,' Fi says as excitedly as she can in hushed tones. 'That's double good news.'

'I don't know about that,' I reply. 'Anyway, I just overheard Cleo talking, and she says they're getting back together for the baby, so …'

'Oh,' my friend replies.

I glance over at the top table. Cleo is back now, and she and Tom look like they're having an intense chat about something.

'Oh, it's fine, our window was ten years ago and we missed it. Nothing we can do about it now,' I tell her. If I keep saying it, I'm sure I'll start believing it.

'I guess not,' Fi replies. 'I want to give you some speech about putting up a fight for him, but if they're having a baby …'

'I know, I know,' I reply. 'I wasn't really entertaining anything happening between us.' I don't think I was, anyway.

'At least you have Pete to distract you,' Fi says. 'He actually came by the table, looking for you.'

I smile. 'Did he?'

'I know that look,' Fi replies. 'That's the look of Luca love.'

'I am excited to spend more time with him. If I ever get chance.'

An uncomfortable feedback noise comes out from the speakers dotted around the room before a hotel official announces that it's time for the speeches.

'After the speeches, go find him, spend some time with him,' Fi suggests. 'Life is short.'

Right on cue, my stomach rumbles.

'Mine *will* be short, if I don't get some food soon. I'm starving.'

'Me too,' she replies. 'I've got an idea, but I'll save it for after the speeches.'

Before I get the chance to ask questions, Kat's dad stands up, ready to give his speech. He's an odd-looking fellow, with a rounded body and the shiniest bald head I've ever seen in my life. He's wearing a tartan suit, for some reason, and red-rimmed glasses.

'Good afternoon, friends, family, countrymen,' he jokes. 'For those of you who don't know me, my name is Martin. I'm Kat's dad – I'm also a performer, available for all occasions, parties … I've left some cards by the door.'

Everyone laughs dutifully.

'I thought, rather than deliver the usual, boring, father-of-the-bride speech, I'd write a little poem, which I'd like to share with you all now.'

'For fuck's sake,' Clarky says under his breath. 'Not poetry. I'd rather eat the vegan food than listen to poetry.'

'Shut up,' Fiona snaps at him under her breath.

'So, here we go.' Martin takes a deep breath. 'Kat saw Matt, and Matt saw Kat – it was love at first sight, and that was that.'

Oh God.

'Their first date was rocky – I think Matt wore a hat,' he continues. 'And he arrived late to meet her, in his banged-up Fi*at*.'

A chuckle echoes around the room.

'But dinner at the restaurant was not to be sneezed at, and Kat's friends inform me they went back to *her* flat – Matt's friends says his wasn't tidy, or something like that.'

I'm cringing a little. I'd be mortified if my dad did this at my entirely fictional wedding that is probably never going to happen. That does sounds like Matt though, his room was always just a sea of clothing, CDs and games.

'Still, the two fell in love and that's worth a shot at, and now it's their wedding we're all eating stew at.'

I laugh, mostly at his use of poetic licence.

'I'm a really proud father of my Kitty Kat, with her poise, and her grace – like an aristocrat. And now Matt's in our family and I'm pleased about that, even though sometimes, he's a bit of a twa—'

'OK, thanks very much,' Matt says, standing up, cutting Martin off before he gets to the punch line. I'm not sure if his interruption was rehearsed, or if he's trying to keep things PG in front of his own parents. 'My turn now.'

Poor Matt, he looks a little embarrassed. Still, he dusts himself down and removes his speech from his pocket, before taking a deep breath, ready to start.

'Thank you so much to everyone for coming today – I know a lot of you have had to travel, which Kat and I both really appreciate. We're so glad we can share our day with you. And, er, thank you to Martin, for that wonderful poem. He's already touched upon when Kat and I met but, I'll tell the story properly – and it won't rhyme, you'll be pleased to hear.'

'Wahey,' Clarky shouts. So far audience participation has been strictly quiet laughter where appropriate.

'Cheers, Clarky,' Matt says, looking down at his notes with a chuckle. 'So, I'm sure you've all noticed Tom, my best man – my best friend – the beautiful man sitting down the table from me.'

There are a few excitable noises from female guests which make me slightly, but uncomfortably, jealous. Someone wolf whistles, but I don't notice who.

'I have a confession to make ... I've always owed my love life, to Tom's love life. I'm sure anyone who knew me back when I was at uni will know that people used to say I bore a striking resemblance to Olive Oil from Popeye, probably because I had longish black hair and really skinny, long arms and legs. I didn't exactly have girls throwing themselves at me, until this guy came along. You'd think it might hurt your chances with the chicks, looking like Olive Oil when your best mate and wingman is a regular Bluto ...'

I can't help but laugh. Tom is very much a Bluto type, with his big, muscular frame and his dark hair and beard. He's just a much friendlier looking version.

'But it didn't actually hurt me at all,' Matt continues. 'It really helped me. Standing next to the guy all the girls want to be with is actually the best way to meet all the girls – who knew? So, when Tom got a girlfriend, when he met Cleo ...'

Cleo gives him a playful wave.

'I thought I'd run out of luck,' Matt says. 'I thought I'd lost my wingman. But what actually happened is that Tom and Cleo introduced me to Cleo's sister, Kat. And, mate, thank you, because this beautiful woman sitting here next to me is the best thing to ever happen to me. I'm not usually one to think that everything happens as it's supposed to – fate and all that – but ... well ... who knows? I am the happiest man in the world, and I hope that one day you get to feel what I'm feeling. No one deserves it more than you, man.'

If looks could kill ... Cleo doesn't look very impressed with Matt's speech. She's got a face like thunder.

Tom, who has been beaming a smile at his best friend up until now, suddenly looks pensive. But Matt's audience lap up his words, and coo, applaud, and toast the happy couple.

'You'd think it was Tom he'd just married, with that speech,' Zach says.

'However …' Matt is still speaking. 'Now it's time for my best man to give his speech, and I'm not sure I'll be talking about him so warmly after.'

The audience laughs as Matt sits back down. There's an uneasy look on his face, and a knowing look on the faces of everyone in the audience. They've all heard best man speeches before, they know how this goes. The best man pokes fun at the groom, shares embarrassing stories, makes inappropriate jokes, and all while the happy couple squirm and everyone else laughs.

Tom stands up, but something isn't right. Tom has always been the class clown, you'd think this would be right up his street. For some reason, he looks anxious, like there's something on his mind.

'Wow, thanks mate,' Tom says, sounding taken aback. He runs a hand through his hair before removing a few sheets of folded up paper from his pocket. He carefully unfolds them, before glancing over each page. He opens his mouth, as if he's about to start reading, but then he stalls. A few audience members laugh, thinking he's trying to create suspense or something. After a few seconds Tom meaningfully folds the paper back up and returns it to his pocket.

'I suppose Matt is right,' he finally starts. 'He did only meet Kat through Cleo, but, technically, I only met Cleo through Matt, so I can't take the credit for this. Back in the day Matt was trying to pull Cleo's friend, which is the only reason I met her. So, you see, Matt, you were always in charge of your own future.'

So it was Matt who invited Cleo's friend – and Cleo – to the party? I never knew that. He never told me. Then again, why would he? He probably had no idea how crazy I was about Tom, even if we did have this obvious will-they-won't-they thing going on, and even if he did, what would've been the point in telling me? Anyway, this is all so high school and I don't have the energy for it.

'Anyone can tell you're perfect for each other,' Tom continues. 'And I don't believe in fate or destiny but if a few things had happened differently, we wouldn't all be here today. Everything happened in the exact way it needed to so that you two would meet and whether it's a coincidence or not, it's amazing. And, maybe you're part of something bigger. Maybe we're all here today so that the rest of us can get our lives back on track.'

I notice Cleo reach up and place a hand on his forearm supportively. She thinks he's talking about her. Is he talking about her? Is there any chance at all he could be talking about me? No, I'm being stupid. I'm letting my imagination run wild.

'A relationship like yours is a real blessing' Tom continues, much to the delight of the women in the room. I think everyone was expecting a lewd, borderline-offensive best man's speech. Instead, they're getting this off the cuff, heartfelt speech that goes way deeper than any wedding speech I've heard before. I would be as weak at the knees as the next girl in here, were I not so salty at the fact he's probably talking about Cleo.

'Maybe we can all get our destinies back on track today.' Tom is practically talking to himself. He lifts his glass to make a toast, pulling his arm from Cleo's. She picks up her glass of water – obviously she can't drink – but it is at this point I decide that, balls to it, I might as well have a drink. 'To destiny.'

'Destiny,' the room echoes.

'Well, that was shit,' Clarky says. 'Isn't he supposed to talk about how small Matt's knob is and how he's punching above his weight?'

'No, we're saving that for your wedding, pal,' Zach replies.

Clarky gives him the finger.

'I thought it was grutiful,' Ed says, raising his empty glass. He thinks for a second and then laughs. 'Ha, I think I was going to say great and then I was going to say beautiful and I just mashed them together.'

'Christ alive,' Fi says, rubbing her temples. 'I think I blocked out what it was like when we all used to get together.'

'It's only today,' I tell her quietly – the same thing I keep telling myself. 'Soon you can go back to your life and you never have to see us again. Until your wedding, obviously.'

'If that goes ahead, we need to talk about what food you're going to serve,' Clarky interrupts, with all the seriousness of dad giving his son a talk on contraception. 'We don't want any accidents like today.'

'You're the bloody accident,' Fi replies.

'That's what his mum told me,' Zach jokes.

Fi isn't impressed. Ed cackles.

'Of course our wedding is going ahead, why wouldn't it?' Zach asks him, suddenly serious.

I glance over at Fi, who looks a little rattled, before turning to our vegan friends who don't know what else to do but stare.

'I told you we weren't going to get better,' I say.

Chapter 14

Then – Valentine's Day 2009

I have Tom and Cleo sitting on the sofa across from me and four DVDs sitting on the table in front of me, but I can't quite make my mind up which movie is the right one for tonight, as soon as I have the house to myself. It's Valentine's Day and not only am I oh-so single, but I'm also the only one at home this evening. Everyone has plans but, most notably, Fifi and Zach are going on a double date with Tom and his girlfriend Cleo. As if it isn't bad enough that she stole him from me, I get to see them not only together all the time, but also hanging out with my best friend and her boyfriend. Yay!

Pretty Woman is my first option. After all, if a smart businessman can fall in love with a random prostitute that he picked up at the side of the road, then there might still be hope for me. My second choice is *Closer* – a personal favourite of mine, because I watch it, and it makes me so, so happy that I'm single. My third choice is *When Harry Met Sally*, asking that age-old question: can men and women be just friends? Can they? I don't know. Technically Tom and I are friends, but with me wanting to be more than that, are we friends really? It's so hard being his friend, especially on days like today when he's sitting in my living room with his girlfriend, waiting to go on a double date with my friends. Finally, there's *Moulin Rouge*. I figured I might as well throw that one into the mix too, to serve as a perfect example of how love can go terribly, terribly wrong – perfect viewing for Valentine's Day.

'Is it a bit unusual, to go on a double date on Valentine's Day?' I ask, making conversation because it's so awkward sitting here in my *Nightmare Before Christmas* pyjamas with Tom and Cleo sitting on the other sofa, all glammed up, while they wait for Fifi and Zach to finish getting ready.

'Not usual, I guess,' Cleo starts as she fidgets with one of her brown ringlets with one hand and holds Tom's hand tightly with her other. 'But my dad is a sound tech, and he's on tour with Coldplay at the moment. He has these spare access-all-areas passes for their show tonight, so he gave them to me.'

'I see,' I reply. God, I just want them to go so I can put my film on, eat the heart-shaped chocolate I bought myself – like the strong, independent woman I wish I were – and feel sorry for myself in peace.

'Do you like Coldplay?' she asks. 'Everyone likes Coldplay, right?'

Erm, actually, they don't. They really don't. I honestly think I'd rather listen to the unidentifiable and frankly disturbing noises that I hear coming from Clarky's room on a night for two hours, but I probably shouldn't say this out loud because it might just come across as jealousy.

'Not really,' I say tactfully.

'You into metal or something?' she asks with distaste.

'Something,' I reply.

'Such as?'

Ergh, why is she talking to me? She really doesn't need to talk to me.

'Luca is a rock chick,' Tom says with a smile.

'But not Coldplay?' she asks.

'Yeah, they're a bit too heavy for me,' I joke.

She smiles.

'So, movie night is it?' She persists with the small talk.

'Yep,' I reply.

'What are you watching?'

'*Closer*.'

'What's that?' she asks.

I mentally roll my eyes. God, I just want to be left alone. This is torture. I toss her the box.

'This doesn't sound like something you should be watching,' she insists, examining the box.

As much as I want the conversation to end, I can't help but rise to it. 'Why not?'

Cleo shifts uncomfortably in her seat. 'Well … it's Valentine's Day … and you're single. This isn't the right film for that – how about I pick you one?'

'Cleo, I am watching *Closer*,' I say. 'But thank you.'

'Erm, *The Passion of the Christ* disc is in the box,' Tom points out after taking the box from Cleo and looking inside.

'Well then I guess I'm watching *The Passion of the Christ*,' I reply with a sigh. 'I haven't seen that one before.'

'Oh, don't spoil it for me,' Cleo says quickly, playfully covering her ears. 'I really want to see that one.'

Is she kidding me? Not only have I not watched it before, but doesn't everyone know how the story goes?

'Right,' I reply.

'Sorry, sorry,' Fifi says as she rushes into the room, closely followed by Zach. 'Someone had five-aside and had to have a shower when he got in.'

'No one said you had to join me,' Zach says cheekily.

Fifi blushes.

'Oh, don't worry,' Cleo reassures her. 'We're pretty much at it all the time too.'

Kill me. Kill me now.

'One of the lads is popping over to get his wallet,' Zach says. 'I told him he could put it in my bag while we played and forgot to give it back to him. Then we can get off.'

Great. I can't wait. I just wished they'd be quicker.

The gang sit enthusing about Coldplay as they wait for Zach's football buddy to arrive. I sit waiting for them all to leave so I can get on with my night. I've been thinking about it, and perhaps *Moulin Rouge* is the film for me tonight because it pretty much sums up my love life – hopeful, but ultimately tragic. Plus, who doesn't love a Baz Luhrmann movie?!

There's a knock at the door. Zach is tying his shoe, so Fifi jumps up to answer.

'Your friend is here,' she says.

Fifi is closely followed into the living room by a buff guy in a grey tracksuit. Under his open hoodie he's wearing one of those low-cut vests that guys like to wear to show off their muscle cleavage. He's undeniably attractive, with his toned body and his shaved head – he's the big, strong bad body women are supposed to fall at the feet of. I suppose I've always liked my men a little softer though.

'Alright mate,' he says. 'Sorry, I hope I haven't made you late.'

'No worries, pal,' Zach says, tossing the guy his wallet.

'You guys off anywhere nice?' he asks.

'Off to a gig, mate,' Zach replies.

'Are you going like that?' he asks me.

'I'm not going,' I reply, fairly sure he was joking. These are so very blatantly my pyjamas.

'Luca is alone tonight,' Cleo says.

'Thanks, Cleo. I'm looking forward to it more and more by the second.'

'What gig are you going to?' buff guy asks.

'Coldplay,' Cleo replies excitedly. She seems to have a little glimmer in her eye. Blinded by muscle, I'd guess. 'My dad is a sound tech, he got us all tickets.'

'Coldplay for Valentine's Day? I'm so jealous,' he says.

Maybe he does have a sense of humour because, y'know, it's Coldplay.

'You not got plans, Alan?' Zach asks him.

God, his name is Alan? That's not a very sexy name, is it? He looks like a Chad or a Brad or something. If this were an American romcom movie, Alan would definitely be playing the most popular guy in school, the one that absolutely isn't going to ask you to the prom.

'Nope, no plans,' he replies.

'Why don't you hang out with Luca,' Zach suggests.

I subtly shoot him a dirty look, telling him to leave it.

'I didn't bring my pyjamas,' he says cheekily.

'Pyjamas optional.' Zach wiggles his eyebrows, clearly not taking my telepathic hint.

'She's watching *The Passion of the Christ*,' Cleo tells him, and I'd swear she was trying to put Alan off.

'Actually, I think I'm going to watch *Moulin Rouge*,' I say.

'Oh, sweet,' Alan replies. He picks up the box and examines it thoughtfully. 'Who doesn't love a Baz Luhrmann movie?'

He doesn't pronounce his name right but, still, it's kind of cute. And those were my thoughts exactly … Perhaps I've got Alan all wrong.

'You're welcome to watch it with me,' I say. 'I'm just going to order a pizza, watch movies, and chill.'

'I'm cutting at the moment,' he says, sitting down next to me. 'But I'd love to join you.'

That suits me just fine – more pizza for me.

'You two behave,' Zach says, all smug, unable to hide his pride in his matchmaking skills. 'Or not.'

'Come on, let's go,' Cleo says, taking Tom by the hand, pulling him from the room.

As she drags him, he holds eye contact with me. He looks like he wants to say something, but he doesn't until he reaches the door.

'Bye, Luca.'

'See you around,' I call after him.

Playing the cards I've been dealt, I turn to Alan and smile.

'Luca is a lovely name,' he says.

'Thanks,' I reply. I'm not exactly sure I can return the compliment.

'Well, let's get this movie on,' he says. 'It's one of my favourites.'

I smile before heading over to the shelves to grab the DVD. This time I check it is in its box – thank God, it is. Someone in this house is terrible at putting DVDs and games back in the correct boxes.

Maybe Alan isn't the guy I thought he was at first. When he walked through the door, I might have decided he was a dim meathead. Now it seems like there may be more to Alan than meets the eye.

Perhaps I'm not going to have such a rubbish, lonely Valentine's Day after all …

Chapter 15

Now

We have finally, formally been released from the confines of the seating plan, which means we can leave our sweltering hot table (and our reluctant table mates) in the marquee and sit outside where there is a nice cool breeze to take the edge off the baking hot summer sun.

Sitting around one of the wicker tables in the gardens, the five of us have gathered to hang out, drink and enjoy the sunshine. We're sitting at the table nearest the outdoor bar, which means the boys don't have to move as far to get drinks, although there's still quite the queue, because what else do people do at weddings, apart from drink? Why is it that people get so drunk at weddings? Perhaps it's a 'grass is always greener' thing, where those who aren't married drink to forget that they aren't, and those who are married drink to forget that they are.

As people are getting drunker, they're getting chattier. Well, I think it's safe to say that my lot were already pretty chatty, but now their lips are getting looser, and we all know what that means.

'So, how was the stag do?' Ed asks the other boys.

'Didn't you go?' Fi asks him.

'Nah, Matt's mates were rubbish at organising it, they didn't let me know the date until the last minute, and then it was too late to get the time off work, and—'

'More like your missus wouldn't let you,' Clarky interrupts.

'I'm a paediatrician, I can't just pop over to Amsterdam last minute,' Ed replies defensively. 'I can't ask kids to stop being ill so I can get pissed with you muppets.'

It did sound a little like he was making excuses – maybe – but who could blame his wife for not wanting him to go on a stag do in Amsterdam? While I'm sure it does have its cultural worth, there is no way they went there to visit the Anne Frank museum and admire the canals, is there?

'It was good,' Zach says. 'Just, y'know ... the usual stag stuff.'

I don't feel so tense now that it's just me, Ed, Fi, Zach and Clarky. We're all used to each other. We all know to take everything with a good sense of humour and a pinch of salt. I can finally relax, because I don't think there is anything this lot could say that would shock me.

'It took ages for my infection to clear up though,' Clarky muses.

Suddenly all eyes are on him.

'Your infection?' I ask, instantly wishing I hadn't.

'Yeah, the strip club we went to, it wasn't exactly five-star, and there was a little audience participation,' he replies casually.

I briefly glance down at his lower half before meeting his gaze again.

'What? Not down there, Luca,' Clarky says in disgust. 'Where is your mind?'

'Gosh, what was I thinking?' I say sarcastically. 'I hear something as innocent as "audience participation" at a strip club and my mind goes to the gutter. Classic me.'

'I know, right?' he replies, oblivious to my sarcasm.

I look over at Zach, who was also in attendance. The colour has drained from his face and he's sheepishly staring down at his nearly empty glass.

'He had an eye infection,' Fi says.

'That's the one,' Clarky replies.

'How on earth do you know that?' I ask her.

'Because Zach had it too,' she replies angrily. 'He told me he got hit by a paint ball. I knew that wouldn't cause conjunctivitis.'

'It's not as bad as it sounds,' Zach starts in his defence. 'It wasn't a sex thing, it was just a dance club.'

'Nah, the sex show was rubbish,' Clarky chimes in.

'You went to a sex show?' Fi squeaks angrily.

Shit. It doesn't sound like Zach has been all that honest with her about what happened while the boys were in Amsterdam.

'Yeah, but it was crap,' Clarky continues, obliviously. 'So we went to this club.'

'What is wrong with you guys?' I ask. I'm disgusted with them, speaking as their friend, so I can't even imagine how Fi must be feeling right now.

'What?' Clarky replies. He clearly doesn't think anything untoward happened.

'Ed?' I say. Ed has always been our moral compass.

'I'm glad I didn't go,' he laughs. 'That's messed up.'

'Thank you,' I reply.

'It wasn't as bad as it sounds,' Zach says, sounding a little embarrassed. 'I didn't do anything. I don't think Matt actually did anything either, but he must've touched his eye with dirty hands, and because we were all staying in the same youth hostel, sharing a hand towel, it just spread between us all really quickly.'

'It was definitely from the lap dances,' Clarky chimes in. 'It had to be. Well, it wasn't from the beer, was it?'

'Maybe now isn't the best time to talk about it,' I point out, noting a few glances from passing guests who are noticing the building hostility at our table.

Each to their own and all that, but I cannot believe that a bunch of taken men would do such a thing … actually, who am I kidding? Of course I can. I just thought better of my friends, and I absolutely thought better of Tom, who must have organised the whole thing.

Zach, happy to change the subject, starts telling Ed and Clarky about the time they had a real lion on set at work.

'I'm going for a lie down,' Fi says, knocking back the last of her orange juice.

'Are you OK?' I ask.

'I'm fine,' she says. 'It's just the sunshine, and I'm starving. Maybe there will be some biscuits in the room or something.'

'Are you sure you're OK?' I ask again. She doesn't seem herself at all.

'I'm sure,' she replies.

'See you in a bit, babe,' Zach calls after her before turning back to finish his story.

'Shouldn't you go with her, check she's OK?' I suggest.

'Nah, she'll be fine,' he insists.

'Yeah, you know what women are like,' Clarky tells me.

I shake my head in disbelief.

'Why did you do that?' I ask him. 'Did you do that on purpose? To upset her?'

'Of course not,' he replies. 'I was just being honest.'

'You could've been gentler,' Ed points out.

'Yeah, pal, you definitely didn't put the best spin on it,' Zach adds.

As though there was a way to tell this story in a positive light.

'Luca,' a voice snaps me from my thoughts. I look up.

'Pete,' I reply brightly. 'Hi.'

'How's it going?' he asks. 'I feel like I've hardly seen you today.'

'I know,' I reply. 'Every time I look for you, I can't find you.'

'Are these your friends?' he asks.

Oh, God, I think he wants introducing to them. To my drunk, idiot male friends who could probably find a way to ruin this for me in under a minute.

'Yes,' I start, reluctantly, noticing that the boys are listening now. 'This is Ed, Zach and Clarky. Along with Zach's fiancée, Fiona, we all lived with Matt at uni. Lads, this is Pete, he lived with Kat.'

'Nice to meet you all,' Pete says politely.

The boys all say hello and I relax a little because everyone is being civil and polite.

'Not much single totty at this wedding, is there?' Clarky says to him, in a 'lad banter' way that I'm sure he thinks is a perfectly normal way to speak to other men.

Pete laughs, but he seems far too mature and refined for conversations like this.

'Funny you should say that,' Pete replies. 'I came over to see if I could buy Luca a drink.'

'Luca isn't totty,' Clarky scoffs.

'Erm ...' I start, and I might be about to say something unbecoming of the kind of mature young woman I'm trying to show Pete that I am, but Ed comes to my rescue.

'He just means, because we're all old friends, Luca is like a *shister* to him,' Ed says.

'A what?'

'A sister,' I say. 'Yes, indeed.'

'Oh, right,' Pete replies. 'I see what you mean. Well, I promise to take good care of her.'

'Yeah, whatever,' Clarky replies, turning back to Zach. 'Tell us more about the lion.'

'Don't get her pregnant,' Ed calls after us as we walk away. He's a fine one to talk. I think someone needs to stop him drinking because without his wife around, I feel like we're getting flashbacks to uni Ed, who was absolutely fine until he got absolutely hammered. No one wants to see that guy again. He was probably the worst one out of all of us. I definitely prefer Ed as our designated sensible friend.

We walk towards the pond as we chat. It's quite big, with a beautiful wooden bridge that stretches across the widest part.

'Your friends seem funny,' Pete says.

'They definitely think they're funny,' I joke. 'I suppose I could've lived with worse though.'

'Yeah, I used to tell myself that,' he replies. 'I think every house has someone who makes bad jokes, someone who doesn't do the dishes, someone who makes too much noise …'

'Exactly,' I reply as we take a seat on a bench, just far enough from the buzz of the wedding party to get some privacy. 'We became this weird little family unit, with everyone taking on the different roles and, without even knowing it, playing them perfectly.'

'Who was who in your house?' Pete asks, amused.

'Clarky is like an annoying little brother. He was always getting in trouble, he had no idea how to look after himself, and he would annoy us all twenty-four-seven. Zach and Matt were the cool, older brothers – a bit too cool for their own good, perhaps. Fiona was your typical girl next-door type, sensible sister in a house full of annoying boys. And Ed and I were lumbered with the parental roles, taking care of the rest of them, helping them with their work, getting them out of trouble, cooking for them, cleaning up after them …'

'That doesn't sound like much fun,' Pete says.

'You don't realise at the time, that you're looking after everyone,' I admit. 'Anyway, I was lucky, I had two roles. Because when I wasn't playing the mum, I got to be the weird sister, the one who dresses in alternative clothing and listens to loud music. I was positively uncool at uni – by society's standards at least.'

'Spoken like a true alternative,' Pete says with a chuckle.

I laugh.

'I suppose I'm still a bit weird,' I admit in the interest of full disclosure, just in case it wasn't obvious.

'I was a bit of an oddball too,' Pete confesses, pausing to sip his beer. 'I was into trains.'

'Trains?'

'Trains,' he says with a knowing look. A look that suggests he has been met with this type of unimpressed reaction before. 'Everyone else I lived with studied cool, sports-y subjects, and I was writing my dissertation on strategic change in the UK rail network.'

'Oh wow, you *were* a train nerd,' I tease.

'I was,' he says. 'It was weird, being the only person in the house studying engineering when everyone else was studying sports subjects.'

'Yeah, I can imagine. We all studied media, apart from Ed, who did medicine. But of all my kids, he's definitely the one I'm the most proud of,' I joke.

'You've raised him well,' Pete replies.

'Thank you,' I say like a proud mamma, placing a hand on my chest.

It's fun to joke around with Pete, but I do like to think I played a part in Ed turning out as well as he has, and I am actually really proud of him for getting the job he wanted and the family he's always dreamed of.

'Well, you seem cool now, and I'm cool now,' he points out. 'I save the planet.'

'Well then, you're practically a superhero now. I think I speak for the entire planet when I say thank you.'

'It's a tough job, but someone has to do it,' he says in what I'd imagine is his best superhero voice. 'We have a lot in common, don't we?'

'I guess we do,' I reply with a smile.

Pete twists his body so that he's facing me. When I look at him, he slowly raises a hand and places it lightly on the side of my cheek. We hold eye contact for a moment before Pete closes his eyes and leans in to kiss me. I'm just about to meet him in the middle when I notice something out the corner of my eye …

Chapter 16

Then – 15th May 2009

First of all – and this is something I need to make crystal clear – I don't think I'm fat. Sure, I'm not the skinniest girl in the world, they're not going to be putting me on any Victoria's Secret catwalks anytime soon, but I would say that I was appropriately curvy for a girl of my height, and completely happy with it. Sure, I might not be very strong and, OK, I'm probably softer to the touch than I ought to be, but I'm happy as I am.

However … in the interest of making an effort with my boyfriend, I am on a strict diet with a hardcore exercise regime. Alan says the workout we're doing isn't actually hardcore at all, but it feels hardcore to me, so that's what I'm calling it. The thing is, I'm only doing it to make him happy, to try and find some common ground between us, so when Alan isn't around, I'm pretty much eating whatever I want. I know, that makes me sound bad, but this way everyone gets what they want. Alan feels like he's helping me be a better, healthier person and I am exercising more, but still eating a bit of what I like when no one is looking.

Tonight, what I like is Maltesers, but as I gleefully toss them into my mouth, I knock the bag over and watch as they all spill out onto the floor and roll under the sofa. Alan is coming over later to pick me up on the way to the gym, and if he sees Maltesers all over the floor, he's going to know I've been breaking my diet. At first I think, so what? I don't even need to be on a diet. But then I think again, and I know that he's only trying to help me be a better person. I should absolutely pick them anyway, because what kind of housemate leaves food on the floor? (Spoiler: Clarky)

I pull the sofa out a little more, enough so that I can crawl behind it and begin scooping up Maltesers, placing them back in the bag. Such a waste. If I didn't know for a fact that no one has vacuumed this carpet since we moved in, I might still eat them. I'm about to crawl back out when I hear the living room door open.

'Just take a seat in here,' I hear Zach say. 'I need to pop upstairs and get changed.'

It can't be Alan already, can it? It's way too early.

Terrified of being caught with chocolate, I decide to stay where I am

'So are you just going to ignore me all night?' I hear Cleo moan.

'I'm not ignoring you,' I hear Tom reply. 'I just don't know what to say to you right now.'

'Say you forgive me,' she says.

'Why would I need to forgive you, if you're telling me nothing happened?'

I feel my heart jump up into my mouth. No matter what, I absolutely cannot come out from behind the sofa now, not now I've heard this much of their conversation. They'll think I stayed here to earwig – or even if they do believe my contraband chocolate story, they'll still think I'm a weirdo for listening.

'Because you seem to think I did something wrong,' she replies angrily.

It's so weird, hiding behind the sofa, only listening to their voices. Cleo sounds irritated and exhausted from having to explain herself. There isn't much sincerity in her voice or conviction in her argument. Tom on the other hand sounds upset, a little angry, and completely suspicious. I imagine him narrowing his gorgeous brown eyes and furrowing his brow as he tries to work out if he's buying what she's selling. Cleo, I imagine, is doing that thing she does, that gentle bat of her hand. I've noticed her use it a lot, to dismiss suggestions or people or facts. She's probably combining it with that eye roll of hers, the one that really makes you feel small when it's for your benefit.

'You were sitting on that bloke's lap,' he reminds her.

'Nathan? I was just asking him where we should visit in Bali,' she replies, as though there's nothing wrong with that.

'Did you need to sit on him to ask that?' he says angrily.

'Why are you acting so jealous?'

'I'm not acting jealous, I'm being angry. You can't just go around sitting on other blokes, flirting with them. Not just because it's upsetting for me – your boyfriend – but because you were leading him on.'

'It's 2009. Women can sit on whoever they want, without being obliged to have sex with them.'

'That's not what I'm getting at and you know it,' he replies. 'What would you say if I, I don't know, I went upstairs, grabbed Luca, and sat her down on my lap?'

A jolt travels through my body at the mention of my name. Why would he say *my* name?

'I'd say you must have strong legs,' she says dryly.

I feel the anger prickling away inside me. What I want to do is jump up from behind the sofa and have a go at her, but I can't. With every second I stay hidden, it gets harder for me to come out.

'Don't,' Tom replies. 'Don't do that.'

'What?' Cleo says casually. 'You brought her into this … for some reason …'

'She's my friend,' he says in a long, drawn-out way that makes it seem like this is something he says a lot.

'And this guy was just my friend,' she points out. 'You're not the only person allowed friends of the opposite sex.'

'Are you jealous?' he asks her.

Cleo doesn't say anything, but her silence speaks volumes.

'Cleo?' he persists.

'The other night, when we were talking about Luca, you said—'

'Right, we're ready to go,' Zach interrupts them. His sentence starts off upbeat, but halfway through he realises he's walked in on something. 'Oh, er ...' He pauses. 'I can go away for a bit, give you guys a minute to finish your conversation?'

Yes! Please! I need to hear the end of this sentence.

'No, it's fine,' she insists. 'Tom is just being silly, aren't you?'

Another pause.

'Yeah, no worries mate, we're fine,' Tom insists.

'OK then, let's go,' Zach says.

I wait until I hear the front door close before popping my head up slowly from behind the sofa. Satisfied I'm alone, I walk around and plonk myself back down.

I can't believe my name came up while they were arguing, but what was Cleo going to say? What did Tom say when they were talking about me?

As I ponder their argument, I realise I've started eating the Maltesers that I picked up from the floor. It serves me right for breaking my diet, I suppose.

Chapter 17

Now

There is a toddler on a mission charging towards the pond, at full, wobbly toddler speed. I think she has her eye on one of the ducks on the water, and she's heading straight for it.

I don't even think about it. I snatch myself away from Pete and race towards the child, snatching her up just before she hits the water.

'Whoa there,' I say, even though it's a child and not a horse. 'What are you doing here?'

'Chocolate,' the pink-tutu-clad girl replies. Ahh, a child after my own heart.

'OK. Let's find your mummy or daddy.'

As we make our way back towards the party, we bump into Fiona.

'Wow, you two haven't wasted anytime,' she jokes.

'Har-har,' I reply. 'Do you know who this little monster belongs to?'

'No idea,' she replies.

'Well, whoever it is, they weren't keeping a very close eye on you, were they?' I say to my new best friend, in that weird voice adults only use for talking to kids. I suppose this is the first airing mine has had. 'She was trying to join the ducks in the pond.'

'The kid was near the pond?' I hear a voice coming from behind me.

'She's fine, Alan. Don't worry.'

I keep forgetting Alan is lurking around.

'It's Al now, not Alan,' he reminds me. 'And she shouldn't be near the water, I was talking to the old chap behind the bar who says they have natrix natrix here.'

'They have what?' I ask. I don't even know what words he is saying to me.

'Water snakes,' he replies. 'Around this time of year, the babies will be hatching.'

'Are they dangerous?' Fi asks in a weak voice. She's like me, she doesn't like creatures. We spent many a night in the old house armed with cans of hairspray and rolled up Cosmopolitan magazines after spotting a spider.

'No, they're not dangerous,' Al explains. 'But they do secrete a garlic-smelling fluid from their anal gland if they feel threatened.'

'Oh my God, why did I have to ask?' Fi says softly to herself.

'Erm … I'm just going to go check in with a few people,' Pete says. It sounds like he can't wait to get away from this conversation. I hope he doesn't think I am affiliated with Anal Alan in any way.

'Oh, OK,' I reply.

'We're just not meant to spend time together, are we?' Pete says with a half-hearted chuckle. 'I'll find you later?'

The fact that he hasn't written me off yet puts me at ease.

'That would be great.'

Once he's gone, Al doesn't waste any time.

'You know, I always thought we'd have kids,' he tells me.

'Wow,' Fi blurts.

'Al, we were together for a few months when we were like 20,' I remind him. 'We haven't even spoken in ten years.'

'Well, I did try and add you on Facebook *years* ago,' he insists.

'I didn't see that.' I absolutely did see that. I just didn't accept it.

'Do you know what your problem is?' Al starts, but I don't let him finish.

'We need to get this one back to her parents,' I tell him. 'Can this wait?'

Al shrugs his massive shoulders.

'I don't know, Luca. *Can* it wait?' Al asks this question like it's the most profound, philosophical thing.

I push the little girl further up on to my hip. I hadn't realised she was slipping down. These things are heavy, when you hold them for too long.

'Christ, Al is still so boring, isn't he?' Fi says once he's gone.

'What, you don't find garlic snake butt secretion fun?' I reply sarcastically.

I suddenly remember the toddler in my arms might be listening, but she's oblivious, her eyes fixated on the clouds as we walk.

'Hey, I thought you were going for a lie down?' I say.

'I was going to get a break from Zach,' she replies. 'And to try find some food, but there's nothing in the rooms. No mini bar, no complimentary biscuits – nothing. I'm so hungry I'm dizzy.'

'That's rubbish. I'm starving too. I'm also worried about the boys drinking so much when they've hardly eaten,' I reply, as my mother mode kicks in. 'Tell you what, I'll meet you back at the table and we'll figure something out, I'll just go return trouble to her parents.'

'OK, sure,' Fi replies. 'I thought kids weren't invited? That's what Ed said.'

'Oh yeah,' I reply. 'Maybe don't tell him.'

'Sure,' she replies with a giggle.

'Right, you,' I say to my new friend, as I rotate in the centre of the lawn. 'Can you show me which one is your mummy or daddy?'

As I twirl, the little girl looks like she's giving real thought to my question – that or the twirling is making her feel sick.

'Are any of those people your mummy and daddy?' I ask, pointing to some adults sitting at tables.

The little girl looks over but there isn't a glimmer of recognition on her face.

'What about over here?' I say as we head towards the bar.

I notice us catch a woman's eye. She looks at us for a second before hurrying over.

'Hello,' she says. 'Is there a reason you have my child?'

'I found her,' I reply, unsure of the woman's tone.

'You found her?' she asks. It suddenly occurs to her to take the child from me.

'She was about to fall in the pond,' I say bluntly. 'And apparently there are snakes in there.'

I don't think this woman needs the gory details.

'Well, she's supposed to be with her nanny. I don't know, you can't get the help,' she says, muttering to herself as she wanders off with her child.

And … you're welcome.

As I approach the toilets in the bar, I can't help but overhear a heated conversation. I stop at the end of a corridor and peep down. Tom and Cleo are arguing, and I know that I should mind my own business, but I can't resist lingering behind the wall, trying to hear what they're talking about.

'… because I'm realising now, more than ever, that life is short,' Tom tells her. 'Don't you think?'

'Yes, I do,' she replies. 'Now, more than ever, I care about being happy, about Sunny being happy.'

'I need to do what's right …' he starts, but I don't get to hear what he says before someone invades my personal space. I don't suppose I needed to hear much more, I should be happy, that he's doing the right thing. He has a child to think about. And I didn't want him anyway, did I? I don't want someone who plans a stag do where everyone comes back physically – and purposefully – mutilated, do I? What a liability. And then there's the fact that he drives like an idiot, in his environment-killing car. With every new thing I learn about the new Tom, I realise he isn't the Tom I thought I was in love with all those years ago. He's no Pete. He's barely an Alan. Speaking of which …

'Luca,' he sings as he places a hand on each of my shoulders and shakes me, I imagine in some kind of weird attempt at dancing with me, but it's just uncomfortable. 'You can't avoid me all day.'

'I'm pretty sure I can,' I say with a laugh, although I'm not kidding.

'The way we ended … it never quite sat right with me,' he starts. 'I think you were hasty, breaking up with me when you did – like you did. I always thought you'd call.'

'Alan, that was years ago,' I say.

'Al,' he corrects me. 'Al Atlantic.'

'Right.'

'Don't you think it's fate, that we're here together now?' he asks. 'Like Tom said in his speech.'

'It isn't fate – it isn't even coincidence,' I tell him. 'We're both friends with Matt, it's his wedding …'

'Look, I know we had our problems back then, but we're both adults now and—'

'Hi,' Tom interrupts us.

'There you are,' I say. 'We've got the thing to do, with the others.'

It only takes Tom a split second.

'Yeah, the thing. We doing it now?' he replies.

'Yeah, let's go.'

'Wait,' Al says, placing an arm in front of me. 'Please can we talk about this?'

'I don't think she wants to talk about it, buddy,' Tom says.

Alan is no threat to me, I know that, but it's nice to see that

Tom is still willing to protect me.

'Says who?' Al asks, squaring up to him (or down to him, I suppose).

Oh God, here we go. I'm trapped here, between the devil and the shallow blue sea, and they're going to start fighting if I don't do something. Tom and Alan never did get on.

'OK, right, we need to go do this thing,' I say, pushing in between them. 'But Alan – Al – I promise we will talk about this later, OK?'

'OK,' he says, giving me a firm nod. He turns to Tom. 'But I'm keeping my eye on you.'

'Oh please,' Tom says as soon as Al is out of earshot. 'The only thing he's keeping an eye on is the mirror.'

'Wow, you're so brave when he can't hear you,' I tease.

'That's true,' Tom says. 'He could kill me easily with one punch, or just his fake tan fumes to be fair.'

I laugh. 'Thanks for the excuse,' I say, turning to walk away.

'Luca, wait,' he says. I stop in my tracks. 'You've got some brown stuff on the back of your dress.'

'What?' I say, spinning around like a dog chasing its tail, trying to get a look at it. I can just about see it. 'Oh my God, I really hope that's chocolate.'

'How would you get chocolate on your back?'

'*How* would I get the alternative on my back?' I ask.

'I saw you slink off with that guy earlier ...'

'And did you also see me carrying a toddler around?' I ask angrily. 'Seeing as how you're keeping an overly close eye on me.'

'I did actually, yeah. I saw you dancing on the grass with her. You looked cute together.'

Tom smiles, and I puff air out of my cheeks because not only do I struggle to keep the butterflies in my stomach calm when I see that smile, but it feels like he is really messing with my head today.

'We weren't dancing, we were trying to find her mum,' I insist.

'Whatever, you were dancing. You might've been looking for her mum, but you were being cute.'

I ignore him, grab my phone from my bag and punch a quick message to Fiona to tell her I need to pop into the ladies' to clean my dress but that I'll be right there.

'I need to go clean this,' I say.

'Need a hand?'

'No thanks.'

'How are you going to reach?' he ask with a cheeky laugh.

'Just fine.'

'Show me,' he suggests, knowing full well I can't reach my own back without taking my dress off.

I sigh.

'Just check there's no one in there; I'll pop in, clean it for you, and then I'll leave you alone,' he suggests.

'Thanks,' I say, annoyed to be accepting his help, but appreciative none the less.

I step into the loos first. Thankfully there's no one there – the other toilets, nearer the outside area, are much busier – so I open the door and tell Tom that the coast is clear.

'Oh my God,' he shrieks with horror as he begins to dab my dress clean.

'What?'

'It's just chocolate,' he says, his face dissolving into a smile. 'And now that I look at it, it looks like a little handprint.'

'Occupational hazard,' I tell him.

'Working in PR?'

'No, being a bridesmaid – and the only one who isn't pregnant. I'm getting lumbered with all sorts of jobs when, really, I should just be sat, getting drunk, moaning about being single.'

'You're not seeing anyone then?' Tom asks casually.

'Only the Deliveroo guy.

Tom looks confused by my joke.

'I made that sound like I'm banging the Deliveroo guy, didn't

I?' I laugh. 'It was supposed to be a joke about how single and lonely I am … like, the only person I see is the person who drops off my food.'

Tom laughs, but then his face falls.

'I'm fine though,' I say. 'That came out wrong. I'm not lonely.'

'Hello,' Fi says, amused to be walking in on the two of us alone in the toilets. 'Gosh, I feel like I'm at uni again.'

'Tom is just cleaning my dress,' I tell her.

'I haven't heard it called that before,' she jokes. 'Anyway, we were thinking of sneaking out for half an hour to grab a quick McDonald's – there's one at a service station not too far from here.'

'You're sneaking out of a wedding to go to McDonald's?' Tom asks.

'It's not as bad as it sounds,' I assure him. 'Bloody Clarky spiked our food with chilli and ruined it. We're all starving.'

'Can I come?' he asks.

'Of course you can,' says Fi. 'I'll buy your silence with nuggets.'

'Throw in a McFlurry and you've got yourself a deal.'

'How are we getting there?' I ask.

'Well, I'm sober, so I can drive, but now that Tom is coming there's too many of us to fit in my car,' she says.

'I can drive as well,' Tom says. 'I haven't actually had a drink yet.'

'Oh, great,' Fi replies. 'Well, I'll take the drunk boys, in case one of them throws up. You can take Luca. She's usually clean. We'll meet you in the car park. Just as soon as you're done "cleaning her dress".'

If I didn't know better, I'd think Fi was setting me up.

Chapter 18

Then – 17th April 2009

'You know I'll always love you, no matter what,' Alan assures me.

'Right,' I reply.

'And you know I'd never want to offend you,' he continues.

'OK …'

Why do I feel like he's about to do just that?

'I just don't want to see you get fat.'

I feel my jaw drop in astonishment.

'You don't want to see me get fat?' I say back to him, just in case I've made some kind of mistake. Did he really just say that?

'Why don't we go for a run?' he suggests.

'First of all, because you always tell me that cardio kills your gains – whatever that means – and second of all, because it's 9 p.m. on a Friday night, it's chucking it down with rain, I've spent all day working on a stressful group project, and now all I want to do it order a pizza and curl up in front of a movie.'

'A pizza here, a cheeseburger there … Combined with a sedentary lifestyle, you'll get fat. It's a certainty. And all you want to do is watch movies.'

When I first started seeing Alan, his passion for fitness was something to be admired. Now, it's starting to get on my nerves. At first it was just small annoyances, like I'd want to spend time with him but he'd have plans to go to the gym. Then he started refusing to go to places to eat if they didn't serve food that didn't 'fit his macros', whatever that means. But now I feel like the camel's back is about to break, because he's doing things to embarrass me or make me feel fat – like telling me to watch how many calorific drinks I consume at parties or when he begrudges me a pizza and a sit down.

On the night we met, I thought maybe we had some things in common, but as time has gone by, I have realised that I was wrong. One of the first things that impressed me about Alan was the fact that he was a Baz Luhrmann fan. It has since come to my attention that he was faking it, and simply read his name off the DVD box to try and impress me – which explains why he couldn't pronounce his name, and why he seemed so confused by people knowing all the words to an Elton John song in France in 1900.

'And don't think I didn't see that bar of chocolate in the fridge,' he continues. 'I'd bet everything I had on that being yours.'

'So what if it is mine?' I reply. 'I'll eat whatever I want. I'll eat the whole bar if I feel like it. I'll eat everything in the fridge.'

'I'm just pointing out that maybe you eat too much, and you definitely drink too much.'

'I'm a student,' I remind him. 'It comes with the territory.'

Alan rolls his eyes.

For a few minutes, we sit in silence. I aimlessly scroll on my phone, avoiding talking to him, before I realise that, you know what, in his own way, I'm sure he only has my best interests at heart. He thinks he's looking out for me, so maybe I shouldn't be so hard on him.

'There's this food festival thing in town tomorrow,' I tell him. 'Loads of pop-up street food vendors, bars, entertainment. A few of us were talking about going if you fancy it?'

'I've got a big day in the gym planned tomorrow,' he says.

Still, I persist. 'Can't you sack it off just for one day and come and have fun with me?' I say, in my flirtiest voice. 'I'll give you a cardio workout that won't kill your gains, if you know what I mean.'

I absolutely don't know what I mean, but it sounds kind of sexy, and even if it doesn't, the fact that I'm running my hand slowly up and down his chest should be a big giveaway.

'Luca, do you think Lou Ferrigno got to where he is by taking days off?' Alan says, pushing my hand away.

'Honestly, Alan, I have no idea who that is,' I reply. 'To be completely honest, I rarely have any idea what you're talking about.'

'That's why I'm trying to educate you,' he says.

'Or maybe, that might be why we shouldn't be together,' I blurt.

Before Alan has chance to say anything, Matt and Tom walk into the living room.

'Oh, sorry,' Matt says when he notices us sitting on the sofa. 'You two having a quiet night in? I'm just getting changed, then we're heading out. I told Tom to wait for me in here but …'

'Don't be daft, it's fine,' I insist.

'Won't be long,' Matt says, before dashing off upstairs.

'So, how are you two?' Tom asks, taking a seat on the sofa opposite us.

'Not too bad,' I reply. 'How are you?'

Awkward, awkward small talk. I hate it.

'I'm not bad. Matt has talked me into a lads' night out.'

'No Cleo?' I reply, and instantly wish I hadn't. It makes me sound like I care – which I do, but I don't want him to know that. But maybe they've broken up, and this is Matt's way of cheering him up? Recently, Tom and Cleo have been over here a lot. It's like they're inseparable, and between Matt being Tom's best mate, and Zach and Fifi going on double dates with them, I am sick of the sight of them. The jealousy eats me up in side. Seeing them together, all over each other, hanging out in my house, with my best friends, is as horrendous as it sounds.

'She's visiting a friend at Leeds,' he says. 'She's staying over there, rather than catching the last train.'

'Ah, OK.'

'Why don't you come for a drink with us?' Tom suggests. It seems like he's only talking to me, until he quickly glances over at Alan. 'Both of you.'

'I thought you said it was a lads' night?' Alan says.

'Luca can be an honorary lad,' Tom replies with a laugh.

'Nah, Luca already said she doesn't want to go out this evening,' Alan replies.

'No, I said I didn't want to go for a run. I'd happily go for a drink.'

Alan shoots me a look, as if to say: I told you that you drink too much.

'Nah, don't fancy it,' Alan says.

'No worries,' Tom replies. 'You guys coming to the food festival tomorrow?'

'Nah, got the gym,' Alan says.

My God, even his voice is boring.

'Are you coming, Luca?' Tom asks.

Now there's an enticing thought. Going with Tom, who I'd actually have fun with, rather than going with Alan, who would just complain the whole time and try to convince me not to eat anything.

'I know Cleo won't mind if you hang out with us,' he adds.

I cannot think of anything worse than hanging out with Tom and Cleo for the day.

'Sorry,' I say. 'I said I'd go to the gym with Alan tomorrow.'

'You did?' Alan replies in disbelief.

'I did,' I insist, even though I absolutely didn't. 'You were just telling me how I need to go.'

I probably shouldn't have made that little dig in front of Tom, but I'm still seething over it.

'Mate, you told her she needs to go to the gym?' Tom replies.

'I want the best for her,' Alan tells him. 'And you … I'm happy to help you work on that emerging beer gut.'

I see Tom raise his eyebrows.

'You know, I think I'm going to wait for Matt outside,' he says, pulling himself to his feet. 'See you around, Luca.'

'Yeah, see you later,' I call after him. I wait until he's gone before ticking Alan off. 'Alan, that was so rude.'

'I was just trying to be helpful.'

'No, you were being rude,' I correct him. 'There is absolutely nothing wrong with the way Tom looks. He's tall, he's fit – he's absolutely gorgeous.'

'Oh, well, if you're so in love with him, why am I your boyfriend and not him?' he snaps.

I honestly ask myself that question every single day.

Chapter 19

Now

When it comes to men, it takes a lot to impress me. Muscles don't do much for me – I learned that being with Alan. And expensive clothes don't mean much to me, because a lot of money doesn't always equal a lot of style. It's very rare that a man's job impresses me either, unless it's something he has worked hard for, that makes a huge difference to society … but that's not exactly something that is gender specific, is it? That's just a good quality for a person to have anyway, male or female.

I'm sitting here, in the passenger's seat of Tom's flashy car, waiting to set off on our quick trip to McDonald's so that we can enjoy the rest of the day without our stomachs rumbling. But before we set off, Tom reaches for a button in between us, and as he holds it down I watch the roof of his car start to disappear. Does he honestly think showing me his convertible will impress me? Because – I hate to admit it – he's absolutely right. When I first saw his car, I couldn't believe what a tosser he was, but now that I'm in it, watching the roof disappear inside the car, feeling the warm sun on my head, and eventually the cool breeze as we get moving, I can't deny it, I love it.

I glance at the speedometer, to see if we're going fast, or whether it just feels like it on these quiet country roads. It's such an adrenaline rush, driving fast, feeling the change in sensation that you get with a convertible. It's the breeze, it's the sun, it's the fleeting shade of the trees. I've got goose bumps.

'So, what do you think?' Tom asks, quickly glancing at me to gauge my reaction before turning his attention back to the road.

'Meh,' I say casually, with a shrug of my shoulders.

'Meh?' he echoes. 'I even put you a power ballads playlist on.'

I did notice that the (also impressive) sound system was pumping out some vintage Whitesnake, but does he really think I'm that easy?

'Sure, you look cool ... but do you even care what you're doing to the environment in this thing? Like, oh, girls think you're so dreamy because you have a flashy car, but do you really need a car this powerful? Unless you're overcompensating for something ...'

Tom snorts with laughter.

'Three things, Luca,' he starts, pausing for a second to laugh again. 'First of all, this is an electric car – so the environment is safe. Second of all, I don't own this car. I couldn't afford a car like this, it's a prototype that I'm driving for work, so that I can write a review. That's why I was stretching its legs last night, because I thought the road would be quiet. And finally, you got pretty up close and personal with me that time we slow danced, so you know I'm not overcompensating for anything.'

'Oh,' is about all I can manage to say. I feel every drop of blood in my body rush to my cheeks. I look out of the window to hide my red face.

I remember that night, back at uni, when we danced together. It was the night I thought we were finally going to get our relationship back on track. Spoiler alert: it didn't happen.

'Not that I drive an old banger, I do have a cool car – not a red Polo with a dinosaur decal on the back,' he adds quickly. 'And it's a hybrid, so you and your newfound passion for the environment don't need to worry …'

I ignore his blatant swipe at my car. I don't care what he says, I love my red Polo. And I bought it used, so it came with the dinosaur sticker on the back. I removed one of his claws, to test the waters, but it's been on there so long the paint has discoloured underneath. So that's that, they dinosaur is staying.

'I have always cared about the environment,' I remind him.

'Oh yeah, I remember the six days you were a vegetarian at uni.' He laughs.

'Erm, it was nine days, actually, and it was your fault I failed. It was the day before we all went home for Christmas, when you took me to McDonald's for chicken nuggets.'

'And here we are again,' he points out. 'On the way to McDonald's, for chicken nuggets.'

'Yep, my life is one, long, cruel Groundhog Day.'

'And here we are again,' he jokes, chuckling to himself. 'On the way to McDonald's, for chicken nuggets.'

'Hilarious,' I reply.

'So, I had a chat with Fi, and the plan is to nip through the drive-thru and then head straight back to the hotel before anyone realises we're missing,' he says, changing the subject. 'Although if Matt keeps drinking at the rate he is, I'm not sure he'll be able to see straight enough to realise we're not there anyway.'

'Yeah, or maybe if he gets another eye infection,' I reply, 'he won't realise we're not there because he won't be able to see. Or you can say you have an eye infection, and that's why you wandered off in the wrong direction.'

I hate myself as soon as the words leave my lips. I hate saying and doing anything that makes me seem like I care about him, or about what he does. If he wants to plan a debauched stag party where everyone goes to sex shows and comes home with conjunctivitis, then that's his jam. It is nothing to do with me.

'Weird,' he replies.

'Erm, yeah, it *is* weird,' I say.

Tom frowns.

'I feel like I'm missing something ...'

'I heard about the stag do,' I admit.

'So ...' he replies.

'So ... I suppose I thought more of you.'

'I couldn't really help it, could I?'

'What?'

'It's not like I did it on purpose.'

'How do you wind up going to an "audience participation" strip club by accident?' I ask, confused.

'Luca, what on earth are you talking about?' he asks.

'The stag do,' I say slowly, starting to get annoyed.

'Yeah, I didn't go, I had to work,' he says.

'Ohh,' I reply. 'I thought you organised it.'

'You thought *I* organised "audience participation" for a man who was about to get married?' he asks, a combination of amused and offended. 'You don't think much of me, do you?'

'I try not to,' I reply.

Tom laughs.

'Well, I would say I'm sorry I missed it, but it sounds like it was weird.'

'It was,' I reply, completely mortified.

We make the last minute of the journey to the drive-thru in silence.

'Right, what can I get you?' he asks.

'Some chicken nuggets would be great,' I reply.

'Wow, it really is just like old times,' Tom replies. 'Maybe this time I won't bottle it when it comes to kissing you.' He laughs, to let me know that he's joking.

'You wish,' I snort.

Five minutes later we're parked up outside McDonald's, wolfing down our food so that we can hurry back.

'I kind of do,' he says.

'You kind of do what?' I reply as I suck ketchup off my fingers in a rather unladylike way.

'Wish I'd kissed you,' he says.

'Tom, don't,' I say. 'Don't start.'

'Luca …'

'Come on, it was years ago. Let's not talk about it.'

'I know, but—'

'Tom,' I say, cutting him off. 'Stop it. We were kids, it was years ago, we've both moved on.'

'Oh,' he says. 'So you *are* seeing someone?'

'I am,' I lie, although I don't know why. I think just the thought of him getting back with Cleo has rubbed me up the wrong way again, and with that in mind, for him to be sat here, saying he wishes he'd kissed me … that's despicable really, I'd be gutted if I were her.

We both reach for the same chicken nugget at the same time and awkwardly bump hands. Our hands stay touching for a few seconds more than is normal before I quickly pull my hand away.

'If you hadn't just told me what you told me, I might've tried to kiss you,' he says.

And the worst thing is that, if I hadn't just told him what I told him, there's a chance I might've let him.

Chapter 20

Then – New Year's Eve 2008, 7.45 p.m.

'Thanks for picking me up,' I say.

'You are absolutely welcome,' Zach replies.

'Am I?' I laugh. 'Even though you're only stuck in this traffic because you came out of your way to get me, because I wound up arriving much later than planned?'

Being late may seem like an unreliable quality, but for me, I think my constant lateness is what makes me consistent. You can always count on me to be late and, as such, you always know when I'm going to arrive – when I said I would, just a bit later.

So, obviously I'm late arriving back in Manchester after Christmas (even though I only live on the outskirts). My train was late (which actually is completely out of my control), and now I'm late picking up my costume from the fancy dress shop I hired it from.

'What's your costume?' Zach asks me, making small talk while we're stuck in the traffic that always surrounds the station.

'Catwoman,' I tell him. 'I need to pick it up from the costume shop on Park Road.

'Don't they close at 8?' he replies.

'Yep,' I reply. 'I'm even late for a shop that is staying open late.'

Zach laughs.

'Matt said he was going there to grab something – something about not having any red spandex, although you know he's got all the other colours. Shall I ask him to pick up your outfit for you?'

'That would be great,' I say, sighing with relief. I was so worried I wasn't going to make it in time. I know it's not important, that it's just a silly costume, but tonight is the first time I've seen Tom since before Christmas and I want everything to be perfect. I want to be the Catwoman to his Batman because that's what we said we'd do and, who knows, maybe I'll just go for it, and pin him down and lick him a la Michelle Pfeiffer in *Batman Returns*.

'He says he'll do it,' Zach says after tapping a few buttons on his phone, holstered by the radio in front of him. As his hand hovers near the button, he decides to turn some music on. 'This will get us in the party mood.'

'"I Kissed a Girl?"' I say as Katy Perry blasts out of the speakers. 'It's not going to be that kind of party, buddy.'

'Well, maybe it will for me,' he laughs. 'A little bird told me that maybe you and Tom might be hanging out tonight …'

'We're just going to see what happens,' I say, a little embarrassed. Fifi must have told him.

'But you want him to be your N-Y-E kiss, right?'

'Maybe,' I reply. 'Speaking of little birds, when are you going to grow a pair and kiss Fifi?'

I notice Zach's jaw drop.

'Wh-what?'

'Don't "wh-what" me,' I reply. 'You're obviously crazy about her.'

'Is it that obvious?' he replies.

'Only if you have eyes or ears,' I reply.

'Well, it's funny you should say that, but I did tell her there was a girl I liked, and that I was going to find her on New Year's

Eve and tell her exactly how I felt …'

'Aren't you brave?' I tell him as a smile spreads across my face. 'But, wait, you told her it was her, right?'

'Well, it's obvious, isn't it?'

'It might not be,' I tell him. 'I would have made it crystal clear.'

'I was trying to be romantic and sexy,' he replies, before pausing for thought. 'I should've told her it was her, shouldn't I?'

I nod my head. 'Well, we're nearly there,' I tell him.

'Maybe we'll both get what we want tonight, eh?' he says.

'I'll drink to that,' I reply.

I feel my phone vibrating on my lap.

'It's Ed,' I tell Zach before answering. 'Hey Ed, how's the party going?'

'Luca,' he sobs. 'Luca, you've got to come quick. You've got to help me.'

'Ed, slow down, what's wrong?' I ask.

Zach looks over at me, worried. I shrug my shoulders.

'I've made a terrible mistake,' he says. 'I … I think I've hit someone.'

Chapter 21

Now

The men I met at university have a lot to answer for.

First of all, there were my housemates. Between them they've made enough girls shed enough tears to fill an Olympic swimming pool. Matt was a player, always with an eye on one conquest or another (the other was usually her friend). Zach, before he got together with Fiona, had some major commitment issues, which is why they took so long to get together. And then there was Clarky, who wasn't exactly a hit with the ladies, but he wanted to be one of the boys, so he was always happy to move in on the 'unattractive' friend.

The bottom line is that, on a daily basis, I was watching them all try to pull, by any means necessary, with the most unromantic intentions. This kicked off my trust issues with men, for sure.

Then there was the guy who invited himself into my room one night during a house party – he didn't exactly show his gender in a positive light.

And then there's Tom. Tom is responsible for my biggest problem at all … I can't trust a man not to hurt me, and it's affected every single one of my short-lived relationships since.

I know, it was ten years ago, but we had a slow and meaningful build up. He saved me, he didn't take advantage of me, he was nothing but an incredible guy. He told me he had feelings for me and I let myself fall for him. I was crazy about him. I stopped telling myself it was just wishful thinking. I *knew* we were going to be together and then Cleo came along ... Tiny, squeaky, pretty little Cleo, with her whimsical ways, her lust for traveling the word, her easy confidence, her undeniable sex appeal. Next to her I felt like this giant, damaged weirdo. He might not have known who she was when he kissed her, but he did after, and he chose her over me. That's the bottom line. He chose a girl he had just met, who kissed him without even knowing him, over me, and then, just to stick the knife in a little deeper, he stayed with her, no matter how much they argued, or how controlling she would be over his life.

That's why I have trust issues, because the men in my life have always been so untrustworthy.

I can't seem to help myself, painting this picture of Tom as the big, bad wolf in my head. Without really thinking about it, I naturally assume the worst of him – but it's his fault.

I hate that I can feel myself softening towards him. I hate that I get upset when I think badly of him. I hate that I feel even more upset when I realise that the good guy I fell for at uni is still in there. I hate that I'm beginning to thaw out and then I find something else that makes me mad at him again. I hate that he's getting back with Cleo. I hate that I think he's flirting with me – I hate that I can't tell for sure if he is or he isn't. I hate that I care that he's getting back with Cleo. Most of all, I hate how much hate is in me right now.

All this goes to show that Tom bloody Hoult is still under my skin, still stuck in my head, and I have no idea how to get him out. I feel like a stupid, deluded teenager again, and I'm a 31-year-old woman. This is ridiculous.

I get out of Tom's car, with a quick thank you, a swift goodbye, and the intention of avoiding him for the rest of the day. Because it is just a day, and then I get to go back to my life. So what if he's in Manchester now? It sounds like he has been for a while, and it's a big city. It's not like I'm going to run into him.

My thoughts stop me in my tracks for a moment, because I'm counting down the seconds until I can get back to my life, but there isn't really much waiting for me. I don't do much apart from work – and work doesn't exactly leave me feeling fulfilled – or spend time at home, alone, binge-watching boxsets. I have no romantic leads, I don't have any real friends, not really. I can't even get a pet to keep me company, because it goes against the terms of the lease on the flat that I'm working all the hours God sends to be able to afford to stay in. Still, I'm a grown woman, and my life can still get better, if I work hard, and try harder to meet new people (but, come on, it's pretty much impossible to meet new people as an adult). I'm sure it beats being here though, and I'll be home before I know it. Then maybe I'll tackle how I can change my life … or I'll just say I will, like I do after every setback, or on every New Year's Eve, and then do nothing about it. That one sounds more like me.

Maybe it's time to give in, to start drinking like everybody else. Perhaps that's the only way to get through a wedding with your sanity intact.

'I'll get this,' Pete interrupts as I attempt to pay for my drink at the outdoor bar.

'Thank you,' I say.

Gosh, it feels nice to see a friendly face.

'But only if you hang out with me. I feel like you're avoiding me,' he says with a playful frown.

'I will absolutely hang out with you,' I reply. 'And I promise you, I am not avoiding you.'

Pete buys himself another beer before we find an empty table and chairs in the garden. The only free spot is at a low table, with beanbag chairs.

I wiggle around on my beanbag for a moment, trying to get comfortable and protect my modesty.

'This is all so much easier without heels,' I confess.

'It's nice to see that you've taken them off,' he tells me. 'So many women are a slave to their heels. Everyone here would have a lot more fun if they were more like you and took them off.'

I don't correct him, I just smile. Well, right now he's commending me for wearing trainers, but if I tell him the truth – that I took my heels off and lost them – it's going to make me look like an idiot.

'Are you having a nice time?' I ask him, changing the subject.

'I am,' he says. 'It's lovely here, isn't it?'

'Gorgeous,' I reply.

It's been a long, hot summer so far. Here in the hotel gardens, the grass is a vivid shade of green. The flowerbeds are beaming with colours, the pond is glistening under the bright sun – everything is stunning. You couldn't ask for a nicer location, or a nicer day for your wedding. I wonder what my wedding day will be like … a cold day in hell, I imagine.

'I hear the giant is your ex-boyfriend,' Pete says.

I laugh. 'Yep. But that was a long time ago, and he wasn't quite so giant then.'

'He must be a hard act to follow,' he says, and I wonder if he's worried he can't quite measure up to Al.

'You'd be surprised,' I reply. 'We weren't together long, we didn't have much in common … You know when it's not right, right?'

'Right.' He smiles. 'With Tom here too, this must be awkward for you?'

'Nah,' I say, playing it down. 'Tom was only an almost-ex. Al is my only actual ex. And I'm doing my best not to speak to either of them.'

'How's that working out for you?' he asks, swigging his beer.

'Not great.' I laugh. 'There always seems to be one of them

annoying me.'

'Well, people are friends with their exes.'

'I've heard of that. But I've never known that to be true. What about you?' I ask. 'Any weird exes knocking around?'

'Not really,' he replies. 'I stayed with the girl I met at uni for a long time, but it didn't work out in the end.'

'Wow, I'm surprised how many people stick with the person they were with at uni for so long,' I say. 'I don't think I was sure of anything at uni, least of all what I wanted for the rest of my life.'

'It's all good,' he says. 'Your almost-ex made sense in his speech. Maybe I was supposed to meet Kat at uni, so that I'd be here at her wedding, so that I'd meet you.'

I smile. I hadn't thought about it that way.

'Anything can happen,' he reminds me.

'So people keep telling me, but I don't know that to be true either.'

'Are you happy?' he asks, taking the tone of the conversation from light-hearted to something a little more serious.

I am taken aback by his question. I wasn't expecting this conversation to get to heavy so quickly.

'Erm …'

'Sorry, I shouldn't ask you questions like that,' he quickly says. 'We hardly know each other.'

'No, it's OK.'

'It's just … I'm not sure if I am,' he admits. 'It feels like something is missing from my life, you know?'

'I know exactly what you mean,' I reply. 'My life is fine but … I'm so bored. I work a lot, my social life isn't what I'd like it to be, my love life is *nothing*.' I pause for a second. Should I really be telling him all this? He did ask, right?

'I hate my job,' I continue. 'I want to be doing something worthwhile, but I've been working in PR for so long, and it's almost exclusively a damage control job. I want to do something good, something that makes a difference. I want to be the person making a fuss over the use of real fur, not the mug on the end of the phone trying to pass it off as an accident so that my bosses continue to be rich. My mum tries to convince me to quit my job, sell my flat, and move to the south of France to live with them. I think she thinks she can get me a job in a boulangerie, find me a nice French husband, get me popping out some little *enfants* …'

'Do you fancy a fresh start?' he asks.

'Erm … I don't know … maybe. I have nothing to keep me in Manchester … but I don't want to move to France.'

'What about London?'

'I don't think I'd be any happier just doing what I'm doing in a different city.'

'Probably not,' he replies. 'But what if I told you the charity I worked for needed a new PR person …'

'Do they?' I reply, sitting up as much as my beanbag will allow me to.

'They do,' he replies. 'And I could put in a good word for a specific applicant, if I wanted to …'

'You'd do that for me?' I reply. I'm not a hundred per cent certain that is what he's suggesting, but if he is, I'm not about to let this opportunity slip through my fingers.

'Of course I would,' he replies. 'It sounds like you really want to change your job, and your life. If I can help you do that, then I'm more than happy to do it. And, who knows, maybe we'll get to spend some real time together.'

I think for a second, trying to pace my thoughts. Would it really be so simple, to move to London, start my dream job, maybe start something with Pete …? And maybe, if I had a boyfriend, it would be easier to make friends too. We could have couples friends. Maybe that's the key to making platonic connections when you are an adult – couples friends or mummy friends. No one cares about the singles in society. My heart is racing – so are my thoughts. I think being a single girl at a wedding might be messing with my head because all of a sudden I'm planning couples activities for me and my hypothetical boyfriend. I'll be making a frantic dive for the bouquet next.

'I don't know what to say,' I tell him.

'Say you'll think about it,' he replies.

'I'll absolutely think about it.'

I don't want to seem too keen, but I also don't want him to think that I'm not considering it. It would be crazy, to move to London, change my job – and all because of a man I just met … but what if this is what is going to make me happy? What if this is what I'm supposed to do? Everyone keeps banging on about fate and how we're all here again for a reason (other than the wedding, apparently) – what if this is *my* reason? I was supposed to come here, meet Pete, take this job and leave my sad, lonely life behind me. There's got to be more to life than spending your days working to pay your mortgage, and spending your nights watching TV until it's time to go to bed so you can get up for work in the morning.

'Luca, there you are,' Kat says, scurrying towards us. I don't know how else to describe the way she has to walk to accommodate for her wedding dress. 'I've been looking all over for you.'

'I've been sat right here,' I say quickly and perhaps a little too defensively.

'Well, come with me,' she demands, jerking her neck in the direction of the hotel.

'Is it urgent?' I ask, desperately not wanting to leave Pete's side, especially given the potentially life changing conversation we're having, but I should have known this question wouldn't go down well.

'It's like you don't know how being a bridesmaid works,' she says with exasperation.

No, it's like *she* doesn't know how being a bridesmaid works. I'm not technically a bridesmaid. She never asked me to be one,

I never agreed to be one, I'm just a girl in a dress that happens to match the rest of the bridesmaid dresses. I never signed up for guestbook duty or grandma hunting or whatever job she's got for me to do now.

'Sorry,' I mouth to Pete, as I pull myself up from my beanbag.

'It's OK,' he whispers back. 'To be continued.'

I smile at him, before dutifully following the bride into the bar.

'So, what can I do for you?' I ask her.

'I need your help,' she says, picking up the pace a little.

'With?' I ask, hurrying along behind her.

'With something the other bridesmaids can't help me with,' she tells me as she holds a door open for me to follow her through.

That's when I realise we're heading into the toilets.

'Oh,' I say.

Kat, a woman who I am meeting for the second time today, is expecting me to help her pee while wearing a wedding dress. I imagine it is a tricky thing to do, so she has my sympathy there (I myself am wearing a pair of tights that suck your stomach in, so I know the struggles of hurrying out of complex garments when you really need the loo, even if it's on a much smaller scale) but do I really have to be the person who helps her? Are we really on peeing together terms?

'How were you planning on doing this before I stepped in as a bridesmaid?' I ask curiously.

'I hadn't really thought about it,' she replies.

'When my sister got married a few years ago, she wore this thing under her dress that sort of pulled up and hooked over her arms, scooping her dress up with it, so she could go to the bathroom on her own.'

'And how does this information help me?' she asks.

I bite my lip.

'Wow, you must really need to pee,' I say. 'OK, fine, let's do this.'

Kat and I squeeze into a cubicle together and I round up her dress and hold it in a big clump behind her back.

'Be careful with the material,' she says. 'It's very delicate.'

Again, I bite my lip. I just stand there holding her dress, and as Kat uses the toilet, I forget about where I am. Instead, I think about Pete's job offer. There's no way I could get a job like this without his influence. My CV alone would put a charity off, knowing I worked for one of the most unethical retailers in the country, and then there's the fact that it's all the way in London. Without a good word from Pete, there's no way I could afford to waste the time and money needed to go down for interviews for what would feel like such a long shot.

I really do feel like there's something between me and Pete. Maybe something special could happen between us if I just put aside my distrust in men and went for it. But even without that in mind, this job feels like too good an opportunity to miss. If Pete is willing to take a chance on me, and help me get my foot through the door, then maybe I need to take a chance on Pete.

Chapter 22

On my way back to the garden, I bump into Ed. He's looking a little worse for wear as he walks out of the toilets, shaking his wet hands around like he's on acid at a rave.

'Bloody dryers aren't working,' he tells me as we walk back to our table outside.

'Ay,' Clarky says when he sees us together. 'Where have you two been, eh?'

'Do you honestly think anyone not in your eye line is off having sex?' Fi asks him. 'Never mind that Ed is married and Luca is …'

I feel my eyebrows shoot up as her sentence trails off.

'Luca is …' I prompt her.

'Nothing,' she replies with a laugh.

I wonder what she was actually going to say. Luca is … not interested in Ed? Luca is … still hung up on her not quite ex? Luca is … completely repellent to the opposite sex? Hmm, it's probably best I don't push for an answer.

Everyone else goes back to their conversations, so I take the seat next to Ed.

'So, how are you doing, buddy?' I ask him.

'Me? I'm great, I'm amazing, I couldn't be better.'

'Yeah?'

'Yeah,' he replies. 'This day off, it's doing me the world of good. In fact ...'

I watch as Ed loosens his tie and unbuttons his top shirt button.

'Oh wow,' I tease. 'You really are letting your hair down.'

'Balls to it,' he says. 'It's time to have some real fun. No one calling me daddy, no one telling me to clean the floor.'

'Sounds like the opposite of a porno I saw once,' Clarky jokes as he stands up. 'I'm off to the bar, who wants a shot?'

'Me, I do,' Ed says.

'Yeah, I'd love a shot, thanks,' Zach replies.

'Nothing for me,' Fi says.

'Me either,' I reply.

'OK, five shots,' Clarky says, completely ignoring us.

'Unbelievable.' Fi sounds really annoyed.

'What's wrong?' Zach asks her.

'I said I didn't want one,' she replies.

'So what?' he says. 'Don't drink it, *I'll* drink it.'

'You'll drink it, and probably start swapping infections with Clarky,' she snaps back. I don't think she's going to forgive Zach for what happened on the stag do any time soon.

I turn to Ed, trying to block out the domestic Fi and Zach are having across the table from us.

'How drunk are you?' I ask him.

'Hmm.' He thinks for a moment. 'Too drunk to drive, but not so drunk I can't work out which one of you said that.' Ed goes bog-eyed and shakes his head. I laugh.

'Sober enough to talk about something?' I ask him.

'Sober enough for the serious conversations and drunk enough to probably not remember tomorrow,' he replies. 'The perfect combination.'

I'm sure he's kidding, but that would actually suit me just fine.

'I met someone last night ... a boy ...'

Ed gasps playfully.

'A boy?'

'Well, a man,' I correct myself. 'And he seems really nice and ... he's offered to put me forward for a job – my dream job – but it's in London.'

'Luca, that's amazing news,' he replies.

'Is it?'

'Of course it is. Do you like him?'

I nod.

'Do you *like* like him?'

'This is just like uni.'

'I know, it's kind of nice,' he says. 'But, honestly, you deserve to be happy. Take a chance.'

'I'll think about it,' I reply, before changing the subject. 'How are the kids doing?'

'The kids are doing great. They're a lot of work but Stella is amazing with them.'

'I can't imagine having four kids,' I tell him. 'I can't imagine having one, to be honest. I still feel like a kid myself.'

'They completely change your life,' he tells me. 'They take all your time and your money and your energy. And, you know what, they're not even grateful.'

'I mean, they're probably not old enough to be grateful, right?' I reply.

'Nah, 25 years old, I think, is when gratitude kicks in.'

'Yeah, 25 at the earliest,' I agree.

'Do you know what you want from life?' he asks me.

'I'm scared of life.'

'Well, remember, it's just as scared of you as you are of it.'

I'm not sure if he's joking or just too drunk to make sense.

'I'm just so proud of you. You've always known what you wanted, and you've done whatever you've needed to do to get it. And here you are, you've got your dream job, your wife, your kids ...'

Ed takes me by the hand and squeezes it tightly.

'Luca, don't think I don't still think about how I owe this all to you.'

'Don't be daft,' I tell him.

'I'm serious,' he says, staring straight into my eyes. The fact that he isn't blinking is making me feel tense, rather than appreciated. 'I owe so much to you, after everything you did for me. Zach too.'

'What about me?' Zach asks, hearing his name.

'We were just talking about how we're all maturing,' I say. 'Ed especially.'

'Well, Ed's always been mature,' Fi replies.

Clarky returns and sets a tray of shots down on the table in front of us.

'Shots,' Ed bellows.

'What were you saying about him being mature?' I ask Fi with a chuckle.

'Do you think it's all men, who are crap or just ours?' she asks me.

The three boys argue over which two of them get the extra shots. As Ed makes his case, Zach knocks back his shot, followed by both of the extra ones.

'Maybe it's just our men,' I reply light-heartedly. 'But we're stuck with them, right?'

'You speak for yourself,' she says under her breath.

Chapter 23

New Year's Eve 2008, 8.25 p.m.

The flashing lights are the first thing I notice. The rhythmic blinking of the hazard lights in the dark, cold night air.

'Oh my God,' I say as we pull up behind the car.

'It's going to be OK,' Zach reassures me. 'Don't look, OK? I'll go see what's happened.'

I nod. I'm so grateful he's going first because after what I heard on the phone, my imagination is thinking up all sorts.

I watch as Zach approaches the front of the car. As he looks down at the ground, I watch him run a hand through his hair and exhale deeply. I can see the anguish on his face from here. He looks terrified.

I can see that he's talking to someone, but I can't tell what he's saying. As he approaches my car door, I take a deep breath and brace myself for what he's about to say. This can't be good news …

Chapter 24

Now

Today has felt like the longest day of my life so far, and it's only 3 p.m.

Wait, no, it can't be. I tap my Apple watch, but nothing happens. It's a smart watch – smart watches aren't supposed to stop, are they? I suppose, technically, it's frozen, which I can't help but find amusing, because it definitely feels like time has stopped moving today.

Perhaps it's because it's summer, and it doesn't get dark until quite late, which is making it feel like the day isn't ending, or maybe it's my circumstances. I can't help but feel I've been thrown back into my old life, and now I'm trapped here, in some sort of purgatory for millennials.

I just want this day to be over, I just want my life to finally get going … but both are as frozen as my watch.

I leave the cool breeze of the gardens to pop my head inside the warm bar where there's a large clock on the wall. You're in no danger of losing track of time in here, every minute passing you by is always in your peripheral vision.

So, it's actually 6 p.m., not 3 p.m., which may be three hours along the line, but it's still a long way away from midnight, when the invitation said the wedding would end. I know there's no law that says you have to stick around until the end, but when you're staying in the hotel where the wedding is, with nowhere else to go, it's hard to come up with a good excuse to scarper.

I find my friends, still at 'our' table outside, and plonk myself down in the chair next to Fi. I open my mouth to speak, only to be interrupted by Kat.

'Luca, there you are,' she says.

'Yep, here I am,' I reply.

Why is it, as soon as I try to relax, someone comes along to stop me?

'I have another job for you,' she says.

Of course she does. God, I really hope she doesn't need the toilet again.

As I stand up from the table I notice the number of empty shot glasses has significantly increased. The boys seem merrier too – and Ed has popped another shirt button open. That's two buttons open now. To a regular person, that's the equivalent of doing two lines of coke – it really must be party time.

'No rest for the wicked,' Fi says as I head towards my master's voice.

'What's up?' I ask.

'Tom is looking for you,' she tells me. 'Wedding business – I'm not allowed to know, apparently.'

'Right. Do you know where he is?'

'He's over there,' she says as she points across the garden, to a gang of groomsmen standing around, looking shifty.

'Great,' I reply.

As I approach them, I notice they're crowded around a bag for life, all peering in, discusses the contents.

Given what I know about the other groomsmen and the stag party, it's probably a bag of sex aids.

I join their circle and peer down into the bag.

Oh.

I was totally joking about the sex aids, making a little dig to myself about their stag do antics, but that is exactly what is in the bag.

'Luca and I have it covered,' Tom tells them. 'Don't worry.'

The shifty group disperse.

'Thanks for helping with this,' Tom says, holding the bag up. 'Come with me.'

'Where?" I ask.

'Upstairs,' he replies.

'Erm ... are you not even going to buy me dinner first?' I joke cautiously. Cracking jokes is my number one coping mechanism for awkward situations, but I am low-key concerned about where we're going and what we're going to do when we get there.

Tom laughs.

'Are they party favours?' I persist. 'Those beads you've got there don't look like the kind the mother of the bride would be interested in.'

Then again, she did seem to have a major hot flash while she was lying on Alan's back, when he was doing press-ups for the crowd earlier.

Again, Tom just laughs at my joke.

We step into the lift together – I've never seen anything like it.

'Oh, wow,' I blurt.

'Oh, you won't have seen this if you're staying in the cottages, will you?' Tom replies. 'It's cute, isn't it?'

'It's ... something,' I reply.

I suppose it's kind of cute, but it makes me feel uneasy. I'm used to metal lifts, with polished doors, mirrored walls, and an eloquent and calming female voice telling me whether I'm going up or down. The lift here is older than I am. It has a wooden door – just a regular door, with a small window at the top – and inside, the walls are covered with carpet. Tom presses a button, to take us up, and as we travel from floor to floor, I realise we've left the door behind us. Instead of doors that are part of the lift, that move with the lift, we are passing each floor and door as we go up – we could even reach out and touch them.

'Maybe we'll take the stairs back down,' I say as we step out.

'Perhaps,' he replies. 'I did notice a sign in reception saying what to do if you got stuck in it.'

'Yeah, that doesn't fill me with confidence. So, are you going to tell me what we're doing now?'

'I have been tasked with the very important job of decorating the bridal suite,' he tells me as I follow him along a corridor that wouldn't be out of place in *The Shining*. 'You're the only person I trust to help me.'

'So ...'

'So the boys have put together this bag of tricks,' he says. 'The idea is, we leave these sex toys all over the room, leave the sexy underwear hanging in the wardrobes – there's some tools in here, to loosen the bed, so that it collapses when they get on it ...'

'I'm the only person you trust to help with that?' I ask.

'Yeah,' he replies. 'Well—'

'You think I'm the person to dismantle a bed and dot dildos around?' I interrupt him, unable to hide my disbelief. 'That will absolutely ruin their night.'

'Yeah, it will,' Tom says. 'So—'

'So, no way am I helping you,' I tell him. 'In fact, I've got every mind to warn them.'

'Luca.' Tom rolls his eyes and laughs. 'Just listen to me, OK? The guys got all this stuff together and they came up with the plan. I insisted on implementing it – with your help – because you're right, it's not funny. It would definitely ruin their night.'

'So ...'

'So I brought some other stuff with me,' he says, nodding towards a different bag on the floor outside the bridal suite. 'I snuck it up here earlier.'

'So you said we'd do it, so you can put nice stuff in their room,' I say, finally catching on.

'Exactly,' he replies. 'You're so quick to think the worst of me.'

'I am. Second nature, I guess.'

Tom hovers with his key in the door.

'So, are we doing this?' he asks.

'Let's do it.'

As Tom smiles at me, I watch the wrinkles around his eyes pull together. He doesn't look old, he looks like he's spent a lifetime smiling, laughing, being happy. When I look at his face, it's like finding a picture that used to hang on your wall, that you put into storage and forgot about. You forget how much you used to admire it, how much it used to make your day when you looked at it.

'OK then,' he says, opening the door.

I step in the room and I'm taken aback.

'This is gorgeous,' I say. I feel a little crackle in my voice but I can't pinpoint the origin of it.

It's a large room, with tall windows and an even higher ceiling. Rather than modernise this one, they've kept it classic. Unlike other parts of the hotel, it looks like it's filled with antiques, rather than old tat. The walls are simple, with a plain cream paper. The colours come from the peach of the carpet and the curtains, which ordinarily I would hate, but in here it looks just right. Like something out of a fairy tale. The pièce de résistance is the king size, four-poster bed in the heart of the room. It's so grand, with its dark wooden frame and delicate white curtains and sheets.

'It is,' Tom agrees. 'I personally think the dildos would've ruined it.'

I laugh. 'I agree.'

We decorate the room with candles (ready to be lit when it's time for the happy couple to come up) and scatter rose petals around. Tom even has a rose petal air freshener in *his* bag of tricks.

'I thought this might be a nice touch,' he says proudly as he places a small speaker on the chest of drawers. Upon closer inspection there's a small MP3 player plugged into the back of it. 'A romantic Eighties playlist, for a man who has shaped his love life around Eighties music.'

'Matt was always more Mötley Crüe than Michael Bolton,' I joke.

Tom presses play and starts playfully grooving to the song that is playing. I giggle as he bops towards me, inching closer to me until our bodies are touching.

'Can I give you some advice?' I say, looking up at him.

'Go for it,' he replies casually.

'You might want to take "I'll Never Fall In Love Again" off the playlist.'

Tom pauses for a second, taking in the lyrics of the Deacon Blue song currently playing.

'Oh,' he replies with an embarrassed chuckle.

He skips the track. Foreigner's 'Waiting For a Girl Like You' plays.

'Much more like it,' I reply.

'Would this seduce you?' he asks.

'You're getting warm,' I tell him, but then I catch myself for flirting with him.

'What about if we wrap these fairy lights around the bed frame?' he suggests with a wiggle of his eyebrows.

We both kick off our shoes and climb onto the bed. Tom carefully wraps the lights around the wooden frame as I feed him the wire to make sure he's doing it evenly.

'It's really is so nice of you to do this,' I tell him.

'It's the least I can do,' Tom replies. 'He's my best mate, he deserves it. Plus, I know he'll do the same for me.'

I smile to myself. It must be nice to have a best mate. My friends these days feel like little more than acquaintances. It's not that there is anything wrong with me, it's just so hard to make friends in your thirties. A few of the women at work are quite close, but it's mostly the ones with kids. They've got this yummy mummy group that, obviously, I can't be a part of. Most of the other people I work with are either young and hip, or older and married. I just seem to fall between the cracks. It's sad because with a few taps of my phone, I have access to countless dating apps that will bag me anything from a quick hook up, to a long term relationship, to a financial arrangement that we're all only a few bad decisions away from contemplating, even if there's no way we'd have the bottle to go through with it. I can pretty much order a man like an item from a catalogue (although, in a similar way, you can't tell if it's good quality or not until you see it in person) but there's no equivalent for making friends.

'Are you getting married anytime soon?' I ask him.

'No,' he laughs. 'You?'

'Not today.'

'My dad keeps telling me I need to settle down,' he says.

'My mum is of a similar opinion,' I tell him. 'She's always reminding me that she'd had me *and* my sister before she was my age.'

'It was one of the last things my mum said to me.'

You know when you hear something and it confuses you because it doesn't make sense with your version of the facts? Then it hits me.

'Your mum passed away?'

'She did,' he replies. 'Sorry, when I said my dad remarried, I didn't think to tell you why he wasn't with my mum anymore …'

'Don't apologise,' I insist. 'I'm so sorry.'

'She … she, erm …'

Tom's voice crackles, just a little. I don't think about it, I just wrap my arms around him and squeeze him tightly. The problem is that, because we're standing on such a soft mattress, we fall down. I hit the bed first with Tom landing on top of me a split second later. Realising that we're both OK, we burst out laughing.

'Did you just attack me?' he asks.

'I think I might've,' I reply. 'But I was only trying to hug you.'

'Are you hurt?'

'Only my pride,' I tell him. 'I'm sorry.'

'Don't apologise to me, apologise to Matt and Kat. They won't be happy with us trying out their bed before them.'

'No, I suppose not.'

I don't move though. Neither does Tom. He rests on one hand as he brings the other one up to my face to remove a piece of hair from my eyes, gently tucking it behind my ear.

It's such a cliché, when people say they get lost in someone else's eyes. I don't feel lost in Tom's eyes, I feel home.

Is his face moving closer to mine or am I imagining it? And is the bed moving?

'Wait, is that my phone?' I ask, noticing the faint sound of it vibrating in my bag.

I feel around on the bed for my clutch and take out my phone to see that I have a missed call and a text from Fi.

'Oh, we're going to miss the first dance,' I tell him. 'We'd better hurry.'

'I'd better get off you then,' he says. If I didn't know better, I'd think he sounded a little disappointed.

We finish putting up the lights in awkward semi-silence before making our way back downstairs – via the stairs this time. Because there's only one thing more dangerous than this hotel lift and that would be lying on that bed with Tom on top of me for a second longer.

Chapter 25

It's a real sign of the times (or perhaps it's more a sign of my fitness levels) that rushing down the stairs is tiring me out. I thought weddings were supposed to be fun but, honestly, this has been nothing but hard work since I got here.

'What do you think their first dance will be to?' Tom asks me.

Tom doesn't seem to be having too much trouble tackling the stairs. He's a couple of steps ahead of me, and not at all out of breath. It did occur to me to blame it on my heels, but then I remembered that I'm not wearing them anymore.

'If Matt has his way, it will be something classically Eighties,' I reply. 'If Kat picks, it will be something modern. Probably something naff.'

'Because the Eighties were so cool,' he laughs.

'Erm, they were,' I correct him. 'But you know Kat … as far as I can tell, she's very poppy and mainstream, right? She loves Ed Sheeran and Little Mix.'

It's amazing, how much you can tell about a person from their Facebook feed.

'So?'

'So, Whitesnake's "Slide It In" isn't going to hit the spot, is it?' Tom sniggers at my choice of words.

'Well, I think Kat will get her way,' he says.

'My money is on Eighties – bloody hell, how many flights of stairs are there? This place is like a labyrinth.'

'These are the last few steps,' he tells me. 'Actually, there's a door here that leads straight into the marquee. I've seen the staff using it.'

'We're probably not supposed to use it,' I reply. 'Let's just walk around.'

'Listen though, music ... it sounds like we're missing their dance.'

'But if it's closed ...'

'Luca, it's just a door,' Tom says, followed by one of his easy laughs. 'What's the worst that can happen?'

'OK,' I say as we approach the door. 'If you think it's better for slinking in ...'

I follow Tom through the doorway, which leads straight onto the dance floor. It only takes me a second to realise that we are just a few feet away from Matt and Kat, who are currently in the middle of their first dance. We are so close to them, in fact, that we're actually standing in their spotlight.

Everyone's eyes were on them; now, they're on us too. Our audience looks confused, seeing us burst onto the scene like this. And Tom thought we were so clever, sneaking in through the staff door ... that's the last time I listen to him.

I just stand there, awkwardly frozen on the spot. I don't know what do but it doesn't matter, Tom has this. He takes me by the hand and places the other on the small of my back.

'Are we ... are we crashing their first dance?' I ask him quietly.

'Looks like it,' he replies. 'But if we own it, it will look like it was on purpose.'

'Will it though?' I reply in disbelief.

'I'm the best man and you're the only bridesmaid without swollen feet,' he whispers back as we slow dance. Finally Matt and Kat notice us next to them. For a moment they look confused, but they carry on dancing. To be honest, I don't think they care that we've joined in. They look so in love and so happy.

'It's practically a requirement that we dance together.'

'Hmm,' I reply with a smile. 'I daren't even look at our audience. I'm so embarrassed.'

'Don't be,' Tom says, pulling me closer. 'Have you noticed what song we're dancing to?'

For a second, I forget my embarrassment, or how fast my heart is beating being so close to Tom (coupled with the four flights of stairs I just hurried down) and I listen to the music. We're dancing to a cover of REO Speedwagon's 'Can't Fight This Feeling' and, as soon as I realise, I take a deep, sharp breath.

'It's …'

'It's our song,' he replies with a smile. 'You remember that night?'

'I do,' I reply. How could I forget it? Tom pulled me close – close like we are now – and slow danced with me. I remember melting into his arms, feeling so safe and happy, until we were interrupted. Then it was like someone pulled the rug from under us. But this time we're on a dance floor – we're supposed to be dancing. There's nothing to stop us this time.

'Ladies and gentlemen, erm … the bride and groom would like to invite you onto the dance floor with them,' the DJ says. He sounds a little confused, reading the announcement when he's supposed to, because we've definitely jumped the gun.

As soon as we're joined by plenty of others, I feel myself relax. Without really thinking about it, I rest my head on Tom's chest. He gives me a squeeze. We couldn't be physically closer right now if we tried. It's a shame we feel so far apart otherwise. It's a horrible thing, to run into the person you've always believed you're supposed to be with when you're both with other people … it's even worse when only the other person is probably going to end up with someone else, and you're so very, very alone.

'Tell me this isn't fate,' he whispers into my ear.

'Everyone keeps talking about fate today,' I reply with a sigh. 'Like everything happens for a reason, and everything happens exactly as it is supposed to, to ensure we all end up where we're supposed to be.'

'What if that's true?' he asks.

I lift my head to look at him. He's deadly serious.

'Where's my sceptic, atheist, cynical friend gone?' I ask him.

'He's under the influence of an Eighties power ballad,' he replies. 'Or a cover of one, at least. Hey, I suppose we were both right.'

'We were?'

'Yeah. You said Eighties, I said modern. This cover sounds like both, so we're both right.'

'That's the key to a perfect relationship, right?' I reply.

'What, us both being right?' he asks.

I laugh.

'No, compromise. They compromised on a song they'd both love.'

'Well, I didn't expect you two to be dancing with us,' Kat says.

I was so caught up in Tom, I forgot there was anyone else in the room. But the song has ended and Matt and Kat are standing next to us.

'We wondered through the wrong door,' Tom says. 'Best cover-up I could think of.'

Kat smiles. I'm relieved she isn't mad at us for ruining it.

'Luca, what did you think of the song?' Matt asks.

'One of my favourites,' I reply. 'I hadn't heard the cover before though.'

'It's from *Glee*,' he laughs. 'Kat loves *Glee*, I love the song … you'd never know, right?'

'Wow, you wouldn't,' I reply. Well, I definitely wouldn't, because I haven't seen any *Glee*.

'Buddy, maybe don't tell anyone else that,' Tom tells him with a chuckle.

'Right,' he replies. 'Well, I think we're going to have another dance, so we'll catch you two later.'

'Fancy another dance?' Tom asks me.

The DJ is playing 'I Wanna Dance With Somebody' by Whitney Houston.

'Erm ...'

'Go on,' he says. 'What if we don't see each other for another ten years?'

There's something about his face, about his smile, about his eyes ... I can't say no.

'OK,' I reply.

'Unless you do want to go for that drink with me in Manchester,' Tom eventually says as we move to the music.

'We'll see.'

'Did you always play so hard to get?'

'I might be moving to London,' I tell him.

'Since when?' he asks, taken aback.

'It's a recent development,' I admit. 'Pete said he'd put me forward for a job.'

'Oh.'

I watch the smile fall from his face and the colour drain from his cheeks.

'So, you're just going to leave? Just like that?'

'I mean, it's of no concern to you and yours, is it?'

Tom pulls me close to him again. I feel like he's about to say something when, for the second time in ten years, our dancing is interrupted by the rug being pulled from under me, but this time it's literal. I catch a glimpse of Tom as I slowly and clumsily make my ungraceful descent and I see the look on his face change. He reaches out to grab me, and I try to grab his hand but it's no use, he can't get a hold of me – and isn't that just the story of my life? As I'm about to hit the ground I wonder to myself just how much more embarrassing this scenario can get. And then I hit my head on the speaker on the floor next to us.

Chapter 26

Then – 2nd June 2009

I'm never convinced I've been to a party, unless it ends with me in my room, alone and in tears. 'What am I upset about today?' I hear you ask. What am I always upset about? Men. It's always – *always* – bloody men.

Things with Alan just aren't working. It's not that he isn't good-looking, or that he isn't a nice guy, deep down, when he's not telling me I'm getting fat. It's just … something is missing, and it isn't just that he isn't Tom. I've been going with the flow, waiting for the strong feelings to kick in, but they haven't yet, and if they haven't four months down the line, I think it's safe to say they aren't going to, are they?

With our third year coming to an end, and Alan planning on moving back home to Norwich, I've been forced to think carefully about what I want, and I just don't want Alan. This relationship doesn't work anyway, so it definitely doesn't stand a chance long distance. I gave it my best shot, but I just don't think he's right for me, and I don't think I'm right for him either.

When I told him we were having a house party tonight, he had absolutely no interest in coming – which wasn't surprising, but it felt like the motivation I needed to break it off with him. I brought up the fact that we had nothing in common, ready to break up with him, but then he did something that caught me completely off guard … he said he'd come to the party. I was taken aback and quickly lost the nerve to break up with him – well, my whole break up speech was based on the fact that he's never interested in doing the things I wanted to do, and there he was, suddenly saying he would do something that I wanted to do.

Flash-forward to now and the party is well and truly over, both here in the house, and between Alan and me.

You can tell the house party is over by the bodies littered all around the room, like the end of a battle between two sides. The music is still playing, but there isn't a sign of life anywhere. It's just me, walking through the hallway, like the lone survivor of a zombie apocalypse.

It's amazing really, that there are people crashing here, because Matt's Eighties playlist is still going strong. You know it's been a good party when the guests stay so long, and have such a good time, that they happily fall asleep.

It's coming up to 2 a.m., but while we're pretty late in the day (or early in the morning, if that's the way you operate) this is a relatively early night for us, and our parties.

Tonight's theme, selected by Matt – the only other housemate who shares my passion for the decade – was the Eighties, and we definitely partied like it was the Eighties, that's for sure.

I was having a great time … until Alan showed up. For someone who was supposedly making an effort, he made no effort at all.

I know that not everyone likes to participate in fancy dress, but Eighties-themed attire is not exactly a bizarre spectacle to behold if you don't want it to be. Sure, some of us have gone all-out, but simply wearing jeans and a T-shirt would've done the trick. And if he didn't want to dress up, he could've at least dressed nice. Instead, Alan turned up in his gym gear.

I definitely went all out for this one, and I'm so glad that I did, seeing as though this is probably the last party we'll have before we all move out. I made my newly peroxide coloured hair absolutely massive and I got into my Madonna groove with a heavily accessorised black outfit, topped off with a black bow in my hair.

Everyone else came dressed up too … everyone but Alan. And then he did nothing but complain. He didn't like the music, or any of the party games. He complained about the food (what kind of student complains about free pizza?) and he even complained about the Eighties décor for the evening because, all around the house, we'd made these near little lines of sherbet, to give the party a real Eighties vibe. But it was just sweets. It was just a bit of fun. The whole night was fun, but Alan was having none of it. As far as I'm concerned, it seems like Alan just doesn't know how to have fun. Fun to Alan is three sets of fifty reps, followed by a protein shake – and you don't get much of either of those things at house parties.

Maybe because he was being especially boring, I had more to drink that I usually would at these kinds of gatherings. I think it was that, coupled with the fact that Tom and Cleo were here, both looking amazing in their Eighties gear, both all over each other. The last time I saw them, they were cuddled up on the sofa together. I was jealous anyway – of course I was. I still feel like it should be me on that sofa with him, not her. But seeing them together and then walking into the kitchen, where Alan told me off in front of everyone for eating a slice of pizza … well, that was it. I'd had enough.

'Are you really going to eat that?' he asked me.

'I am,' I told him. 'I'm going to eat this, and then maybe another one, and if you have a problem with that I'll eat you too.'

'Chance would be a fine thing,' he replied. A blatant dig at the fact that there hasn't been much going on in the bedroom with us recently but … I guess I just don't fancy him. Something is just missing, and it's something that I need to be happy.

At that point, it really felt like there was no turning back, so I took him to my bedroom and sat him down, ready to lay my cards on the table. At first I tried to be subtle, gentle even ... but the big, dumb, meathead assumed I'd taken him up there to shag him, after he made that little dig about our sex life. I didn't want to hurt him or make him feel bad, but the last thing I wanted to do was sleep with him. I didn't want to be intimate with him. I didn't want to be with him at all ... but I just couldn't bring myself to be cruel to him. I felt so heartless, dumping him, but that was no reason to stay with him, unhappy ... so I lied to him to spare his feelings. I told him that it wasn't him, that is was me. That I had a problem with commitment.

I might have spared his feelings a little, but Alan still got upset. Very upset, in fact. He shouted at me, told me I was making the biggest mistake of my life, that he was going to be someone someday, and I was going to be single forever if I kept pushing people away. Before storming out, his final words to me – or rather, about me – were him musing about what my problem was, but I know what my problem is. No matter how hard I try to convince myself otherwise, my problem is that he isn't Tom.

I take a sip as I hover in the kitchen for a second, debating whether or not to poke my head into the living room, to see if Tom and Cleo are still there. I'll bet they are, snuggling on the sofa, fast asleep together. I don't know why I want to look – it would be painful to look – but I just can't help myself.

I brace myself as I look through the door, but the last thing I'm prepared to see is Tom, sitting on the sofa, wide awake and alone. I jump out of my skin.

'Oh my gosh, you scared me,' I say.

'Sorry,' he replies with a half-smile.

Tom is wearing a cream suit (with the sleeves rolled up on the jacket, of course) with a pink T-shirt underneath. His hair, which is usually spiked up as tall as gravity will allow, is straight and flat, and hangs down around his face – something I've never seen before and it makes him look so different. But the thing that stands out the most is the glum look on his face, and the fact that Cleo is nowhere to be seen.

'Look at you,' I say to him. 'You look fresh out of *Miami Vice*.'

'That was the idea,' he replies. 'You look … well … not too different to usual.'

'You know I love the Eighties,' I say. 'The clothes, the music. It's the main thing Matt and I have in common. He says he was born at the wrong time, that being born in the late Eighties meant he was too young to enjoy it.'

I feel a text message come through on my phone. It's from Alan, saying that he thinks we can make it work, that we can both change, that if I reply to him right now, he'll come back and he'll make things right. I consider whether I'm being too critical of him … perhaps half our problem is that I just can't help but compare him to Tom. Am I going to do this with every man I meet?

'You had a good night?' he asks.

'Yeah,' I lie. 'You?'

'Erm, I've had better,' he says. 'I think Cleo and I are over.'

Those are the last words I expected to hear him say. I feel my eyebrows shoot up and my eyes widen.

'Oh no, what happened?' I ask, sitting down next to him.

'I'm just not sure we're right for each other,' he says. 'I think we want different things. She wants to go travelling, pretty much as soon as we finish uni, but I've got this summer work placement at Manchester Live. I'll probably make more cups of coffee than I'll write articles for the website, but it's a foot in the door and I've been really looking forward to it.'

'I totally get it,' I assure him. 'Alan and I just broke up.'

'Luca, I'm sorry,' he says. 'Are you OK?'

'I'm fine, really. We wanted different things too.'

'You don't think you can work it out?' he asks.

'Sometimes people are just wrong for each other and there's nothing that can be done to make it work,' I reply. 'But I'll be fine.'

'Cleo and I argue a lot,' he confesses, but I already knew that. I think everyone knows that. They're always having these big arguments … but then they always make up again. 'But I think this is just too much this time, expecting me to give up my placement to travel. We could travel after, or years from now – but no, it has to be now, because Cleo says so.'

'I'm so sorry,' I say.

'What a sad pair we are,' he replies with a big sigh. 'Let's not wallow, let's dance.'

'Now?' I laugh.

'Now.' He stands up and offers me his hand.

REO Speedwagon's 'Can't Fight This Feeling' starts playing. Isn't it funny, how life always has a way of imitating art … or is art imitating life?

I wrap my arms around Tom's neck as he places his hands on my waist.

'How did we end up in such a mess?' he asks. 'I thought we were the sensible ones? Well, after Ed, at least.'

'Yeah, no one is as sensible as Ed,' I reply. 'I don't know.'

'It's weird how things play out, isn't it? I didn't think things would end up this way. The way I ended up with Cleo …'

'Ah, don't worry about it,' I say. Well, what's the point?

'Maybe I shouldn't have ended up with her,' he says softly as he nuzzles his face into my neck. As we slow dance, I feel Tom's hands move from my waist to my bum. I have my face pressed into his neck, so close to him I can smell his aftershave. He's so warm and he smells so good. I press my body against his and he holds me tight. I didn't think that things with Alan felt right but here, now, feeling this … this feels right.

We're interrupted by the bang of the front door. We quickly separate.

'Hey honey,' Cleo says, in the sickly sweet voice of hers, as she enters the room.

'Hi,' he says awkwardly.

'Oh, hey Luca,' she adds, noticing me.

'Hi,' I reply, equally as awkward.

Cleo pulls a face, like maybe she's picking up on something, but she quickly lets it go.

'I'm glad you're still here,' she tells him. 'I tried your flat and when you weren't there … anyway, you were right, of course. It was wrong of me to expect you to give up the chance to write, when it's what you want to do. So … I have a surprise for you.'

Cleo pulls two envelopes from her bag.

'In this envelope are two tickets to Thailand that, I admit, I might have been a little premature in buying. But in this one is the URL for the website I'm having built for you. You'd be wasted at that job you were going to take. Start a travel blog, be your own boss – I believe in you.'

Bloody Cleo, with her endless supply of her parents' money, with her sudden tickets out of nowhere. I wouldn't be surprised if she'd booked them ages ago, without waiting for Tom's approval, and this is just some stunt to cover up how controlling she can be. She always has to have her way.

'I'll leave you two to it,' I tell him.

'Luca,' he says.

'It's OK,' I tell him. 'Enjoy your trip.'

Chapter 27

Now

Well, I've found my shoes.

I know they say that things you have lost will always be in the last place you would think to look for them, but this is ridiculous. It must be true though, because the last place I expected to find my missing shoes was under my feet on the dance floor.

I don't know who moved them from the toilets, where they've been, or how they ended up on the dance floor, but, hey, at least I've found them. Although there is quite a significant scratch in the red sole on one of them, so I doubt I can return them now. I suppose I'll try and cover it up with a red Sharpie, before returning them to their box, and putting them away until the next wedding.

There's also quite a significant scratch on my face too, because I broke my fall with my cheek, hitting it on a floor speaker.

I'm currently in the office, trying to catch my breath after my tumble.

'Did you lose consus … consciousness?' Ed asks, spluttering out his words.

I stare at him for a moment.

'Luca,' he shouts in my face. 'It's Ed, can you hear me?'

'I can hear you,' I reply, unimpressed. 'I'm just trying to work out who I'd rather get first aid from: the hotel receptionist who just admitted she didn't pay much attention during her first aid course, or a really good doctor who is absolutely hammered ...'

'Well, you've chosen me now,' he says. 'So, did you lose ... did you pass out?'

'I didn't,' I reply.

I'm sitting on the desk in the office behind reception – just me, Ed, and a first aid kit.

'Well, I don't think you need stitches,' he says as he examines the cut on my cheek.

While I was waiting for him to fetch the first aid kit, I used my phone to take a look at my face. It's bleeding, but the cut is only maybe an inch long. It's not attractive, by any stretch of the imagination, but it could have been much worse. I feel so fortunate that this the extent of my injuries.

'Will it scar?' I ask.

'Nah,' he replies. 'I do need to clean it though. Are you going to be a brave girl?'

I laugh at his baby voice. Kids must love seeing Dr Ed. He's just got this warm and friendly way of making you feel at ease – even when he's drunk, it turns out.

'Thanks for helping me,' I say. 'I bet you didn't think you'd wind up actually working on your day off, did you?'

I wince as the antiseptic touches my cheek.

'It's no trouble,' he says. 'After what you did for me on New Year's Eve ...'

I'm sure it's just the alcohol crying, but I notice Ed get a little bit choked up.

'Ed, listen to me, you have nothing to thank me for. Everything you've achieved, you've done that all on your own. What Zach and I did for you ...'

'It was everything,' he replies. 'No one has ever done anything like that for me. No one ever will. And I'll never get the chance to do something like that for someone.'

'You literally save the lives of children every day,' I remind him. 'It would be worth it, just for that. And, anyway, you're going to make sure this doesn't leave a scar. My looks are all I've got going for me.'

Ed laughs as he places a couple of little sticky strips over my cut. I know I was joking, but did he have to find it so funny?

He takes a seat next to me, so I hook my arm around his and place my head on his shoulder.

'You OK?' I ask him.

'The guilt eats me up – all the time. Sometimes, I'm not even thinking about it, I'm playing with the kids or cooking and … it just pops into my head.'

'You can't let the guilt ruin your life,' I tell him. 'Everything worked out OK – I know, it could've been worse, but you learned your lesson, right?'

'It's not just the accident,' he says. 'I feel so guilty about … the ripples.'

'Ed—'

'I know, I know. But if I hadn't made you late home, maybe Tom wouldn't have even met Cleo – maybe you two would be together now, like you should be.'

'You can't think like that,' I insist.

I can't think like that.

'But if you hadn't been helping me – Zach too. I'll always feel guilty … what happened … Fifi and Clarky.'

'Ed, you need to calm down, buddy,' I say, turning to face him. 'You're not even making sense now – and to think, I let you give me medical treatment.'

I laugh to lighten the mood, but I can see something bubbling away inside him. A dangerous mixture of guilt, upset and alcohol, making one hell of a strong cocktail. One that's about to come back up.

'When we got back that night ... I just wanted to get showered and get to bed. Someone was in the house bathroom, so I went into Clarky's en-suite.'

When we moved in we drew straws to see who got the bedroom with its own bathroom. I really, really wanted it, but Clarky got it, and he wouldn't let anyone else use it, even if the house bathroom was occupied and his was not.

'Everyone was busy partying so I snuck into his room,' he says. 'I didn't think he'd mind – I didn't really care. But when I came out of the bathroom, he was in bed ... with Fi.'

'Oh!' I say. 'I didn't know that. She never told me that ...'

I can't believe she didn't tell me – we told each other everything. I suppose, looking back, it looks bad for her. That night, Zach was going to tell her that he had feelings for her and when he didn't show up, she must've been upset. I guess she thought that sleeping with his friend would make her feel better.

So much makes sense now. On New Year's Eve, Ed and I arrived home long before Zach did. So when he finally got home, I suppose the damage had already been done – Fi had already slept with Clarky. Then, after Fi found out Zach had 'been in an accident' she threw herself at him, and that's how they finally wound up together. I suppose we'll file it under fate, like we are doing with everything else today. But she can't have been out of Clarky's bed more than an hour before she ended up with Zach ...

'I feel bad for never telling Zach – he's supposed to be my friend. I just feel like everything is my fault,' Ed sobs.

I thought he was supposed to be looking after me, not the other way round. I wasn't expecting emotional drunk Ed, but I can't stand seeing him so upset. We all make mistakes, but we can't let them define us.

I take his face in my hands, holding his head so that his gaze has to meet mine.

It's weird, Ed has always looked like an old man. He's always dressed sensibly, he's never done anything wild with his hair. In a way, he looks his age but, on the other hand, he looks no different to how he looked at uni. The only real differences in his appearance, that I imagine only comes once you have actual kids, are the dark circles under his eyes and the dad bod he's sporting now.

'You need to listen to me,' I say, still holding his head. As drunk as he seems, I'm not even sure he'll take this in, but it's worth a shot if he really does still feel guilty. 'We are all perfectly capable of making a mess of our own lives. Me, Tom, Fi, Zach … nothing you did changed anything. You're an amazing, amazing man.'

'Do you really think so?' he asks.

'I do. I really do.'

One minute he's smiling at me, the next his lips are on mine.

'Whoa, Ed.'

I push him away by his chest. He stands up and stumbles a little on his drunk feet.

'Shit,' he says.

'It's OK,' I assure him. 'You're drunk. We just got our wires crossed.'

'Shit,' he says again. 'Why do I keep messing up? I need to put things right.'

'Wait,' I call after him as he makes a bolt for the door.

Shit! Shit, shit, shit.

I hop down off the table and run after him. I need to get to him – or at least to Fi – before he says something that will ruin everything.

Chapter 28

Then – New Year's Eve 2008, 8.30 p.m.

I undo my seatbelt and open the door.

'What's happened?' I ask Zach.

'Ed's had a car accident,' he replies. 'I don't want you to panic …'

But I do panic. I've been panicking since he called and asked us to hurry over and help him. I jump out of the car and run to the scene of the accident, where I find Ed, sitting on the floor with his head in his hands. Then I look in the middle of the road and see what he hit, just laying there in his headlights.

'Oh, God,' I say, rushing towards the dog in the middle of the road. 'Is it dead?'

'I don't know – I think so,' Ed cries.

'Mate, what happened?' Zach asks him. 'What are you doing in Matt's car?'

I glance around. We're on a relatively quiet road, but on the end of a residential street. I don't know what order events happened in, but it looks like he hit the dog, and then crashed the corner of the car into the wall.

'Are you hurt?' I ask him.

Ed hugs his knees, to try and steady the full body shakes he's having. He must be in some kind of shock.

'We need to call the police,' Zach says.

'No,' Ed says quickly.

'Mate, it's an offence not to report hitting a dog.'

'Oh, is it really?' he asks, agitated.

Something about him doesn't seem quite right.

'Ed, are you drunk?' I ask him.

'I don't know,' he cries. 'I could be … I had a few drinks before I left. Everyone was worried we didn't have enough food, so I said I'd go to the shop. I didn't see any harm in taking Matt's car … but I don't know, I might be over the limit.'

'Mate,' Zach says, his disappointment apparent in his sigh.

'I felt fine,' he snaps back. 'I … I thought I felt fine.'

'Listen, someone will have heard you hit the wall,' I say. 'It's a miracle no one has passed you already.'

I'm trying my absolute hardest not to think about the poor dog, lying dead in the middle of the road. I can't bear to think about it, it makes me feel sick. That's someone's pet. Someone's baby, practically.

'I … I made a mistake,' Ed sobs. 'I can't believe I did it. Will I be in a lot of trouble? I'm not even insured to drive this car – I didn't even ask for permission to borrow it. And I'm supposed to be learning how to help people, not kill things. I think I'm going to be sick.'

'Look, calm down, mate,' Zach says, but it's too late. Ed is having a full-blown panic attack, panicking about what will happen if he is under the influence, panicking about what his parents will say, about whether or not this will have any effect on his future.

'Oh my God, it's still alive,' I say, noticing the dog moving.

I run over to it and crouch down.

'Hello you,' I say to the golden retriever. He doesn't look very old but he isn't a puppy. He doesn't move – it's like he knows he's hurt – but he looks up at me with his big, brown eyes.

'Ed, come here,' I say.

I look at the ID tag on his collar. His name is Monty.

'Hello Monty,' I say brightly. When I talk to him, even though he doesn't move, he wags his tail, and it absolutely breaks my heart. 'You're going to be OK, cutie. I'm going to get you some help.'

Ed doesn't listen to me, he's still panicking. He's on his feet now, pacing back and forth in the car headlights.

'Ed, get over here, now,' I snap. 'Look at him.'

Ed reluctantly comes over and examines the dog.

'I don't know, I don't know,' Ed panics. 'He needs a vet. Soon as possible.'

'We need to call the police and we need to call the owners,' I say. 'Poor little thing, he needs help.'

'I'll do it,' Zach says.

'Give me your phone,' I say. 'I'll key the owner's number in.'

'No, I mean, I'll do everything,' Zach says to me quietly.

'What?'

'Just get him out of here,' he says.

'Zach …'

'He was driving, probably drunk, in a car he didn't have permission to borrow, without insurance, and he's hit a dog,' he points out. 'He'll be in so much trouble, Luc.'

'But what about you?'

'I'll be fine,' he says. 'I'm in my car, I'm sober. Get him in Matt's car, drive him home. You haven't had a drink, right?'

'I haven't.'

'Does your insurance cover other cars? I've seen you borrow Matt's car before …'

'Yes, but—'

'Ed has a brighter future than any of us – especially me. He's going to be a brilliant doctor one day … but maybe not, if this one mistake defines him. So hurry up.'

'Zach, we just need to get this dog to a vet, and you need to stop being crazy.'

'My mind is made up,' he says confidently.

I kiss him on the cheek as I hand him back his phone.

'You're going to be just fine, Monty,' I reassure the dog as I blow him a kiss.

I grab Ed, who is over by Matt's car dry heaving.

'Get in the car,' I tell him, ushering him towards the passenger seat.

'What?'

'Get in the car,' I say. 'We've got to get you out of here.'

'Why?' he asks.

'Because you have one of the best friends in the world,' I tell him. 'And he's got your back, but you have to swear to me, you'll never pull a stunt like this again.'

Ed sinks into the passenger seat and sighs with relief.

'I don't know how I'll ever repay him – or you,' he says.

'Just … don't do it again. Please.'

My voice finally wavers. I feel a lump form in my throat. I can't get the image of poor, little Monty out of my head.

This is definitely not the way I thought my New Year's Eve was going to play out.

Chapter 29

Now

If there's one thing I know, it's movies. I have watched a lot of movies in my 31 years.

When I was three years old, I had chicken pox. Apparently, the only way my mum could get me to sit still and stop scratching, was to put on the movie *Tom Thumb* – the 1958 version. I'd watch it again and again, and then, as I grew older, my love of movies only grew stronger.

As a student, studying media from the age of 14 until I graduated at 21, I had to watch a lot of movies over the years.

Finally, as a single adult with subscriptions to Sky, Amazon and Netflix, I fill my empty nights with movie after movie. So, I think it's safe to say, I've seen more than your average person.

The point I'm trying to make is that, I've seen a lot of fictional weddings take place. In movies, it always kicks off at weddings, but people don't usually make a scene in real life, do they? God, I hope they don't. Because in all of the weddings I've watched on screen, when things kick off, they *kick off*.

The chances of this wedding playing out normally (well, as normally as it can with this guest list) will be greatly increased if I can find Ed and stop him from saying something stupid, or at least warn Fi about what he's saying, so she can be ready for it. I suppose there's a small chance that it might not be true. That Ed might just be drunk and rambling, or he might have made a mistake at the time. There's no sense in everyone falling out and creating a bad atmosphere at Matt's wedding because of a decade-old misunderstanding.

I scan the bar for Ed, Fi – anyone really. I notice Pete chatting with a couple of men at the side of the room. When I catch his eye, he runs over to me.

'Luca, are you OK? I've been looking everywhere for you since I saw you fall.'

'I'm fine,' I say. 'Just a cut. Have you seen any of my friends?

'I haven't, sorry,' he replies. 'Listen, you've done enough today. Isn't it about time you relaxed?'

'Oh, it's impossible for me to relax at this wedding,' I tell him, not that he could even begin to imagine the full extent of why.

Pete places his hands on my shoulders and gives me a soothing smile.

'We need to get you out of here,' he says. 'Why don't we bail, go watch some trash TV in my room – we have fully stocked mini bars upstairs, I've heard a rumour that the smaller rooms don't have them. We can relax, talk more about jobs and futures ...'

'God, that sounds good,' I tell him. 'But I need to find my friends first, avert a crisis.'

'Luca, there you are,' I hear Tom's voice behind me. He grabs me and he hugs me tighter than I think I've ever been hugged before. 'Are you OK?'

Tom loosens his grip on me, just enough to hold me at arm's length, to look over my injuries.

'I'm fine, thank you' I say. 'It's just a cut.'

For a second, I wonder if this is genuine concern, or because he doesn't like to see me talking to Pete, but I get mad at myself for questioning his intentions like that.

Tom takes a thumb and brushes my cheek gently, just under my cut.

'It looks sore,' he says. 'What did Ed say?'

Ed said way too much.

'He says I'll be fine,' I tell him. 'It shouldn't leave a scar. It's just a glorified scratch, really.'

Pete clears his throat. I'd kind of forgotten he was standing there and I feel bad for making him feel like a third wheel. It's so easy to get caught up in the attention Tom gives everyone he talks to. He truly makes you feel like the most important thing in the world and – especially at times when you need it – it is such a huge comfort. I can't let myself get caught up in it though, because tomorrow he'll go home with Cleo, and in a few months they'll have a child together. I am almost certain I can't compete with that, but I am absolutely certain I shouldn't try. I can't do another second of this, I need to move on with my life.

I turn to Pete.

'Pete, everything you said before – that sounds great.'

'Well, OK,' he replies with a big grin. 'Room 312. I'll see you there after you find your friends?'

'See you there,' I tell him.

Tom waits for Pete to walk off before he says anything.

'What's that all about?' he asks, sounding just a little bit annoyed.

'That is nothing to do with you,' I tell him. 'I've got to go.'

Tom gently takes me by the arm, to stop me walking away. It occurs to me, to call Fi, but I've left my phone in my bag in the office.

'What?' I ask him. 'What do you want? What do you want from me?'

'You're going to his room? You just met him.'

'I literally knew you for years,' I tell him. 'Doesn't always work out though, does it?'

'Tell me you're not feeling something between us today and I'll leave you alone,' he replies.

'I don't have time for this, I need to find Fi.'

'I've seen her. I'll tell you where, if you just answer me,' he practically begs.

'Tom.' I look him in the eye and muster up as much faux confidence as I can. 'Whatever you're feeling between us – it's entirely one-sided. After the way you treated me when we were younger, I'll never, ever trust you again. OK?'

In the five seconds before Tom says anything, I watch my words wound him and I feel sick with myself. The truth is, of course I've felt something between us today. I've felt something between us since that first conversation I had with him in my bedroom all those years ago. But it is true that I don't trust him. And without trust, what have you got?

'I saw her arguing with Zach outside,' he tells me. 'By the pop-up photo booth and the sweet cart.'

Perhaps the greatest tragedy of all today is that I am only just learning about the sweet cart. Maybe I'll raid it after I sort out this mess, before I go to meet Pete.

'Thank you,' I tell him. 'Now go find the girlfriend you chose over me all those years ago, and make things right with her. You made your bed, Tom. It's too late now, you've got to sleep in it.'

'Luca,' he calls after me as I head for the door, but I ignore him. It breaks my heart to do it, but what else can I do? I can't get in the way of him getting back with his pregnant girlfriend, even if I'd like to. Before, when he said they had split up, it sounded like he had no interest in being there for his kid, and I don't know if that was true or for my benefit, but either way, it's awful. If he and Cleo are trying to reconcile, I cannot get in the way of that. I have to remove myself from the equation, and perhaps moving to London is the best way to do it.

Chapter 30

I can only see Fiona standing by the sweet cart. As I hurry over to her, the overwhelmingly strong scent of sugar fills my nostrils and I feel intoxicated by it. I feel like, in my position, a normal adult might consider drowning their sorrows at the bar, but I want nothing more than to commiserate with a bag of pick 'n' mix, and maybe one of those two-foot-long jelly snakes I've just spotted. But I can tell that Fi looks upset, and that she needs me. I just need to keep my eyes on the prize. I'll tell her what Ed is saying, make sure she's OK and then I'll get the hell out of here.

'Hey, is everything OK?' I ask her.

'Zach and I were just arguing,' she tells me. A tear escapes her eye, which she quickly wipes away.

'Oh, God, has Ed told him?' I ask.

'Told him what?' she replies.

'Oh, erm …'

Suddenly I feel awkward, and incredibly guilty for taking drunk Ed's word about what happened. This is Fi. Fifi, my best friend at uni, who could never even bear the idea of a one-night stand – especially not with the love of her life's best friend.

'It's Ed,' I tell her. 'He's taken this day off thing way too far.

He's so drunk, he actually tried to kiss me while he was cleaning my cut.'

'What?' Fi shrieks. 'He's married. He's not just married though, he's like, really, really married.'

'I was shocked too,' I tell her. 'But I think he's having some kind of moral crisis … or something.'

'Shit,' Fi replies. 'Is he OK? Where is he now?'

'He's looking for you,' I tell her. 'Or maybe Zach … he was saying some stuff …'

'Like what?' she asks.

She doesn't sound nervous or guilty or like she has a clue what I'm about to say, and now I feel really, really bad. Perhaps I shouldn't even tell her – what's she going to do, go and yell at him? I'm sure that's the last thing he needs right now.

'Luca, come on, what is he saying?' she persists.

'He's … well … he's very drunk, and he's somehow got it into his head that, on New Year's Eve – the one when you and Zach finally got together … Well, he's got it in his head that, before that, before Zach got home, when he'd had his accident …' I pause for a few seconds. Best just to spit it out. 'He reckons he caught you shagging Clarky.'

'Oh … my … God …' she stutters, before quickly raising her hands to her mouth.

'Listen, don't panic, he's just drunk, he's talking rubbish, he doesn't …'

My voice trails off as I notice something in her eye. A little glimmer of … I think it's panic. Fear even.

'He is talking rubbish, right?'

'No, it's true,' she says, her voice crackling. 'Shit, it's true. Luca, no matter what, we can't let him tell Zach because …'

'Because he'll kill him.'

We both jump at the sound of Zach's voice. He's been standing right next to us, listening to our conversation, for God knows how long. Long enough to realise what's going on.

His Glaswegian accent always sounds so charming and fun-loving. Right now, I can hear the anger rumbling inside him, his words coming out in a growl.

'Zach,' Fi says, but he isn't listening. He marches off, looking for Clarky I'd imagine.

I quicken my steps to catch him up. Now I really do feel fortunate to be wearing my trainers.

'Zach, listen, let's just calm down, OK? Let's just stop and talk about it.'

'Luca, stay out of it,' he replies.

'Zach.'

'Listen, as far as I can tell, you and Matt were the only ones who didn't know anything. I have no problem with you. Clarky and I need a little chat though. Maybe me and Ed too, if I've got any fists left.'

Zach marches over to our table looking for Clarky, but he isn't there. Ed is there though, and Matt has finally found a moment to take a seat and chat. He honestly couldn't have picked a worse time.

'Clarky?' Zach barks at them.

'Not here, mate,' Matt replies. 'He's chatting up some bird, they went for a walk around the pond. You know what he's like, he probably thinks she'll shag him.'

Matt laughs, until he sees the anger on Zach's face.

'You OK, bud?' he asks.

Zach doesn't reply, he storms off in the direction of the pond.

'Zach, please, just talk to me,' Fi says running after him.

I suddenly notice how dark it's getting, and how chilly it feels, now that the sun isn't warming the occasion.

With my watch still frozen, and my phone in the office, I can genuinely say I have absolutely no idea what time it is. I've been conscious of the time maybe twice today. I feel trapped in a perpetual state of uni drama. When it was still light, it felt like this wedding might never end. Now that it's getting dark, I can just about imagine the light at the end of the tunnel, but you know what they say: it's always darkest before the dawn.

'Luca, what's going on?' Matt asks me.

'Ed thought today might be the day to mention Fi and Clarky had sex at uni,' I tell him angrily.

The colour drains from Ed's face.

'I only told you,' he insists.

'I though you were going to tell Zach, so I told Fi. Zach overheard,' I reply.

'Shit, we'd better go after them,' Matt says, jumping to his feet. I feel so sorry for him, he really didn't need this on his wedding day.

The three of us run towards the pond, like the world's worst trio of superheroes. We arrive just in time to see the poor girl Clarky was trying to chat up scarper. Zach is currently chasing Clarky around the pond, with a tearful Fi following his every step.

'Mate, it was years ago,' Clarky says, panting as he runs. 'It was before you two even got together.'

'Yeah, minutes before,' Zach shouts back.

Clarky looks momentarily relieved as the cavalry arrives, but Zach sees an ally in Matt. And he'd be right.

'Matt, block him,' Zach shouts.

Matt decides where his loyalty lies. It follows his moral compass. Clarky tries to escape by running across the old, wooden bridge that stretches across the large pond, but it's so long that the inevitable happens, and Zach blocks one end of the bridge, while Matt blocks the other. Poor Clarky just stands in the middle, looking back and forth between the two of them.

'Lads, listen, we just need to talk about this like adults,' Clarky reasons, which is rich coming from him, but the two of them beating him up isn't the answer.

Fi, Ed and I hurry to Matt's side of the bridge and push past him. As the three of us run towards Clarky, so does Zach. Now we're all in the middle of the bridge together, Zach trying to murder Clarky, with only Ed's minimal physical strength and my attempt at words of reason getting in his way.

'You bastard,' Zach yells at him.

'Mate, I'm so sorry,' Clarky says. His eyes widen as he runs a hand through his hair. He looks absolutely terrified.

'Why?' Zach yells. 'Why did you do it?'

'I didn't think you'd care,' he replies, rushing through his words. 'Fi didn't either. She told me that you were going to finally tell the girl you had feelings for all about it New Year's Eve. When you never came home, she figured she wasn't the girl. And it just happened.'

'Oh, for God's sake,' Zach replies. 'I'm late home and you jump into bed with the first willing person?'

'I was upset,' Fi says weakly. 'I didn't know you'd had a car accident.'

'Except I didn't have a car accident,' Zach says. I notice the veins on his temples becoming more pronounced as his anger increases. 'I was covering for this bloody idiot.'

Zach yells this straight into Ed's face. Ed lets go of him. Luckily Zach is too busy spilling the truth, to start spilling Clarky's blood – for now at least.

'What?' Fi says.

'Ed had the car accident. Ed hit the dog. Ed got drunk and decided to take the car for a spin. It was *him* who had the accident.'

'You've got to be kidding,' Matt says.

'Luca and I covered for him,' Zach says. 'We didn't want him to fuck up his career and his future. And how does he repay me for taking the fall for him? He watches my best mate nailing my girlfriend and doesn't think to tell me.'

'I wasn't your girlfriend yet,' Fi insists. It takes a second for what Zach actually said to catch up with her. She turns to Ed. 'You … you actually watched us?'

'Wait, you watched us?' Clarks says, equally as outraged. 'I knew you'd seen us together but I didn't know you'd watched. You're a dog murderer *and* a pervert.'

'Ha, as if you think you have any right to be upset,' Zach fumes.

'I didn't say that I *watched*,' Ed says. 'I couldn't help but see though … and hear …'

Ed has the look of a solider recalling the unspeakable terrors of war.

'Yes you are,' Fi says. 'Luca told me how you just tried to get off with her while you were supposed to be helping her.'

'I'm not the pervert, you're the pervert,' he snaps back. 'I saw what you two did, remember.'

'OK,' I start trying to diffuse the situation, but no one is listening.

'As a doctor, I can't advocate something so unhygienic.'

'You little …' Zach starts, before charging forwards.

Matt pushes past us towards Zach, holding him back from another violent outburst. I'm not sure if this one was intended for Clarky or Ed.

'And, mate, you know it was your car Ed crashed, right?' Zach tells Matt.

Oh, God, it's all coming out now.

'What?' Matt says.

'That night, it was your car that he crashed. He borrowed it without asking you.'

'You covered for him and you let me believe I'd crashed my own car into something without realising?' Matt replies.

I don't think Zach saw himself coming off at all badly with that revelation.

'I knew I hadn't done it,' Matt rants. 'And Cleo said so too, she knew I hadn't hit it that night. I only went out to pick up bloody costumes that night.'

'Cleo?' I say. 'What's Cleo got to do with this?'

'That's where I met her, at the fancy dress shop,' he says. 'I invited her and her mate to the party. The shop had just closed but Cleo didn't have a costume – I'm bloody glad I gave her yours now, Luca.'

'What?' I reply.

'I gave Cleo your costume. And I'm glad – I never thought you'd lie to me.'

Just like I'm on a rollercoaster, my heart jumps into my mouth, before plummeting into the depths of my stomach.

'You gave Cleo my costume,' I repeat back to him.

'Luca, I don't know why you're getting so upset,' Zach says. 'Of everyone that's been wronged, your thing is the least important.'

'You didn't just give her my costume, you gave her Tom,' I say angrily. 'He was looking for Catwoman that night. We were going to finally be together, except he met Cleo first, and he kissed her, and it's because she was wearing my costume. This is all your fault.'

'How was I to know?' Matt asks me angrily.

I bite my lip and shake my head.

'We're supposed to be friends,' Ed says softly.

'Friends?' I reply. 'We're not friends, none of us are. We deceive each other, we hurt each other – we don't have each other's backs. You're all just out for yourselves.'

'Never mind friends,' Zach adds. 'Fiona, you're supposed to be my fiancée. Why didn't you tell me?'

'Because you wouldn't have got together with me at the time if you'd known,' she says. 'And the more time went on, the more I thought it would hurt you to find out about it.'

'You're damn right I wouldn't have got together with you if I'd known Clarky's bed was still warm from you being in it. My God, you slept with me that night too. That was our first night together.'

Fi honestly looks like she's going to throw up. Now she is throwing up, leaning over the side of the bridge.

'Do you know what makes me the angriest of all?' Matt starts. 'It's the fact that it's been ten years, but you wait until now, until today—'

'Matt, shush,' I say quickly.

'Luca, don't shush me,' he says. 'Not now.'

'No, listen. Did you guys hear that?'

For a few seconds, there isn't a sound. Just the quiet buzz of the wedding at the other side of the gardens. But then I hear it again, a clicking noise.

'Did you hear that?' I say.

'Luca, hear what?' Clarky asks angry. 'If this is one of your hippy ways of making people make friends, listening to the trees or—'

It happens again, and this time everyone hears it. After a few seconds it happens again, and then again. And then the clicks start getting louder and closer together.

It's not the trees, it's the bridge.

'Maybe we should get off this thing,' I say, over the loud clicks and subsequent creaking noises.

Everyone makes a move to get off the bridge at once, but that's all it takes. Before any of us can figure out what is going on, the bridge collapses beneath us.

Chapter 31

Then – New Year's Day 2009

'Are you not getting dressed today then?' Ed asks, poking his head around the living room door.

'Nope,' I reply. 'Not today, not tomorrow – maybe not even this year.'

'Well, there's not much I can say to that,' he says. 'Other than we'll all join you.'

Ed comes out from behind the wall, revealing his red and green Christmas pyjamas. They're designed to make the wearer look like an elf – and they're completely adorable.

For the first time today, I crack a smile at my super serious friend in his super serious pyjamas.

'We?' I say.

'It's safe to come in,' Ed calls out.

Fifi, Zach, Matt and even Clarky all come in – and they're all wearing pyjamas too.

Matt is carrying a pile of pizzas. The warm, delicious smell drifts over and my unintentional hunger strike hardly seems worth it now. Maybe I'll just gain loads of weight instead – I'm borderline anyway, I may as well pick a side and own it.

'We thought we'd hang out with you, eat junk, watch movies,' Fifi says.

'But we thought we'd send Ed in first, make sure it was safe,' Clarky adds.

'Oh, wow, so Ed was just the canary you sent in to make sure it was safe?' I joke.

'He owed me one,' Zach says with a smile.

'So, what do you reckon?' Matt asks. 'Pizza, maybe a Will Ferrell movie or two? I might even let you wear my Superman dressing gown, if you play your cards right.'

I feel immediately lighter.

'That would be great,' I reply, sitting up to make more room on the sofa.

I may have lost Tom, but a boy is just a boy. My friends will always have my back. As long as I've got my friends, I know I'll be OK.

Chapter 32

Now

I always thought things like this happened in slow motion – at least that's what the movies led me to believe.

In reality, when you fall down in such a spectacular manner, it's over before you even realise it has happened. You go from arguing on a bridge with your oldest friends to bobbing around in a dirty pond with them in the blink of an eye.

The tension breaks easier than the bridge did, when one of us starts laughing no more than a split second after the water has settled. Soon enough, we're all laughing.

It's amazing, how things appear a certain way until you get to see them from a different perspective. For example, the first time I saw the pond it looked gorgeous; warm, sparkling, deep water – weirdly inviting, in an impractical way. In reality, the water is cold, dirty, and not more than four feet deep.

Clarky tries to get to his feet a little too quickly and slips on something at the bottom of the pond. As he falls backwards he make another splash, which Matt bears the brunt of. He playfully slaps some water back at him. Well, we're all already soaking wet, it's not like anyone can make the situation worse, is it?

'Luca,' I hear a voice bellow from afar. I hear it again, only this time it's louder.

I twirl around in the water to see Al Atlantic charging towards the pond. As he gets closer he rips his shirt open – Superman style – kicks off his trousers, and jumps into the water.

'Al, what on earth are you doing?' I ask.

'I'm saving you,' he replies.

'Al!' I protest as he hooks an arm around my body and drags me to shore.

He puts me down on the grass, laying me flat on my back.

'If you try and give me mouth-to-mouth I will punch you in the face,' I say as he looms over me, so close he's blocking the dim light of the garden lanterns. It's so dark now, without them, his face is hidden in his shadow. It really is getting dark now. Chilly too.

'Are you OK?' he asks me.

'I'm fine, thank you,' I say – not that I needed saving.

Alan takes my hand in his and attempts to take my pulse. I snatch my hand back with a laugh.

'Alan, honestly, I'm fine,' I insist.

'Alright, Alan, calm down,' Clarky shouts over. 'Any excuse to take your bloody top off.'

I lift myself up on to my elbows.

'I'm not showing off,' he protests to me.

I look him up and down as he kneels on the grass next to me. Water rolls down his alarmingly hard body, washing off his fake tan as it navigates the contours of his muscles.

'You're literally making your pecs dance right now,' I point out.

'Luca, I saved you,' he insists.

'From what, a few feet of water? This pond is shallow – even for Clarky,' Zach calls back. Teasing Alan has always come naturally to my friends. I think they knew he was wrong for me from day one. 'What are you saving her from?'

Al turns to the water with a grave seriousness.

'There are snakes in there,' he bellows.

I watch as my friends scramble for the shore, fighting against each other, against the slippery pond floor, against the weight of the water.

They join me in lying on the grass.

'They're only a threat if you're a vampire,' I tell them, remembering what Alan said earlier about garlic.

'You're screwed then, aren't you, goth?' Clarky says before placing a finger to his nostril and blowing the contents out of the other one onto the grass.

'Leave her alone,' Alan replies, jumping to my defence.

'It's OK, Al, he can't hurt me,' I say. 'I don't have a girlfriend he can sleep with.'

'No, you don't have anyone,' he replies.

This rubs me up the wrong way.

'I'd rather have no one than take advantage of someone who is only sleeping with me because she's upset,' I snap.

'OK,' Fi says pulling herself to her feet. 'Let's not get back into this.'

'Yeah, let's pretend it never happened,' Zach says sarcastically. 'Except Luca is right.'

'No, she isn't,' Clarky says, standing up, the anger in his words and the volume of his voice intensifying. 'I'm in love with her, OK?'

'What?' Fi replies, collecting her jaw from the floor.

'Well, at least I thought I was, until now. I always thought there was something between us, but now ... I'm starting to think you were just using me, flirting with me and kissing me to make Zach jealous ...'

'You think?!' Fi replies.

'And then sleeping with me ... forgive a guy for getting the wrong end of the stick. And I didn't dump Bella, she dumped me. She dumped me because I didn't want to marry her, because

I kept thinking about you, thinking maybe you still had feelings for me, and that night, and what might've happened if Zach hadn't turned up.'

'If I'd had the good manners to die in the car accident you thought I'd had, you mean?' Zach replies. 'You don't love her. You don't love anyone.'

'I'm pregnant,' Fi shouts over their bickering.

'What?' Zach says weakly. If he weren't already on the floor, he'd be straight back down there.

Fi doesn't answer him, she runs back towards the party.

'Wait,' Zach calls as he struggles to his feet on the slippery, wet grass.

He runs after her, leaving the rest of us in stunned silence.

Clarky slowly begins to walk away too.

'Where are you going?' Ed calls after him.

'I'm going to put in a complaint about that shitting bridge,' he calls after him.

'He'll be fine,' I tell Ed. 'He's always happy when he's complaining.'

'My new wife won't be happy with me when she gets invoiced for a bridge,' Matt says as he stands up. 'Or when she sees that my £600 suit is ruined.'

He storms off too, leaving me, Ed and Al.

'I feel … responsible,' Ed says softly.

'Doubt it, mate,' Al replies.

'Yeah, you didn't tell Zach what happened,' I point out. 'He overheard me talking to Fi about it.'

'Plus, you've always been kind of boring – no offence,' Al adds. 'What could you have done?'

'I'm boring?' Ed replies. '*I'm* boring?'

'Right, OK, we're not doing this,' I say, using Al's arm as a handrail to pull myself up. 'I'm not doing any of this shit anymore.'

'Luca, wait,' Al calls after me.

'Nope,' I reply. 'Nope, nope, nope.'

I've had enough. I've really, truly had enough.

I expected to come to the wedding and – worst case scenario – feel like crap about my life and be reminded of all my failures as a woman. This though … this is too much. It's like everyone has reverted to being a student and everything is trying to go back to how it was then. You know what, my life might not be up to much now, but it's certainly better than it was back then. I'd rather be a sad single than a messy twenty-something changing her significant other more often than I changed my hair colour. We're supposed to be adults – adults don't all end up angry and wet at the bottom of a pond. I'm sure most students manage to graduate without doing so too.

I feel the dirty water squelching in my trainers as I meaningfully tread the ground back across the lawn to where the party is. With my eyes fixed on the door that leads into the hotel, I march through the party without so much as peeping to see if anyone is staring at me, the drowned rat in the designer dress she can't afford, with water leaking from her trainers and a face like thunder. I really, really don't care what people think of me, all I can think about now is making a change – a big one. I have emerged from that pond a whole new woman, and as I crawl from the grass, drip through the party, and finally strut through the bar, I feel myself evolving into something better, something lighter. Someone who grabs life by the balls, instead of being repeatedly kicked in her own metaphorical ones.

'Luca, oh my God,' I hear Tom's voice behind me.

'Not now,' I reply.

'Wait, what happened?' he asks, taking me gently by the arm, stopping me in my tracks.

I turn to face him. Great, Cleo is with him.

'Look what the cat dragged in,' she says. 'Because … you look like something a cat dragged in.'

'Hilarious,' I reply sarcastically. 'I'm sure normally I'd be annoyed or upset or blah blah blah.'

'Lord, she's drunk,' Cleo says. 'Why are you wet?'

'I've been in the pond,' I reply, as my only explanation.

'Do you have spare clothes with you? I'd lend you some of mine, but I doubt they'd fit.'

I roll my eyes.

'Because I'm pregnant and you're not, duh,' she points out.

Maybe it was a fat joke – maybe it was a boast about her being pregnant – I. Don't. Care.

'Luca, you're bleeding,' Tom says, rushing towards me, raising his hand to my neck.

He reaches up to touch my wound, but as he pulls his hand away I notice something.

'That's not blood, it's orange – it's fake tan from Alan, from when we were in the pond.'

'Ooh, Luca and Alan in the pond,' Cleo sings.

'Mmm,' I reply insincerely. 'You'd love that, wouldn't you? Nope, nothing going on between me and Alan. But I am going upstairs to shag Pete's brains out and accept his job offer in London. You two have nice lives.'

My parting gift to my dear, dear frenemy Cleo, is to give her the finger as I head for the stairwell. I *am* going to make an active effort to be more mature … just, starting now I guess.

I was so annoyed with myself when I left my clutch in the reception office earlier – it just felt like another crappy feature of the unreliable Luca Wade brand – but now I'm so happy I did because it would've been ruined in the water.

I arrive at reception and ring the bell, but no one appears. I wait a few seconds and try again … still nothing.

I glance at the door. I don't think you need anything special to open it – I'm pretty sure Ed and I walked freely through it. Oh, I don't have time for this. I'm just going to grab it. Well, it's my bag, right? I can't get in trouble for stealing my own bag. If they are in any doubt as to whether it is my phone, I'll just show them the thirty-five failed selfie attempts I took this morning. I'd hoped for at least one belter, even if it needed a little 'postproduction' to make it acceptable, but they were all duds. Still, those kinds of selfies are arguable the ones with the best likeness to our real faces, right?

I open the door slowly and pop my head through to make sure no one is around. If they are, I'll pretend I was poking my head through the door to ask for it, rather than just helping myself.

'Oh God,' I blurt, more than announcing my entrance.

'Oh, hey Luca,' Clarky replies.

He's standing there, in the middle of the office, in nothing but a towel. The receptionist – the one who sassed him earlier – is kneeling on the floor in front of him, patting his legs dry with a towel.

'I've got us some compo, for the bridge thing,' he says.

'Us, or just yourself?' I reply nodding towards the receptionist.

'All of us,' he replies.

Wow, it's been fifteen minutes. That's got to be a new consumer complaint record for Clarky. It's probably a new record for him getting a girl to touch him too.

I grab my clutch and my shoes and turn to leave. I just have my Everest (AKA the stairs) to conquer and then I'm done.

It is definitely harder climbing up the stairs than it is walking down them, and I don't suppose my waterlogged clothes are helping. Perhaps I should have gone to my own room first, but I don't plan on keeping these clothes on for long anyway.

When I get to the top, I pause for a few seconds to get my breath back. As I steady my breathing, I notice my reflection in the glass of the door. Wow, I look like a swamp monster. It will be a miracle, if Pete even lets me through the door.

I walk along the corridor and take one last deep breath before knocking. It might sound pathetic to some, but this is a big deal for me. I don't take chances like this with my job, my life or, least of all, my heart.

Now all I have to do is wait for Pete to open the door.

Chapter 33

I shuffle awkwardly on the spot. My wet, smelly clothes are really starting to make me feel uncomfortable, and every second I stand here increases the urge to retreat.

There's no answer, so I knock again. I give it another thirty seconds, but there's still no sign of life.

Well, that's that then. So much for my big gesture. I guess Pete is still at the party, so I'll have to go back downstairs. This absolutely isn't me retreating, it's just a short detour.

When I reach the stairwell doorway, I notice Tom through the window, almost at the top of the stairs. I don't want to speak to him anyway, but after my big speech about coming up here to see Pete, I definitely don't want him to see me skulking around without him.

I hurry back towards the lift. I think I'll take my chances in that death trap, rather than face Tom right now.

I step inside the lift but, just as I'm pulling the door closed, Kat's mum emerges from her room and gives me a wave, signalling for me to hold the lift for her. I can't exactly ignore her, can I? We're looking right at each other.

'Thank you,' she says as I hold the door for her. 'Oh, hello Tom.'

'Hello Susanna,' he replies. As he turns to face her, he clocks me.

'There you are,' he says.

'Here I am,' I reply.

The three of us squash into the lift. With the room service cart that's in here already, it's a tight squeeze. Much to Kat's mum's credit, she doesn't mention the fact that I'm soaking wet or kind of smelly.

'I'm only going down two floors,' she says. 'I'm taking my mum her medication, she's calling it a night. Are you two ...?'

'I was just looking for Luca,' Tom says.

'And I was just looking for Pete,' I reply.

'Oh, Pete,' she says, her smile beaming. 'Such a lovely boy.'

'He is, isn't he?' I reply.

'Well, I suppose I shouldn't call him a boy, even though I've known him since he was one,' she muses. 'He's a man now – a lovely man. It's a shame his wife and kids couldn't make it.'

'It is,' I reply politely. Then her words sink in. 'What?'

'They couldn't make it,' she says. 'I don't think it has anything to do with Lucy being pregnant, it was her stepdad's 60th birthday, I believe.'

The lift grinds to a halt on the second floor.

'See you both back down at the party,' she says as she steps out.

Without a single word or a shred of emotion, I pull the door closed and press the button for the ground floor.

'Luca,' Tom starts softly.

'Don't,' I reply. 'Please don't.'

'Luca, listen.'

'I said don't,' I snap angrily, right as the lift slams to a halt.

The lights flicker for a few seconds. I wait for the lift to move again, but it doesn't, and I can tell that we're trapped between floors because there is mostly wall in front of us, with a little bit of door at the top.

'Oh, wonderful, brilliant, amazing,' I rant. 'Of course the lift gets stuck, and of course I'm stuck in here with you.'

'Listen, don't panic,' Tom says soothingly. 'It said this sort of thing happens all the time. It's nothing to worry about.'

'So, what do we do?' I ask. 'You said you saw a thing in reception saying what to do if the lift stopped.'

'Oh,' he says. 'I *did* see that … I didn't read it though.'

'Wonderful, brilliant, amazing.'

I scan the buttons on the wall. 'There's no alarm.'

'There's no signal either,' he replies, putting his phone back in his pocket.

'Why didn't I get changed?' I say to myself.

'Well, there are towels in here,' he says as he roots through the room service cart.

'I'll be fine,' I tell him. 'Someone has to come soon.'

Ten minutes later, I glance at my watch, but it's still frozen. It doesn't seem like anyone is coming to our rescue.

'We really need to get you out of those clothes,' he says.

I shoot him a look.

'No joking or flirting,' he says. 'That water can't have been very clean.'

Tom takes two towels from the cart. He also takes a bottle of water and soaks one of the towels.

'Use this one to clean the sludge off you, and this one to dry yourself,' he says.

'Is there a change of clothes in there too?' I ask sarcastically.

Tom slips off his jacket and unbuttons his shirt.

'Wha … what are you doing?' I ask.

I force myself to maintain eye contact with Tom, but there's a voice in my head telling me to look down.

'Wear this as a dress,' he says.

'Thanks,' I reply weakly.

I hover for a second, with the towels in my hands.

'Oh, I'll turn around,' he says.

Not only does Tom turn around, but he makes an effort to cover his eyes with his hands too.

'Thank God there are no mirrors in here,' he says with an awkward laugh. 'Let me know when you're done.'

I clean and dry myself as best I can with the tools I've been given. I immediately feel better for taking my dress off, and even better for wiping my skin clean.

'Is there any moisturiser in there?' I ask.

'Yeah,' Tom says.

As he goes to grab me some he opens his eyes and inadvertently glances over at me. My modestly is just about protected with the towel I'm holding up in front of me, but I wrap it round me tighter while I wait for the moisturiser. Tom passes me it and covers his eyes again. I slather myself is as much as possible, not because the pond has made my skin dry, but because I can smell it on my skin still.

When I'm done, I put on Tom's shirt. Buttoned up, it's not unlike a shirt dress I already own, except mine doesn't smell this good. This one smells amazing, like Tom's aftershave. I take a big whiff of the collar before telling Tom it's safe to turn around.

'So, do you want to talk about it?' he asks me.

'About what?'

'Luca, come on,' he starts. 'We both heard what Susanna said.'

'Tom, I appreciate the towels and I appreciate the shirt, but I don't want to talk to you, OK?'

'So we're going to just wait in silence for the lift to be fixed then?'

'Yep,' I reply.

Tom laughs at me like I'm ridiculous.

'OK, fine,' he says. 'If that's the way you want it to be.'

'It is,' I reply.

I just hope someone comes to help us soon, because I'm not sure how long I can hack it in here.

Chapter 34

'Oh my God, it's been hours,' I moan.

'Luca, it's been like half an hour,' Tom laughs.

'Well, it feels longer,' I say. 'I'm going to go mad, stuck in here, in this tiny lift – with *you*.'

'Charming,' he replies with a smile.

God, he's so easy-going and it drives me mad.

We must look so ridiculous. Me, sitting here in Tom's shirt, smelling like a combination of pond residue and magnolia hand lotion. Tom sitting opposite me, without his shirt.

I think the lack of mirrors in the lift makes the situation seem so much worse. It makes it feel even more claustrophobic, and with each minute that goes by, it feels like the lift gets smaller and smaller. I swear, Tom and I are getting closer together – then again, we've always been like a moth to a flame with each other.

'Right, that's it,' he says clapping his hands. 'I'm sure, under the circumstances, this will be completely fine.'

Tom opens up the room service cart and pulls out small packets of biscuits – the kind you usually find with the tea and coffee making facilities – and several mini bottles of alcohol. He lays them out on the floor in front of us.

'Here's what's going to happen, OK? You're going to drink a

couple of these little bottles, you're going to eat a few biscuits, and we're going to talk about whatever you want.'

I sigh.

'OK, sure.'

'OK,' he says in a way more enthusiastic tone than me. 'So, I want to get a good pairing for you … here's a mini bottle of vodka and a packet of chocolate chip cookies.'

I give him a half-hearted smile as I thank him. When my anger starts to dissolve, I forget why I was even mad at him in the first place.

'So, what shall we talk about?' he says.

I shrug my shoulders.

'We could talk about why you and Alan were in the pond,' he suggests. 'I've been wondering.'

'It wasn't just me and Alan,' I say. 'It was me, Fi, Zach, Matt, Clarky and Ed. Alan just jumped in to save me from the snakes. He reckons there are snakes in the pond, but I didn't see any.'

Only the ones I'm friends with.

'You were all in the pond?' he replies in disbelief.

'Have you seen the bridge that goes from one side of the pond to the other?'

'The beautiful old wooden one?' he replies. 'Yeah.'

'Yeah, it isn't there anymore,' I reply. 'We broke it.'

'You broke it? How?'

'We were all arguing on it.'

'You were all arguing on it?'

'There's a weird echo in this lift,' I joke. 'We just … all fell out … with everyone … simultaneously.'

'Can I ask why?'

'Because of stuff that happened at uni,' I say. 'I know, stupid, right?'

'Give me the abridged version,' he says as he tosses back a tiny bottle of Jack Daniels with a custard cream chaser.

I take a deep breath.

'Well … ten years ago, when we had that New Year's Eve party, Zach was finally going to tell Fi that he loved her, except Ed got drunk and crashed Matt's car. Zach and I covered for him, but because Zach was late home, Fi slept with Clarky. Ed saw, and blurted it out drunk today. Zach found out and kicked off. Matt found out Ed crashed his car and didn't tell him, and I found out that Matt gave my costume away to Cleo, which is why you thought she was me, which is why you kissed her and she wound up your girlfriend instead of me – but we don't talk about that, do we?'

'Wow,' he replies.

'And just when you think the day can't get any worse, I go to find Pete, the man offering me a fresh start and a new job and a relationship … and I find out he's married. So I'm going to have to assume none of what he said was real, he was just trying to shag me because his wife wasn't around – his pregnant wife, no less – and I was stupid enough to fall for it.'

I breathe quickly because I think I spat all that out at Tom in maybe two or three breaths. I feel tears prickle my eyes. You know what, I'm going to take my metaphorical hat off to myself, because I've made it this far through the day without crying. But, really, what's the point in playing it cool now, huh?

Tom scoots across the lift floor on his bum. He sits next to me and wraps an arm around me, pulling me close.

'He's an arsehole,' Tom tells me in a very matter of fact way. 'Plain and simple. But you didn't fall for him – you didn't fall for it.'

'I was knocking on his hotel door when you found me,' I point out.

'You would've realised,' he says. 'And if you hadn't, well, I would've been knocking on the door within five minutes with some excuse to get you out of there. I would have saved you.'

'Why, did you know he was married?'

'I didn't,' he admits. 'That would've been much less embarrassing than the reality … I was jealous. I was going to interrupt you and drag you out of there under false pretences … because I was jealous.'

'You have no right to be jealous,' I tell him. 'Cleo wouldn't be happy with you being jealous.'

'Why do you care so much about what Cleo thinks?' he asks me. Now it's his turn to sound annoyed.

'I don't care,' I say defensively. 'She's your girlfriend, not mine.'

'I already told you, she's not my girlfriend anymore. She hasn't been for a long time.'

'I heard her talking about how the two of you were getting back together.'

'Ooh, you got me,' he says sarcastically. 'Luca, Cleo and I are not getting back together. She suggested it today, but I shot her down. Gently, obviously.'

'You won't even get back with her for the baby?' I ask.

'No,' he replies confidently.

'Don't you think that's awful?'

'No?' he replies. 'It's not my job to raise someone else's kid, with a woman I don't love. I feel bad for them, sure, but not to the point where I'd throw my own life or happiness away.'

'Wait, what? Cleo isn't having *your* baby?'

'Of course she isn't,' he replies. 'We broke up years ago. Wait, have you spent all day thinking I knocked her up and bailed on her?'

I feel my cheeks flush.

'Possibly,' I reply sheepishly.

'Why on earth would you think so little of me?' he asks.

'Why wouldn't I?' I reply. 'You spent all Christmas telling me we were going to be together and then you kissed a girl half my height "thinking it was me" and wound up with her instead.'

'Luca, I was young, I was an idiot. If I'm being completely honest, I was scared too. I was so protective of you, I was terrified of someone hurting you. I spent all Christmas thinking about you, looking forward to seeing you, but worrying it was going to destroy our friendship if we got together. I did kiss Cleo thinking she was you, but when I realised my mistake … I was so embarrassed, and I didn't want to tell her that I thought she was someone else. As we chatted, I realise that not only was I scared of someone hurting you, but I was terrified of it being me. Cleo gave me an easy out, and I did like her … I loved you, but—'

'You *loved* me?'

'Is that reaction to the fact or the tense?'

'Both,' I admit.

Tom twists around a little, to look me in the eye.

'Maybe it's a stretch, to believe that we're meant to be, or on some kind of course correction path,' he says mockingly. 'Maybe it's a coincidence that our song was playing when we danced – *our* song with *those* lyrics. And we're both here at this wedding, bumping into each other after all these years. We find out we're living in the same city now. Fate or coincidence – who cares? We both took roads away from each other and look what's happened, they've led us right back to each other.'

'So?'

'So I don't care how or why we've been brought back together,' he says. 'I'm just happy that we have.'

I think for a moment.

'Is it that easy?'

'It's as easy as you want it to be,' he says. 'What do you want, do you want me to beg? I've already given you the shirt off my back – I could take off my pants?'

I smile.

'It couldn't hurt,' I reply.

'Oh, a joke,' he replies. 'She's making jokes, she must be forgiving me.'

'Don't count your chickens too soon,' I tell him.

'Well, how about this … I did love you back then. I still love you now. I'll always love you, if you'll let me.'

Tears escape my eyes again.

'Please don't be upset,' he says. 'I'm sorry. I'll shut up now.'

Before I have a chance to say anything, Tom throws back another mini bottle of booze.

'I'm not upset,' I tell him. 'I ... I love you too. Always have. Always will.'

'Yeah, but I already said that,' he jokes. 'You can't use recycled material on me.'

'OK, well, how about this,' I start, but I don't say anything. Instead, I lean forward and kiss him, and it's exactly the kind of kiss you'd expect after over a decade of build-up. It's messy, weirdly sexy, passionate, and I'm pretty sure I'm still crying.

'Hmm, not bad,' he replies with a cheeky smile. 'Can we try again?'

In one swift move, Tom swipes me into his arms and pins me down on the lift floor. He runs his hands up my body as we kiss, but we're interrupted by a loud noise, which quickly separates us.

Oh, how bloody typical, that I'm going to die in this carpet-covered lift, moments after I've finally got my hands on the thing I've wanted the most, my entire adult life.

'It's OK,' he reassures me. 'They're probably just getting it moving again.'

I squeeze Tom tightly. Why do I get the feeling I'm about to plummet to my death?

It's somehow even scarier when the bottom part of the door that we can see above us is opened slightly, and a horrific looking arm reaches inside and starts aimlessly grabbing at the air.

'Oh my God,' I blurt.

It's massive, with blotchy orange skin covered in green and black gunk. Wait a minute ...

'Luca? Are you in there?'

'Alan?' I call back.

Suddenly his face appears in the gap, like Jack Nicholson in

The Shining.

'My name is Al now.'

Well, like Jack Nicholson in *The Shining*, but with a much less terrifying catchphrase.

'Are you two … are you naked?'

'Tom gave me his shirt,' I say. 'Because I was dirty from the pond.'

I'm scared that if I give Alan any indication that Tom and I have kissed, he won't save us.

'Why are you so dirty still?' I ask him.

'Matt lost his wedding ring down there,' he says. 'I promised him I'd find it before his wife realised.'

'Any luck?' Tom asks him.

'Of course,' he replies. 'I'm Al Atlantic.'

'Very impressive,' I reply and, do you know what? I don't think I'm being sarcastic.

'And for my final trick,' he starts. Alan uses his strength to force open the lift door.

'OK, take my hand, I'll pull you out,' he says.

'What?' Tom replies. He doesn't seem overly happy with this arrangement.

'I'll pull you out, one at a time,' he says.

'I'm sure I could climb, now the door is open,' Tom says.

Alan just laughs.

'Just let me pull you out, chief.'

'God, this is so emasculating,' Tom says quietly to me.

I kiss him on the cheek.

'See you on the outside,' I say.

I reach up and take Alan's hand. In a couple of seconds he's pulled me up and out of the lift, like I'm weightless.

'Come on then, big fella,' he says to Tom patronisingly, although I don't think he means it maliciously.

I hug Alan and thank him.

'Erm, are you two … you know,' he says.

'Are we ...?' Tom replies.

'Are you two finally together?' he asks.

Neither of us says anything. Well, are we?

'I always kind of suspected you'd end up together,' Alan replies. 'Well, you have my blessing.'

I smile and I hug him again – this time like I really mean it.

'The lift mechanics are on their way,' he says. 'I might stick around, see if they need anything lifting.'

'Like the building?' I joke.

'Exactly.' He winks at me.

'I'm going to go and finally wash the pond off me,' I say. 'Night Al.'

'Night Luca.'

We head for the stairwell. I need to go downstairs and head outside to get to the cottages. Tom on the other hand, is back up the stairs.

'Let me walk you to your room,' he insists.

'You don't have to do that.'

'I don't want you going outside alone,' he says. 'My granny always used to say these things happen in fours.'

'I thought things happened in threes?'

'They do,' he replies. 'But you've fallen on the dance floor, fallen off a bridge and got stuck in a lift. I think you've had your three, but I really want an excuse to spend more time with you.'

I smile. 'Well, that's OK then.'

Tom takes me by the hand and we head downstairs together.

'We must look ridiculous,' I tell him, as we approach the bar.

'Just walk with confidence,' he says. 'No one will notice.'

We walk through the bar without anyone batting an eyelid – mostly because it's empty. Everyone is out dancing under the marquee.

Outside, walking across the gravel car park, we bump into none other than Pete. He's talking on his phone but when he sees us, he quickly ends his call.

'Luca, I was looking everywhere for you,' he says. 'You're not wearing clothes ... neither of you are ... and you're holding hands.'

'Technically we're wearing a whole outfit between us,' Tom informs him playfully.

Pete ignores him.

'Luca, you're not getting back with him?' he says. 'After the way he treated you.'

'I mean, I'm not technically getting back with him,' I reply. 'We were never together. Hey, was that your wife on the phone?'

Pete looks mortified.

'W-w-what?' he stutters.

'Your w-w-wife,' I reply.

'Luca, I can explain.'

'Don't bother.'

I start walking towards my room, pulling Tom along with me, but Pete gets in my way.

'Luca,' he says, starting to sound agitated.

Tom immediately drops my hand, grabs Pete by the lapels and pushes him away from me.

'Tom, don't,' I say.

I'm terrified he's going to hit him – it's not that he doesn't deserve it, but I don't want Tom getting in trouble. Tom squares up to him.

'I could hit you,' Tom tells him. 'I could punch you in the face ... but that might get you some sympathy, and I don't want that. I don't want anyone being nice to you. Instead, I want you to go home, and I want you to look your wife in the eye every day, and kiss her goodnight every night, and know what a piece of rubbish you are. You don't deserve your family.'

Tom lets go of him.

'Now piss off,' he says.

Pete, like a frightened little kid, scurries off inside.

'Wow,' I blurt. 'What was *that*?'

'I think they call it psychological warfare,' he says with a laugh. 'I could've hit him, but I didn't want to hurt my hand. I need it.'

'What do you need it for?' I ask, stroking his face.

'This,' he says, scooping me up. 'It's tradition I carry you across this car park.'

'Well, I can't argue with tradition.'

Tom carries me up the steps to my room and gently places me down outside the door.

'OK, well ...'

'Well,' I reply. 'You didn't carry me inside this time.'

'I didn't. Given recent developments, I didn't want you to think I was inviting myself in. I didn't want you thinking I was trying to have sex with you – you could probably do without another person trying to have sex with you, right?'

'Maybe,' I say. 'Or maybe what I need is for someone who I actually want to have sex with to try and have sex with me. Did you think of that?'

'To be honest I've thought about nothing else since I saw you earlier,' he says, biting his lip. 'You looked amazing in that dress – and you look incredible in my shirt. I think the towel was my favourite though.'

'Yeah, I saw you peeping,' I laugh.

'You were staring at my body first,' he points out. 'I was just levelling the playing field.'

I smile as I unlock my door.

'Thomas Oliver Hoult,' I start, in my most formal of tones. 'Would you like to join me in my hotel room?'

'I would like that very much, Miss Wade.'

Unwilling to wait another second, I throw myself at him – literally. I wrap my arms around his neck and my legs around his waist as we kiss. Tom walks through the door, completely unable to see where he's going. As I feel him about to place me down on the bed, I call out for him to stop.

'What? What's wrong?' he replies.

'Twin beds,' I say breathlessly. 'Remember, they're twin beds.'

We both peer down at the gap between the beds where Tom was just about to try and put me down.

'That would've been the fourth thing, for sure,' he jokes.

Tom places me down gently.

'What are you doing?'

'I'm pushing the beds together,' he says.

'Now?'

'Yep.'

'It's late and you're kind of drunk,' I point out.

'That just means I'm motivated and blind to any strain it's going to put on my back,' he replies as he finally shoves them together.

'You think *that's* going to put strain on your back …' I say.

I push Tom back onto the Franken-bed and climb on top of him.

As I lean forward to kiss him, my hair falls in front of my face and I catch a powerful whiff of the pond smell.

'I'm going to have a shower,' I tell him. 'Because I don't want to smell like sewage for our first time.'

'Maybe that's what is doing it for me?' he jokes.

I begin to climb off him before pressing back down on top of him.

'You tease,' he says.

I shrug my shoulders.

'OK, I really am going this time,' I say. 'Make yourself comfortable, put the TV on if you like – I watched *Kitchen Nightmares* around this time last night, it was actually really good.'

Tom laughs.

'I'll wash all this junk off me, and I'll be right back.'

'Don't be long,' he calls after me. 'I miss you already.'

I take off my shirt, run a wipe over my face to remove my smudged make-up, and finally step into the shower. Now that it's a little cooler, the warm water feels amazing and it's just so nice to feel clean finally.

I hear a knock on the bathroom door.

'Erm … come in.'

'I was just thinking,' Tom starts. 'Maybe I'll join you.'

'You'll join me?'

'Yeah,' he says, pulling back the shower curtain before stepping into the bath with me. That's when I realise he's naked. 'I thought I could wash your back for you or something.'

Tom carefully ushers me back under the rainfall shower before we pick up where we left off.

'Plus, I've been waiting ten years to get my hands on you,' he adds. 'I don't want to waste another second.'

Chapter 35

Waking up, being spooned by Tom, with the speaker outside my bedroom window playing Elvis's 'Can't Help Falling In Love' – I feel like I've died and gone to heaven. I don't know when it happened, maybe it was in the pond, or maybe it was in the lift, but this isn't my life. This has to be a dream.

I reach over to the bedside table and grab my clutch. I carefully take out my phone with one hand, making an effort not to wake Tom. I still have a little battery luckily, and I can see that Clarky sent me a message last night.

Compo breakfast at 10 a.m. Whole gang. Meet in the dining room.

I smile at my phone.

I could carefully lift Tom's arm, wiggle out from under it without waking him, but I've waited ten years for this – the last thing I want to do is move.

'Mmm,' Tom says as he squeezes me tightly.

I roll over to face him. Of course he looks amazing on a morning, even with his hair sticking up in all directions and red lines on his face from resting on his arm.

Tom opens his eyes slowly, adjusting to the light in the room. 'Morning,' he says.

'Morning,' I reply. 'So … last night happened.'

'You noticed it too?' he replies with a grin.

'I did,' I say. 'I just wasn't sure if I'd hallucinated …'

'From the head injury?' he replies.

'What head injury?' I joke, acting confused.

Tom smiles.

'Would you be offended if I got up and left?' I ask.

Tom's smile drops.

'Oh, no, not like that,' I insist. 'It's not you.'

'It's not me, it's you?'

'It's Clarky actually,' I tell him. 'He's arranged for us all to have breakfast together.'

'You're all getting together in a room with knives?' he jokes.

'I'm going to take my chances,' I reply. 'I think maybe we all need this.'

'I understand,' Tom says, stroking my cheek. 'I hope you guys figure things out, you've all been friends forever, it would be a shame.'

'It would,' I reply.

I would love to stay here, wrapped up in Tom's arms, enjoying the music drifting in from outside, talking about what happens next. But in twenty minutes my friends – practically my family – will be gathering in the dining room and, even if I didn't think I needed to be there to referee, I want to be there. I want to figure all this out. If we don't, the best-case scenario is that Fi and Zach's wedding will be incredibly awkward but, worst-case scenario, Fi and Zach might not be getting married at all.

I begrudgingly climb out of bed, self-consciously wrapping one of the duvets around my body because now that I've got Tom in my bed (or these two hotel beds pushed together, at least), I don't want to scare him off with my squashy bits – which is silly really, because he probably saw everything last night. I was terrified when he got in the shower with me because we're all capable of a little strategic positioning when we're lying down, but when we're standing up, there aren't too many shapes you can make to disguise a combination of an average thirty-something body and gravity.

I grab a long black sundress, split up to the thigh on both sides, a pair of black caged heeled sandals, and a pair of sunglasses. Well aware I'll have to take the glasses off inside, I layer on the make-up to disguise my tired face. Unfortunately there's no amount of priming, foundation-laying, concealing, baking, or highlighting that can hide the raised cut on my cheek, but I do them all anyway, to try and overcompensate for my injury – my injury, and the fact that going to bed with wet hair has left me with inconsistent natural waves. A quick of spritz of perfume and I'm ready to face the world.

'You look gorgeous,' Tom says when I finally emerge from the bathroom.

'So do you,' I reply.

He's still lying in bed, watching TV. He has the covers pulled up to his waist and as much as I want to get back in with him, I need to go and do this.

'I'll try make it quick,' I tell him.

'Don't worry. I think breakfast finishes at 11, so I'm going to pop down anyway. See you there?'

'Sure,' I reply.

'Good luck,' he calls after me as I walk out the door.

'Thanks.'

I'm going to need it.

Chapter 36

The hotel dining room boasts the same round tables we sat at during the reception yesterday, expect this time, it's just us. Me, Clarky, Ed, Zach, Fi and Matt. I appreciate Matt being here, given that it's the morning after his wedding, but Kat looks more than happy at another table, having breakfast with her bridesmaids – including the one I replaced in the ceremony, who has brought her baby for everyone to meet.

Clarky stands up.

'Good morning, thank you for coming,' he says formally. 'As breakfast is on me, I thought I'd take point.'

'Breakfast isn't on you,' Zach points out. 'It's free.'

'Yeah, thanks to me,' Clarky reminds him. 'So ...'

No one actually has any breakfast in front of them, which is a real turn up for the books. There's a glorious smelling breakfast buffet at the other side of the room – normally, this lot (myself included) would've been all over it the second we walked through the door.

'I've been rehearsing this, so just let me get it all out before anyone says anything,' Clarky says. 'I want to start by saying that I'm sorry. Zach, I am sorry for what happened back at uni. I could try and make excuses – I'm not going to. There's nothing

I can say. We shouldn't have done it, we should've told you … whatever, we didn't do the right thing. Fi, I'm sorry for saying I loved you. I thought I did. It's easy to feel things for people when you don't see them everyday but I've been an idiot. Look at the two of you. You're getting married, you've got a kid on the way. Now that I can see that, I don't know what I've been clinging on to all these years.'

With Zach and Fi apologised to, he turns to Matt.

'Matt, I'm sorry this came out at your wedding. I hope we didn't ruin your day or get you in trouble with the missus.'

He turns to Ed.

'Ed, I'm sorry you had to see what you saw, and that you've been carrying it around all this time. It sounds like you were having a shitty night, you didn't need us adding to your problems.'

For the first time in forever, I see a softer side to Clarky. He's being mature, he's taking responsibility for his actions – things I've never seen him do before. It's nice to see because he can be a real arsehole sometimes. Maybe there is a kind, understanding, sympathetic human lurking in there after all.

'Luca …' I raise my eyebrows expectantly as Clarky turns to me. 'I have nothing to apologise to you for.'

Everyone laughs.

'But sorry anyway, just in case,' he says quickly before sitting down.

'I'll go next,' Fi says. She seems way more comfortable with the conversation, not feeling the need to stand up and address people one at a time. 'Zach has always been the love of my life … when I thought he didn't want me, I was devastated. That's no excuse for sleeping with someone else … but when Zach did show up that night, I felt so guilty that he'd been in an accident, I didn't dare tell him what I'd done. I comforted myself with the fact that it happened before we got together, but that's no excuse. The more time went by, the harder it got to tell him, but the less I thought about it. I've been so preoccupied with the wedding and then I found I was pregnant and … I was too scared to tell you.'

Fi is looking at Zach now, holding his hand.

'I was going to tell you this weekend but you said something to Ed about going back to misery, meaning his wife and kids, and you said you were pleased there were no kids at the wedding because kids were annoying. It occurred to me that, even though we talk about having kids, that you might not actually want them, and I panicked.'

Zach squeezes her hand.

'I overreacted,' Zach says. 'I'd had too much to drink and I let my ego get the better of me … but as soon as Fi said she was pregnant, nothing else mattered. It snapped me out of my rage and reminded me just how much I love her, and how much I can't wait to spend the rest of my life with her – and the bump. The future is all that matters.'

It's amazing really, how a cold dip in a pond and a night spent sleeping on it has allowed everyone to see things in a new light. Last night, I felt like we all could've kept arguing forever, today we're all figuring stuff out. Time passing does change everything …

My attention drifts away as I start thinking about Tom. I'm wondering if, after a night sleeping on it, he feels differently about me this morning. I'm not sure how I feel. After ten years of foreplay, sleeping together felt like something that was inevitable, like we had this unresolved tension between us, but can we really just be together? Tom said what happens next is as easy as we want it to be, but do I want it to be easy?

'Luca,' Ed says, snapping me from my thoughts. 'I'm sorry I tried to kiss you – I barely remember it. I don't know what I was thinking. I think just, being around everyone again, it all came flooding back.'

'Don't worry about it,' I say. 'I totally get it.'

'And I'm sorry about what happened that night. I was a young, stupid idiot, and you guys – whether you knew it or not – saved my life. Not a day goes by I don't think about that poor dog that I killed.'

'You didn't kill him,' Zach says.

'What?' Ed replies.

'Yeah, he was fine, think he broke his leg or something – I've got him on Facebook.'

Ed exhales a lifetime of relief.

'Mate, I wish you'd told me that years ago.'

'We said we'd never talk about it,' Zach reminds him.

'Well, I've learned my lesson regardless. I'm still learning – I need to drink less. When I drink too much, it always seems to end in tears.'

'I'm sorry I didn't let you bring your kids, mate,' Matt tells Ed. 'If I had, Stella would've been here, and you would've behaved. You're terrified of her.'

Ed laughs. 'Perhaps.'

'I'm sorry for any part I played in any of this,' I say sincerely. 'And I'm sorry I didn't do more to get things under control last night.'

'You were doing a great job until I upset you,' Matt says. 'I'm so, so sorry I gave your costume to Cleo.'

'It's OK,' I tell him. 'I think there might have been more to it than just a costume.'

'I think you're right,' he replies. 'But I'm Tom's best mate, remember. He didn't think he was good enough for you – he probably never will, he worships you. Always has.'

I give him a half-smile.

'Honestly,' Matt persists. 'He's asked me about you constantly for the past ten years. I think he thought he was doing you a favour … he always kept one eye on you though. He never quite let go of you.'

'This is nice, isn't it?' Clarky says. 'All friends again.'

'It's a little late but … Fi, congratulations,' I say. 'I can't believe you're pregnant!'

'It's not mine, is it?' Clarky jokes, in the most inappropriately timed inappropriate joke of the occasion.

'Too soon, mate,' Zach tells him, wincing.

'We should get some breakfast,' Clarky says, changing the subject.

'How did you blag this?' Matt asks him.

'Compo, for the bridge,' he says. 'Apparently it was supposed to have signs on it, saying no more than two people at once. And, hey, I didn't just get breakfast, I got that receptionist bird's number too.'

'How did you blag *that*?' Matt asks.

'Well, when I walked in on him, she was down on her knees, drying his legs for him,' I say.

'Do you think Little Clarky swayed her?' Ed asks.

'Can't be that little if she gave you her number,' Matt laughs.

I notice that Zach is being tactfully quiet in all of this. It must be weird for him. Then again, he just seems so over the moon to be becoming a dad, I don't think he cares.

'Well, we're not far from Cambridge,' Clarky points out. I hadn't realised that's where he was living now. 'So we'll see.'

I can't help but smile. I feel like my kids are finally growing up.

'OK, food,' Clarky says.

'Just don't spike it this time, mate,' Zach says as they head for the buffet.

Matt and I hang back for a second.

'Have you seen Tom?' he asks me. 'He disappeared last night, and when I knocked on his door this morning there was no answer.'

'Don't worry, he's in my room,' I say.

'Luca,' he sings. 'Did you ...?'

'We did,' I say, feeling my cheeks flush a little.

'It's about bloody time,' Matt says, and he smiles like he means it. 'So are you two a thing now?'

'I don't know what we are,' I admit. 'We haven't really spoken about it.'

'Well, if we've learned anything, it's that we should grab happiness where we can find it,' he says.

'Erm, I don't think that's right,' I point out. 'People grabbing happiness where they could find it is pretty much the reason we all fell out.'

'Oh. Maybe it's that everything happens for a reason?'

'I'm not sold on that one either,' I laugh.

'No … you're probably right. I'm going to go and get a sausage.'

'I'll be right behind you.'

'You might want to wait a bit,' he says nodding at something behind me.

I turn around and see Tom. He must have been back to his room and got changed because he looks amazing. He's wearing a pair of black jeans and a crisp white shirt.

'Talk to you two in a bit,' Matt says. 'Loving the Eighties hair, Luca.'

'Thanks,' I call after him. 'It's more a product of sleeping with wet hair, rather than a passion for the decade, but I'll take it.'

Tom laughs. It's just him and me now.

'You guys figured stuff out then?' he asks.

'We have,' I reply. 'It was relatively painless too.'

'Well, that's good,' he replies with a smile.

Now that I think about it, it feels like these were conversations we needed to have with each other – some of them ten years overdue. Amazing really, that it took the destruction of a real bridge to start building them amongst ourselves.

'Now we just have to figure out us,' I say, ripping off the plaster.

'Straight on to that?' He laughs. 'You don't even want any Coco Pops first?'

I smile, but the absence of a laugh causes Tom to snap into serious mode.

'We're both living in the same city now, right,' he says. 'So, we can just see what happens when we get back?'

'Oh, OK,' I reply.

'Give me your number,' he says. 'I'll give you a call, and we'll organise that drink.'

Suddenly, I don't feel good about things anymore. I'm petrified, that we've done all of this in the wrong order. First we slept together, next we're going for drinks – shouldn't that be the other way round? What if he's still scared? Maybe he was drunk last night and felt emboldened, or maybe he was just jealous … but now, in the harsh light of day, maybe he's changed his mind again.

'OK,' I say, even though it isn't OK at all.

I give him my number and I suppose I'll wait and see if he calls, but I won't hold my breath. What can I even say to him now, that won't scare him off or put him off?

'Can't wait,' he says as I hand him back his phone. 'So, we'll see each other back in Manchester.'

'We will,' I reply.

I'm not so sure now though.

Chapter 37

I'd like to say the drive home doesn't feel as stressful as the drive here. I'd like to say I have different things playing on my mind. Neither of those things would be true though.

Time is on my mind. How much of it I've had, how much of it I've got left, and how exactly I'm going to fill it.

Everyone around me has grown up. Everyone but me.

The wedding is over, and while everyone else is going back to their lives, I am going back to my … nothing. Sure, Tom has said that we'll go for a drink. Can you think of a more underwhelming response to our situation? It's not like I was expecting him to pop the question or anything, but simply saying 'we should grab a drink sometime' isn't anything, is it? 'We should grab a drink' is what I would say to a friend I bumped into on the street, in an attempt to be polite whilst under no obligation to socialise with them.

It only feels like a minute since my 21st birthday. Where has the time gone? When I was 21, I felt like I had my whole life ahead of me. Now that I'm 31, unmarried, childless, in a job with no prospects for progression, I feel like my whole life is behind me.

My mum had kids when she was my age. Fi is my age and

having a kid now. It probably won't be long before Matt and Kat follow suit. I don't want to be in a rush to have kids – I don't even know if I want kids – but I'm being bombarded with information telling me that, as a woman in my thirties, my clock is ticking, and I'm slowly but surely becoming worthless. Bloody targeted marketing is supplying me with all the info I could possible need (that I really *don't* need), being a woman closer to 35 than 25. I want to say that I have never felt so old and useless, but then I'm sure there are people in their eighties who would give anything to be in their thirties again … I'd just like to make a similar deal, but only to go back as far as uni. I feel like that's where it all started going downhill for me. Regrettably, time travel isn't a thing. We only lose time (by the second – ha), we never gain it.

I'm never going to be younger than I am now … I need to stop wasting my time. Maybe Tom will call, maybe he's just playing it cool. Or maybe he is panicking now, and has no intention of reaching out. Either way, I can't put my happiness in his hands again. It didn't work out for me last time, it won't this time either.

I've wound myself up now, and I absolutely hate driving when I'm stressed. It takes me from nought to Mad Max in a matter of minutes, and that's not the best mood to be in when driving on the motorway. I eyeballed a sign for services not too long ago, probably best I pull over for a bit, go to the loo, maybe buy a drink and try to chill out.

As I drive around the car park looking for a space, someone leaves a great space right by the entrance, just in time for me to pull in to it. It's nice when stuff like that happens, isn't it? On days like these last few days, when it feels like everything is going wrong, it's nice to see a little glimmer of good luck.

After a quick trip to the loos to run my wrists under the cold taps, I pop into Starbucks to grab myself an icy, fruity drink. I browse the weird and wonderful crap you can buy here on my way out – who goes to service stations to buy lawn ornaments or poop emoji cushions? With no need for either, I head back to my car.

Slurping down my drink, I go to open my car door when I notice a note, held in place on my windscreen by one of my windscreen wipers.

I frown as I remove it and read it to myself. Just when you think your day can't get any worse … It says that someone has hit my car. The last thing I need is to get stuck here, or to have to fork out for repair work. I suppose I'm fortunate they left a note. Whoever assaulted my poor little Polo is inside the service station, sitting at a table by the big screen TV, waiting to swap insurance details with me. It's annoying, but at least they're doing the right thing.

As I head back inside, I give my car a quick once-over. It's strange though, I can't see so much as a spec of damage – well, nothing that wasn't already there when I parked at least. Still, I walk back inside and locate the big screen, keeping an eye out for someone who looks guilty, and that's exactly what I find, except it's a familiar looking face.

'Erm … hi,' I say, as a confused but delighted smile stretches across my face.

'Hi,' Tom replies. 'I got you some nuggets.'

I look down at the table he's sitting at, to see nuggets, fries and drinks for two. I take a seat next to him.

'What are you doing here?' I ask.

'I was driving home and I thought I'd stop here for a bit,' he says.

'Same,' I reply suspiciously.

'I was on my way back to my car when I spotted your little red Polo, right outside the door. I recognised the T-Rex on the back,' he says with a chuckle. 'As soon as we said goodbye in Norwich, and I got in my car and drove away, my mind started racing, wondering: did I do the right thing? And, now that I think about it, I'm not sure I did.'

'Oh?' I say.

'I didn't want to scare you or seem too keen,' he explains. 'So, I left things more casual, but then as soon as I started thinking about it, I realised what a mistake I'd made. I shouldn't be playing it cool, I should be making it as obvious as I possibly can.'

'I have to admit, I did perceive your playing it cool as disinterest,' I say.

'And as soon as I left you, I realised that's probably how it seemed.'

'Listen, don't beat yourself up,' I say. 'It's easily done. We've spent ten years getting this stuff wrong.'

'I know you hate the fate talk – I'm sorry, I know you do, and everyone keeps going on and on about it – but come on, what are the chances we'd run into each other here? We set off at different times, there are multiple routes we could've taken, multiple service stations we could have stopped at. But I was thinking about you, worrying that I'd blown it … and now, here you are.'

'So you pretend to bump my car?' I chuckle.

'I thought it might be cute, to leave you a note,' he says. 'Look on the other side of it.'

I turn over the note to see that it's on the back of a receipt for sweets.

'Oh wow,' I say. 'You went all out.'

'Not really,' he admits. 'I'd just bought some sweets. But doesn't that lend to the fate theory too?'

I roll my eyes, but a grin creeps its way across my face.

'Tell me you weren't driving along the motorway, cursing me for doing the wrong thing?' he says.

'Not cursing,' I say. 'Something similar maybe.'

'I messed up,' he admits. 'So let me make this clear: I love you and I want to be with you. Immediately. No more crossed wires, no more waiting. Let's go home and start our lives together straight away. That work for you?'

'That works for me.'

I have been waiting for a literal decade for him to say this to me. It might be late, but it feels like I'm finally getting what I need to be happy.

Tom calling us ending up together fate isn't annoying me as much anymore. The truth is that, we can all use the term fate, peddling whatever lines up with our own agendas. I think Tom, Alan and Pete all suggested that fate might be the reason our paths crossed at the wedding, but the real reason that happened is simple: we were all at the wedding. It can't be everyone's fate to bump into me, only one can be right.

I don't think it is the universe, littering my life with hints that Tom and I should be together. Instead, I think something different is going on. I honestly think it's a combination of circumstance and coincidence that Tom and I reunited at the wedding, and that we've bumped into each other here now. It might not be a magical message from a greater power, but it does remind me of something: no matter why Tom and I have bumped into each other, we have. If we hadn't, we wouldn't be together. Things don't happen for a reason, they happen purely by chance. I am lucky to have found my way back to Tom. I'm not going to rely on fate, to hopefully always keep us together, no matter what happens, I'm going to remind myself how fortunate I am to be with him, I'm going to love him forever, and I'm going to make sure that I never, ever let him go.

Chapter 38

Then – 1st August 2009

'Family meeting,' I hear Matt shout. 'Family meeting everyone.'

I'm currently in my bedroom, packing up my things, getting ready to move out today. I'm cutting it fine – of course I am – so I don't really have time for a 'family meeting' … but I suppose, because we're all moving out today, it might be nice.

I fold the dress in my hands before placing it in a box and heading downstairs. When I get down there, everyone else has gathered in the living room.

'OK,' Matt starts. 'I know we've all got a lot to do, but there's one thing we haven't figured out … who gets the TV.'

The TV in the living room was all we could collectively afford when we moved in. We found a good deal on an already cheap TV and the six of us all put the same amount of money in for it. Now that it's time to move out, we need to work out what to do with it.

'Well, I'm happy with whatever,' I say.

'Same,' Fifi replies.

Now it's just down to the boys to figure out who gets it. I lean forward, to stand up, head back upstairs and finish my packing, but a voice in my head tells me to stick around and mediate.

'The place I'm moving to already has a TV,' Ed says. 'So I don't want it.'

'I guess I've got my big TV in my room,' Matt adds. He recently bought himself a new TV to watch in the privacy of his bedroom, and I won't miss the noise that came from it at night one bit. 'So, yeah, I'm out.'

That just leaves Zach and Clarky. They eyeball each other for a moment, waiting for the other to back down. Neither of them do.

'Well, I think I can make a good case for why I should have it,' Clarky announces.

'The hell you can,' Zach cackles.

This isn't going to be easy.

'Well, you can't share it,' Matt points out. 'You can't cut it in half.'

'I'd rather cut it in half that give it to Zach,' Clarky says.

I can't help but roll my eyes.

'Why doesn't one of you buy the other one out?' I suggest. 'That's kind of like splitting it.'

'Because it's old,' Clarky tells me. 'It's not worth much now.'

'If it's old and worthless, why do you want it?' Zach asks him with a grin.

'Fine,' Clarky says. 'There's only one way to settle this … we wrestle for it.'

'Yes,' Matt says, clapping his hands.

'No,' Fifi says just as quick.

'Babe, it's fine,' Zach assures her. 'He's about as tall as one of my legs.'

'Let's do this,' Clarky bellows.

I sigh. Boys never cease to amaze me. I can't believe they are going to wrestle for an old TV. Thankfully this is my last day here with them. I'll never have to watch them fight again. I am almost entirely relieved but, if I'm being honest, there is a small part of me that is going to miss my weird little family.

Fifi, Ed and I squash up on one sofa, lifting up our legs so that they don't get in the way. Zach and Clarky square up to each other, with Matt standing between them, delighted to be given the job of refereeing.

'Ladies and gentlemen the following contest is scheduled for one fall,' Matt announces in a faux American accent. 'And it is for our crappy old TV. Introducing first, all the way from Glasgow, 6'1", weighing in at 195 lbs ... Zach Anderson.'

'Woo,' Fifi cheers. At first, it seemed like she was dead against this fight, but now she seems more than happy to stand by her man.

'Introducing the challenger, the Scouse Mouse himself, standing at 5'6" tall weighing in at 98 lbs soaking wet ... Mark "Clarky" Clarkson.'

'Whoop,' Ed says unenthusiastically.

Clarky bounces around on the spot. I'm no expert but doing that, with his fists in the air, seems more like boxing to me.

'Nothing in the face,' Zach adds, a little too late.

Clarky reaches up to grab Zach's head but can't reach, so Zach gets him in a headlock. For a minute, the two of them just hold this position, Clarky trying to struggle free, Zach refusing to let him.

This is honestly the worst excuse for a wrestling match I've ever seen, and I went through a WWF phase when I was 11. No one is doing anything, they're just holding each other in a really awkward way.

'Just let me pin you and it will be all over,' Zach says.

'Never,' Clarky replies, his voice sounding all kinds of weird from his neck being squashed.

'Do something,' Matt yells passionately. 'Come on.'

Something does happen. I'm not sure what, but the two of them move all at once, crashing into Matt, before the three of them fall into the TV stand. The TV falls off and, on its way to the ground, the screen hits the corner of the big, black TV stand.

'Well, that settles that,' Ed laughs. 'No one gets it, it's knackered.'

'It might still be OK,' Clarky says rushing to his feet.

'Maybe,' Zach replies. 'Either way, there's no shame in losing.'

'No, there's no shame in losing at all.'

Oh God, from the tone of their voices, it sounds like they both think they won.

'I'll still take it,' Zach says. 'Maybe it can be fixed.'

'You won't,' Clarky tells him. 'I won.'

'No, you didn't,' Zach says. 'I wiped you out, mate.'

'No, I dragged you down.'

Zach scoffs.

They both turn to Matt, the referee, as he climbs up from the floor, rubbing his shoulder.

'I have no idea,' he says. 'One minute nothing was happening, the next we were on the floor.'

'Oh, for God's sake,' Fifi says. 'Are we really arguing over who won a rubbish fight to win a broken TV?'

'Yes,' they both reply in unison.

'We've got bigger problems,' Ed points out. 'Look.'

He points at the TV stand. On the corner, where the TV hit, the black coating has chipped, revealing the wood colour underneath.

'That came with the house,' she says. 'We won't get our deposit back.'

'Shit,' Matt says. 'He texted me earlier, said he'd be over this afternoon to inspect the place. He could be here any minute.'

'Really?' Clarky replies. 'I was really hoping I'd be gone by the time he got here, my room is an absolute tip.'

'You're supposed to clean it,' I tell him.

'Alright, Mum,' he laughs.

'No, I mean you're actually supposed to clean it, if you want your deposit back,' I remind him.

'It's no big deal, the deposit wasn't even that much. Plus, you still all owe me for your share,' he replies.

'Wait, do you think you paid all of our deposits?' Fifi asks him.

'Yeah?'

'Mate.' Matt laughs. 'That was just yours, and you won't get it back unless you tidy your room.'

'I think we're all in trouble, unless we fix the TV stand,' Fi points out.

'I hope you two are happy,' Ed ticks the boys off.

They both sheepishly look at their shoes.

'I have an idea,' I say, before dashing up to my room, grabbing a black Sharpie marker from my desk and hurrying back.

I dab the pen on the wood and, before you know it, you can only tell it's damaged if you look really, really closely.

'That one of your eyeliners?' Clarky jokes.

'Charming,' I say. 'I'm fixing your mistake, and that's the thanks I get.'

'Thank you,' he says quietly.

I smile. 'And now, we need to fix your room.'

'Really?' he says, with a hopeful smile.

'My God,' Ed scoffs. 'We have literally spent the whole year cleaning up after you.'

Clarky's face falls.

'But I suppose we've all cleaned up after each other anyway, so what's one more job.'

'And it won't take us long, if we all pitch in,' Fi adds.

'Yeah, why not,' Matt chimes in.

The only person left is Zach.

'I'll do it … if I get the TV,' he says.

'Not a chance,' Clarky replies.

I roll my eyes. I only need to be patient with Clarky for a couple more hours, and then none of this will be my problem anymore.

'You know,' I start, 'your deposit is actually worth more than a broken TV.'

'I know, Luca, I'm not an idiot … but my pride is worth more,' he replies.

I leave him to think it over for a second.

'OK, sure, Zach can have the rubbish old TV, I'll take the money,' he eventually says.

I don't point out to him that this isn't a game show, and that on top of the TV Zach will be getting his deposit back too. Instead, we all grab cleaning products and plastic bags and head up to Clarky's room to help him get it in a fit state for inspection.

As poor Fifi braves the bathroom, I get to work cleaning out the junk under his bed. Zach is vacuuming, Matt is dusting, and Ed and Clarky are packing up the last on his things, into the flimsy cardboard boxes he's attempting to use to move. Together, we get the room clean in a flash, long before our landlord comes over to check it.

Suddenly, the thought of moving on with my life terrifies me. I like living here, with these weirdos. I know how to handle the problems we have here but, out in the real world, I'm not sure I'm going to know what the hell I'm doing.

'I actually think I'm going to miss you all,' I blurt.

'I'm glad someone said it,' Matt says. 'I've been thinking it too.'

'We'll all keep in touch, right?' Fifi says.

'Of course,' I tell her.

'This is getting bit mushy for me,' Clarky complains, pretending to stick his fingers down his throat.

'We love you too, man,' Zach tells him. 'Even if you lose fights.'

'Erm, I won,' Clarky insists. 'But … same.'

I don't think we're good at this sort of thing. I think that, if we've learned one thing during our time living together this past year, it's that none of us are very good at expressing our feelings.

One thing I know for sure though is that even if it doesn't always seem like it, and even if we lose touch, we'll be friends forever. Five years, ten years, fifteen years … it doesn't matter, I know that meeting up with these guys will be like slipping on an old pair of jeans. You might not wear them anymore but, when you try them on again, you remember how right it felt.

I've spent the past few months convinced that I lost my chance at true love, but maybe I found it after all … just with this bunch of misfits.

Chapter 39

New Year's Eve 2020

'Is it unusual to get married during winter?' Stella, Ed's wife, asks.

'Never mind that,' Ed replies. 'It's New Year's Eve. Who gets married on New Year's Eve?'

It's so strange, being back at the Willows Lodge Hotel in Norwich – but this time during a particularly harsh winter rather than a roasting summer heatwave. The last time we were here we were all relaxing outside. It's far too cold for that today though, so we're all inside, sitting on cowhide sofas, surrounding roaring fireplaces instead of out in the garden, sunning ourselves. It's a definite change of scenery but, still, it brings back so many memories.

'Oh, I'm sorry,' Zach says. 'Were you supposed to be at a wild New Year's Eve party with your wife and four kids?'

Stella winces slightly at Zach's reply. I'm not sure she'll ever get used to the way we all playfully tease each other.

'Oh yeah,' Ed replies sarcastically. 'And which wild party were you, Fi and baby Robin supposed to be attending instead of being here?'

'This is why we got married in the summer, in the sunshine,

away from all the major holidays,' Fi points out with a delicate smile.

She's cradling Robin on her knee. I don't suppose I spend much time around kids, but he seems remarkably well behaved for a nine-month-old. In the movies, babies always seem to be crying, but I don't think I've heard so much as a gurgle come out of Robin yet.

'He's so good,' I point out.

'Barney is eight months, and he just cries all the time,' Kat says, massaging her temples, as though she's stressed out by the mere thought of it. 'It was nice of Al, to take him for a walk around the hotel, give us a break to sit and chat.'

It's weird, seeing gigantic Al Atlantic holding a tiny baby in his massive arms. He seems like a natural with kids though, it's cute. He's like a real life BFG.

'Matt, I was wondering … has anyone called you and Kat out on the timeline of your baby?' Zach wonders.

'No, most people are too polite,' Kat answers sharply.

'Oh, OK,' he replies. 'Not that I can talk about having babies out of wedlock, but … I was just curious about what came first, Matt: you or the wedding?'

I laugh so hard, I choke on my drink.

'Anyway,' Matt starts with a clap of his hands, quickly changing the subject. 'I can't believe we're all together again.'

'This is the third time in seventeen months,' I point out. 'It's nice.'

'We've had three weddings, including this one. Two births. One engagement,' Fi points out. 'I can't help but wonder what is coming next.'

Tom sits down on the sofa next to me.

'What you drinking?' I ask him.

'Martini with lemonade,' he says.

'And how's the menopause going?' Matt asks him. 'My mum drinks those.'

Tom laughs it off, in his usual, easy going way.

'You sure you don't want one?' he asks me.

'No, I'm fine with my cranberry juice, thanks,' I reply.

'Luca, are you *not* drinking?' Fi asks me suspiciously, looking me up and down.

'I'm not drinking, but I'm not *not* drinking,' I reply with a laugh. 'Sometimes people just don't drink. Ed is only drinking lemonade.'

I kick myself as soon as I point it out. I'm proud of him though, for knowing his limit now when it comes to drinking.

'Unpopular opinion, but some people do enjoy being married for a while before they start having kids,' I say.

I'm only teasing, and everyone knows that. There is no longer a right or wrong order to do things in, all that matters these days is doing what makes you happy.

'Who gets married after little over a year together?' Matt asks.

'Two people in love,' I tell him.

'Yeah, but you and Tom are in love – and you've got years behind you as friends too – and you're not hurrying down the aisle.'

'You're just gutted you're not best man,' Tom tells him with a chuckle. He puts his drink on the table and wraps his arm around me, pulling me close. Even inside, sitting in the warmth of the fire, it's kind of chilly in here, so the warmth coming from Tom's body is more than welcomed. 'He went for some star power instead of his oldest friend.'

'Speaking of the best man,' I say as Al approaches the table. If you look closely, you can just about see baby Barney in his massive arms.

'He's flat out,' Al says. 'Hopefully he'll sleep for a while now.'

'Al, you're amazing,' Kat tells him quietly. 'Like some kind of baby whisperer.'

'Hey, didn't I hear you saved a baby from a car accident?' Ed asks him casually, although he's been bursting to ask him about it all day.

'I did, yeah,' Al replies casually. 'I ripped the door of a car and lifted her out.'

'You ripped the door off a car,' Tom repeats, and it's not in disbelief because he doesn't think Al is capable – I think he's just amazed at how often Al gets to play the superhero.

'Yeah, here's the thing though, I don't know how much you know about the hinge on a rear door of a Ford Focus, but just inside the …'

I tune out. It's amazing, how Al can make saving a baby from a car wreck sound boring. He's a great guy though, it's nice to see him doing well. Thanks to his heroics, and his Mr Macho hat trick, Al is somewhat of an internet celebrity now. He has a vlog, where he gives advice on healthy eating and exercise – the kind of unsolicited advice he used to give me, except now he has an audience of adoring fans hanging off his every word.

'I'm going to take Barney to change him,' Kat says.

'For what?' Matt jokes.

Kat just rolls her eyes, but you can tell that she still finds him charming, even when he's making dad jokes.

'Hey everybody,' Clarky sings as he approaches our table. 'Having a good time?'

'Can't believe we're here to be honest, mate,' Matt replies.

'Back where you got married?' he asks.

'No, because I can't believe *you* got married.'

'Hey, when you know, you know,' he replies. 'I've met the girl of my dreams. Couldn't wait to take her up the aisle.'

I roll my eyes at his attempt at a rude joke, but Clarky has a glimmer in his eye that I don't think I've seen before. He seems really, truly happy and content with what he's got. I haven't seen him rubberneck a single girl today – or a married one.

'Married life suits you,' I tell him. 'You've got a real spring in your step.'

'That'll be those heels he's wearing,' Zach quips. 'Don't think I haven't clocked those, pal.'

Clarky looks very smart, in his grey three-piece suit. He wore a top hat during the ceremony, which I'm relieved to see he's taken off now. Now that I think about, coupled with the heels, the top hat was probably a vain attempt at making him appear taller in the photos.

'Hey, they've got a new bridge outside, did you see?' Clarky asks, like an excitable little kid.

'Really?' I reply.

'Yeah,' he says. 'I was thinking we should all go stress test it.'

God, I hope he's kidding.

'Well, you did get a wife out of it last time,' Tom points out.

I can't believe that Clarky is marrying the hotel receptionist he met last year at Matt and Kat's wedding. I suppose he's right: when you know, you know.

'It's only Luca who isn't married now,' Clarky points out.

'Mark!' Fi tells him off.

'It's fine,' I tell her. 'We get this a lot.'

'And what I keep telling people,' Tom says, 'is that if I give any indication of when I plan on popping the question, it will ruin the surprise for Luca.'

'It'd be funny if you did it on the bridge,' Clarky says. 'Even funnier if it collapsed.'

'Nope, I'm going to get her when she least expects it,' Tom says, giving me a cheeky smile. 'No pre-existing memorable dates, no familiar places … Something completely new and completely random, but completely special too. Luca isn't into all that kismet stuff.'

I smile at him. It never ceases to amaze me how well he knows me.

Matt learns forward in his seat. A serious look takes over his face.

'OK, but listen to this,' he says, taking a deep breath. 'What if I was supposed to go to uni with you guys, and Tom was supposed to end up with Cleo, so that I'd meet her sister, Kat, so that we could get married. Then, at our wedding, it was all supposed to kick off, so that Tom could end up with Luca, who he's supposed to be with, and Clarky could fall into the pond, meet the receptionist, and that's why he's getting married today. Because all that happened. What do you think of that?'

'I think this group has never done anything the easy way,' I point out. 'I think we could've got the same happy endings with way less drama.'

'Cynic,' Matt replies, smiling to let me know that he doesn't really mean it.

I still don't buy into the whole fate thing, I think we make our own fate. Whether it's the love of your life, your dream job, or any other goal you might have – sitting back and thinking fate will deliver it to you is crazy, that's never going to work. We have to work hard for the things we want, and even when we get them, we have to keep working hard. Say fate had brought Tom and I together, does that mean I can take him for granted? That I don't have to make an effort to make sure our relationship works? Of course it doesn't. The same goes for my job – I was unhappy, so I changed it. And that's not to say it was easy, I had to land myself a new one before I could leave my old one, but I'm so glad that I did. We decide our own fate. Nothing is set in stone. Life is what you make of it.

If fate isn't the reason we're all sitting around this table right now then it has to be pure luck and coincidence that got us here, and a decision to stay in each other's lives that keeps us here. If that's true, then the slightest differences in our lives could've sent us down completely different roads. One small decision by any one of us, and things could be so different now. That's why I feel so lucky though, to have found exactly what I want, despite multiple roadblocks. The reason Tom and I are together isn't fate, it's love. We're together because we choose to be together, because we love to be together, and I can't wait to see what kind of future we make for ourselves.

Acknowledgements

An extra massive, extra special thank you to my brilliant editor, Nia, who has been an absolute joy to work with on this book. Thanks to you, and to the entire HQ team, for all of your hard work.

Big thanks to my wonderful readers, who continue to read and review my books. When I hear that someone really enjoyed one of my stories, or it got them through an especially hard time, it reminds me of the main reason I do this.

Thank you so much to James, the genius behind my beautiful website (portiamacintosh.com). I had no idea putting together a website could be so much fun, although that may be down to his karaoke throughout.

A special thank you to Aud, who might just be my number one fan. You're one hell of a lady.

Thank you to Kim, for all of your promotion, love and support. I have no idea where I'd be without you.

Huge thanks to Joey, master of the English language. Thanks for listening to me bang on about weird story ideas and for all your proof-reading-work. I promise to always do the same for you (even though your material is way weirder).

Finally, an extra big thank you to Joe. Thanks for always taking care of me. From helping me come up with ideas to proof reading to just generally keeping me sane. I'm not sure if you laugh at my jokes because they're funny, or just because you love me, but I don't mind either way. I love you, chief.

Turn the page for an exclusive extract from
Love and Lies at the Village Christmas Shop …

Prologue – 1998

'Holly Jones, what have you done?' I hear my mum ask through gritted teeth, with enough volume to show that she's angry, but not so much that the shop full of customers can hear her.

I remove my nose from my copy of *Harry Potter and the Philosopher's Stone* to see what exactly my sister has done now. I wouldn't usually jump to conclusions, but this is Holly, and Holly will do anything if it has enough shock value.

We went our separate ways at the school gates no more than a couple of hours ago. Holly wanted to go into town with her mates for a while before tea, but I wanted to come here and read my book, sitting on my stool behind the counter of my mum's Christmas shop. I always enjoy spending time here but now that it's December – and actually Christmas time – the place feels all the more magical.

This afternoon the shop is overflowing with tourists, who have travelled from all over to check out Marram Bay's open-year-round Christmas shop. Christmas Every Day is so much more than just a shop though, it's like a magical Santa's workshop, with wall-to-wall Christmas decorations and gifts, with glitter and twinkly lights everywhere you look. Mariah Carey's 'All I Want For Christmas Is You' is pumping out through speakers around the shop. It's such an infectious song, which you can't help but love and sing along to. I'm not even sure I can name another Mariah Carey song, but this one is a Christmas classic.

Despite the trees in the shop being artificial (they do have to stay up all year round, after all), my mum has these special pine air fresheners which, combined with the locally made gingerbread she's selling at the counter at the moment, give the place a real, irresistible Christmassy smell that I can't get enough of. Perhaps my favourite part of all – and a favourite feature of many of the customers who visit the shop – is the steam train that runs on a track around the shop, over bridges, through tunnels and even around the shop Christmas tree that stays up all year.

From the second you walk through the door there's just this magical feeling in the air. That warm, hopeful, festive feeling you only get at Christmas time. It makes you want to eat gingerbread, sing carols and be happy with your loved ones – and I get to experience it all year round.

But while I might share my mum's love and passion for all things festive, my twin sister Holly absolutely does not. In fact, she has such a strong dislike for the most wonderful time of year that she always acts up around the holidays. And now, here she is, like clockwork, on 1st December, with a drastic new hairstyle that my mum did not sign off on.

Holly's previously shoulder-length blonde hair, along with her hairline and most of her neck, is now bright red.

'It's just like Lisa Scott-Lee's,' my sister says, running both (stained red) hands through her hair, by way of an explanation. I think it's safe to say that her obsession with Steps has reached its peak.

'You're my 14-year-old daughter, you're not Lisa Scott-Lee,' my mum reminds her as she serves a customer. When the shop is so busy, my mum is forced to parent around working – or work around parenting, whichever needs to take priority at the time.

I laugh quietly to myself, although not quietly enough.

'Oh, should I want to be a wizard when I grow up, like Ivy does?' she says mockingly.

I clutch my book to my chest self-consciously.

The customer my mum is serving laughs as she watches our little family drama play out in front of her.

'Sisters, huh?' she says to my mum politely, like perhaps she has daughters of her own, and she knows exactly how tricky they can be.

'Would you believe they're twins?' my mum replies. 'Non-identical, in both appearance and interests. Fascinating really. Can I get you anything else?'

'No, that's great, thanks.'

'Have a very merry Christmas,' my mum says brightly as she hands over a receipt, before turning her attention back to Holly. 'Who did that for you?'

'I did it myself,' she says proudly. 'Only 99p from Boots.'

'Will it come out?'

'Yeah, well, in three washes,' she admits.

'Can you go and get started on the first wash now then, please,' my mum asks gently.

'I thought you'd like it,' Holly persists. 'Red is festive.'

My mum laughs wildly. 'You're not going to convince me you did this in tribute to Christmas – you hate Christmas.' We all know Holly hates Christmas; she's not exactly shy about it.

Right on cue, Wizzard's 'I Wish It Could Be Christmas Every Day' starts playing. Holly rolls her eyes.

'OK, fine,' she whines.

'Oh, Holly,' my mum calls after her. 'Ivy was looking for her boot-cut jeans. Have you taken them?'

'No, burglars broke in, and only stole Ivy's jeans,' she replies sarcastically as she disappears up the stairs.

'Never have teenagers,' my mum tells me once Holly has stormed upstairs. I blink at her. 'You don't count; you're not like a teenager. You're an angel.'

I smile.

'Holly doesn't think Christmas is cool,' I tell her. It's not a very good explanation, but it's all I have.

'Not cool like Steps.' My mum laughs. 'She's going to be mortified, when she's in her thirties and someone reminds her she used to wear a cowboy hat.'

With a moment of calm at the till between customers, my mum takes my natural long blonde hair in her hands, combing it with her fingers.

'It's no surprise your sister is sick of Christmas,' my mum reasons. 'She does live in a Christmas shop that's open all year round. You're lucky you love it as much as I do. For her, it must be torture.'

I replace my bookmark and close my book, setting it down to one side.

'Have you always loved Christmas?' I ask, because I realise I haven't actually asked her that question before.

'I have,' my mum says with a smile. 'This shop is my dream come true. Like now, in December, it's so wonderful to see people coming in, all excited for the holidays, looking for quirky decorations to hang on their trees, or unique little gifts to give their loved ones. I love it in the summer too, though, when tourists come in from the baking-hot sun, usually after a day catching rays on the beach – they literally step into Christmas and that pleasantly baffled look on their faces is one I never grow tired of.'

'I can't wait to work here,' I tell her. Ever since I was little, all I've wanted to do is help out in the shop. My mum sometimes gives me little jobs to do, so that I think I'm working here, but now that I'm a teenager, I'm hoping she'll let me work here properly one day soon.

'And I can't wait for you to help out, but you need to finish school first,' my mum insists.

I smile as I watch a dad lifting up a little girl so she can choose a bauble from the tree. She delicately removes a glass bauble with a white feather inside – a great choice; I've always loved that one. We have the exact same one on our tree in the living room upstairs.

I feel my smile drop as I think about my own dad. It doesn't matter how many Christmases go by since he passed away, I still miss him now more than ever. They say these things get easier with time but every time I see something that belonged to him, someone mentions his name, or I see a happy child playing with their dad, it gets me. I miss him so much.

'You know, apart from you and your sister, this shop is the thing I'm the most proud of. It's practically like one of my kids.' She laughs. 'It's taken a lot more raising than you – probably less than Holly, but don't tell her that.'

I giggle.

'I like to think about when you and Holly are grown up, happily married, with kids of your own. I imagine you bringing them here and then, after I'm gone, I don't know … I imagine the shop being in the family for years, generation after generation. That's silly, isn't it?'

'That's not silly,' I reassure her.

'You're a sweetheart, Ivy Jones, but you know I'd never expect either of you to work here. I'm sure you've got your own big ideas for the future.'

'Mum, I mean it. We'll keep the shop going forever.'

'That's my girl,' she says, squeezing my hand before turning to serve yet another smiling customer, delighted by the armful of Christmas decorations they have selected.

I'm not sure whether or not she believes me, or if she's just humouring me, but I'm serious. I know how much this shop means to my mum. I'll always be here to help.

I hear thudding on the floor upstairs – most likely Holly working on her routine to '5, 6, 7, 8'. Holly might not care about Christmas or the shop, but I do. I know how important this shop is to my mum and I'll always do whatever it takes to keep it going.

Chapter 1

I sit up in my bed and stare straight ahead, as though that might make my ears more efficient. Did I just hear something or was I dreaming?

After a few seconds I hear the noise that woke me again and realise it's a knock at the door.

I grab my phone from next to me and look at the time. Uh-oh, it is 8.45, which means I've overslept – I never oversleep.

I grab my brown reindeer dressing gown (complete with antlers on the hood) and throw it on over my nightshirt before dashing downstairs to answer the door, combing my hair with my fingers and wiping sleep from my eyes as I hurry down the stairs.

As I approach the shop front door, I can just about see Pete, the postman, on the other side of the glass, which, now that I think about it, I maybe went a little too heavy on with the spray snow. The white, frosty edges frame his face, giving him this angelic white glow. I don't suppose I look so festive from where he's standing; all he'll be able to see is me hurrying across the shop floor undressed, with my bed head hair, fumbling with my keys.

He waves at me, all smiles, as I unlock and open the door.

'Hello, Ivy, sorry, did I wake you?' he apologises as he clocks my dressing gown.

'Hey, Pete. I'm glad you did,' I admit. 'I need to open the shop in 15 minutes.'

'It's not like you to sleep in,' he says, handing me a parcel. 'Is everything OK?'

'Everything is fine,' I assure him. I don't tell him that I was up late looking over my finances, worrying a few years' worth of wrinkles onto my face until I finally dropped off some time after 3 a.m. 'I was up late reading.'

'Now that I believe.' He laughs. 'Is that what's in there?'

Is there not some kind of law that prohibits postmen from asking you what's in your parcel? There could be anything in this box – what if I'd ordered some super sexy lacy underwear or something? I mean, it *is* from Amazon, and it is book-shaped, but still. I'm not always so predictable (I am).

'Yep, another book,' I tell him. 'Something to read while I'm working.'

'Business still quiet?' Pete asks.

'Yeah,' I say with a sigh. 'It's December 1st though, so things should pick up a little.'

'I'll be in for a few bits,' he assures me.

'Thank you.'

'I'm sure I had something to tell you,' he says, hovering outside the door. I appreciate that it must be uncomfortable, talking about my difficult livelihood – especially for the man who delivers my bills. I usually enjoy his friendly small talk, but today I just want to get back inside and get some clothes on.

Pete furrows his brow for a second, visibly racking his brain until he has a thought. The second it hits him his face relaxes again.

'Oh, some gossip for you,' he starts, setting his bag down on the floor and taking his phone from his pocket. 'I saw a man in town today.'

'A man?' I gasp, faking shock.

Pete laughs. 'No, like … a mysterious man. He isn't a local, and he doesn't look like a tourist. He's walking around, wearing a suit, carrying a briefcase. Seems like he's scoping the place out.'

'Hmm. For what, I wonder.'

'Indeed,' Pete replies. 'I snapped a photo of him, put it in the Facebook group. Just in case he's one of those white-collar criminals – you know, in case he steals something or what have you.'

'I don't think a white-collar criminal is just a criminal in a suit,' I point out with a laugh.

'See,' Pete says, holding up his phone to show me a photo of a man in a suit, eyeing up a building on Main Street. 'He's weird.'

He's gorgeous – but I don't say this out loud. I study the photo for a moment, as my head fills with fiction-worthy reasons why this mysterious man might be hanging around town. The eligible bachelors in this town are few and far between. All the good ones are taken. This guy is definitely not from round here – take it from a single girl who knows.

'Weird,' I say in agreement, pushing all fantasies of handsome, mysterious strangers from my mind. 'Well, I'd better get on with opening up the shop.'

'Yes, I suppose the post won't deliver itself,' he says. 'Not yet, anyway.'

I don't have the heart to point out that emails are pretty much that.

'Same time tomorrow,' he says as he walks off down the path.

'Yeah, if I don't sleep in,' I joke. 'Have a good day.'

I watch Pete head for his van before he drives off. My lonely little shop is his only stop here. The shop sits alone, on a quiet country road, outside the town. It's an old, stone cottage, which used to be a big house, sitting smack bang in the middle of a massive, beautiful garden. Just like a house, it has a little gate at the bottom of the garden, and a cute little pathway that leads up to the shop doorway.

When my mum took on the place, she converted the downstairs

of the cottage into the shop, with a kitchen at the back, and the upstairs became our living space. It was strange, growing up above a shop when all my friends lived in big houses, but come summer time, when I had this massive garden to play in, I didn't think twice about how cramped things were indoors.

I notice a bill, hiding under my package. I shove it in my dressing gown pocket, to be worried about at a later date – probably tonight, when I should be sleeping.

I unlock the fire exit at the back of the shop before flicking the switch that turns on every fairy light, every musical statue and snow machine. The things that make the shop seem alive, even when there's no real people in it.

I check the shop floor to see if anything is out of place, or if any rubbish is lying around, before turning the sign around on the door to say that we're open ... for all the good it will do. I don't tend to see any customers until the afternoon mid-week – usually tourists in the middle of a hike, or, at this time of year, the occasional local in need of some new decorations or wrapping paper.

I was only standing in the doorway chatting for ten minutes and I'm positively freezing. I'm almost always freezing, sometimes even in the heat of summer. I don't know how long it has been since my last summer holiday, but I'm pretty sure it's a double-digit number of years now. I don't like to think about it; it makes me feel old.

What I need right now is a steaming-hot cinnamon latte, with a generous dollop of whipped cream and a sprinkling of tiny golden white chocolate stars, to make it extra festive. I'll make myself a drink, warm up a little and then head upstairs to throw some clothes on before the lunchtime rush which, yesterday, was a whopping four people.

I plonk myself down on the stool behind the counter and fire up the usual Christmas playlist. The dulcet tones of Mud drift from the speakers, with 'Lonely This Christmas' – not exactly the vibe I need this morning.

I take my phone from my dressing gown pocket and load up the Marram Bay residents' group on Facebook. It's a private group, strictly for locals and businesses in Marram Bay and over on Hope Island, mostly used for selling things, announcements and a good old gossip. People in small towns just love to talk – mostly about each other.

Today's gossip du jour is the 'mysterious man' Pete was telling me about. I see Pete's paparazzi-style photo of a man wearing a suit, and carrying a briefcase, and otherwise not doing anything at all unusual other than being uncharacteristically good-looking. A glance at the comments tells me more about the man. He's been spotted all over town this morning, driving around in his convertible Porsche – some reckon he's a professional athlete buying one of the mansions that sits just outside town, someone else swore blind it was Henry Cavill, while someone else has corrected them that, no, it was in fact Jamie Dornan.

It's only now that I'm thinking about it that I realise Henry and Jamie do actually look quite similar and the thought of this man being a hybrid of the two is, coincidentally, exactly what I asked Santa for this year – well, it would be, if I were remotely interested in having a man in my life.

Hmm, no, he's definitely not a famous actor. I suppose he could be a sportsman. He's got the build for it, but I don't know nearly enough about sports to recognise anyone other than David Beckham.

Perhaps he's a prince, visiting from a sexy European country, looking for a woman to be his queen, or maybe he's a spy, deep under cover in Marram Bay for some Secret Service operation … Perhaps I've just read too many books.

Speaking of which, I unwrap my latest Amazon package to find a copy of *Little White Lies*, the latest Mia Valentina romcom. I do feel guilty, buying books when money isn't exactly great, but the day I begrudge myself a £3.99 book (when reading is my favourite thing to do) is the day I really need to think about selling a kidney.

You can't beat a good book, can you? The way it just drags you in, taking you into someone else's life, into their home, their relationship – into their everything. It's a sneak peek into something you don't usually get to see, and I think that's why I love it so much. Whether I'm walking through the streets in King's Landing in *A Game of Thrones* or being a fly on the wall in Nick and Amy's house in *Gone Girl*, people are living a million lives far more interesting than mine, and with books, I get to live them too.

I have my coffee, I have my book, I'm all snuggly and warm in my dressing gown. I know that I won't have any customers until after lunch at least, because I never do, so there's no harm in starting my book and enjoying my drink before I head back upstairs to get ready. One chapter turns into two, and before I know it my cup is empty and I'm almost four chapters deep. I'll finish this one and then I'll get back to reality.

'Hello,' I hear a man's voice say in an attempt to get my attention.

I glance up from my book to see *him* standing in front of me – the mystery man, the athlete, the Henry Cavill-Jamie Dornan hybrid, (almost) all I want for Christmas.

'I'm so sorry,' I say. 'Have you been here long? I used to do the exact same thing when I was younger, just sit here behind the counter, lost in a book while my mum did all the hard work.'

'Am I in your living room?' he asks with a laugh.

I pull a puzzled face as I close my book and place it down in front of me. It's only as I do that I notice the brown sleeves of my reindeer dressing gown and I remember what I'm wearing.

'Oh, God, no, sorry,' I babble. 'It's a long story. This is a shop and we're open. I run the place. I'm Ivy.'

I hope down from my stool and walk around the counter to shake his hand.

'Nice to meet you, Ivy. I'm Seb.'

Seb holds my hand for a few seconds as he peers over my shoulder.

'Are … are those antlers and a red nose on your hood?' he asks with an impossibly cheeky smile.

I feel my cheeks flush the same colour as the nose on my dressing gown. 'Yes,' I reply with an awkward laugh. 'I wasn't expecting any customers yet and it was cold …'

'No, I like it,' he replies. 'It's cute.'

If it's even possible, my blushing intensifies.

'So, business is quiet?' he asks, walking across the shop, picking up a snow globe from the shelf before shaking it up and watching the flakes fall.

I can't help but stare at him – not watch him, really stare at him. Taking him in. Seb must be over 6 feet tall, and he's so muscular that I feel like an elf next to him, my petite, 5'3" frame resulting in me not even coming up to his shoulders.

He has perfectly neat, swept back dark hair, and a thick but short beard – combined with his sexy blue eyes, his chiselled cheekbones and those gorgeous dimples when he smiles are probably the reasons why people so easily mistook him for a Hollywood actor.

'It's picking up for Christmas,' I assure him.

'It's a strange thing, a Christmas shop that's open all year round,' he muses as he strolls around.

'It's not that,' I insist, following him closely. 'My mum opened the place up when I was a kid and it was always heaving back then. I took over, after she died, and we were busy for a while. It's since satnavs became popular. This road used to be the main way into town, so tourists would always pass the shop on their way in or their way out. These days, satnavs lead everyone along the new road, so no one even knows we're here. We get hikers, and other shops let tourists know we're here, and they usually remember to stop by.'

'Hmm,' Seb says thoughtfully. 'So, is it just you working here?'

'You ask a lot of questions,' I point out.

'I do,' he replies. 'It's been said before.'

'What do you do for work?' I ask.

'At the moment, nothing,' he replies.

I raise my eyebrows.

'What?' Seb laughs, and there are those dimples again.

I suddenly remember what I'm wearing and tighten the belt of my dressing gown self-consciously.

'You do nothing?'

'Nope.'

'How does a man who does nothing afford a suit like that? And drive around in a Porsche?' I ask suspiciously.

'You've got me, I'm a drug dealer,' he says sarcastically. 'No, I'm just between jobs at the moment. Does this train work?'

Seb runs his hand along the track until he reaches the miniature steam train that used to run all around the shop.

'Not anymore,' I admit. 'It needs repairing.'

'Shame,' he says. 'I like it.'

'So, you're just taking a break in Marram Bay then?' I ask.

'Just having a look around.'

'Well, if you need someone to show you the sights,' I start, before my brain has chance to catch up with my mouth and reality hits me. What am I saying? This isn't me; I don't talk to men. Well, I do talk to men, most days in fact, but this isn't Pete the postman, this is a *man* man. I don't know what on earth I was thinking, saying that. There's just something about Seb that is drawing me in. I quickly backtrack. 'I'm sure you don't …'

'I might just take you up on that, Ivy,' he replies with a big smile. 'Do all your customers get this kind of special treatment?'

'What customers?' I joke.

Seb takes the snow globe from the shelf and brings it over to the counter. 'Is this Marram Bay, inside?'

'It is. There's a local guy who makes them – I buy them from him.'

'I'll take it.' He grins, placing it down in front of me.

I can't help but wonder if he actually wants the snow globe, or if he's only buying it because he feels sorry for me, for seemingly having no customers. I can appreciate that, to an outsider, a Christmas shop that is always open might not seem like the kind of place that would get much custom, but things *will* pick up in the run-up to Christmas. Either way, I appreciate him buying something. Along with his cheeky smile, Seb has a glimmer of kindness in his eyes, a glimmer that I can't help but notice twinkling when I look at him.

'That's £9.99, please. Would you like me to wrap it up for you?'

'That's OK, I'm going straight to my car,' he says, before furrowing his brow. 'How did you know I drove a Porsche?'

'What?'

'You know what kind of car I drive ...'

'Oh, just a guess.'

Seb laughs. 'Is that your party trick? Guessing what kind of car people drive?' he asks.

'Is it even possible for anyone to be able to do that?' I reply.

'Sure,' he tells me. 'Hold out your hand.'

I place my hand out in front me, which Seb takes in his hands, examining my palm. It's amazing, just how warm his hands are compared to mine.

'Let's see ... you drive ... a Honda HR-V,' he says.

Spooked, I snatch my hand back.

'A gold one,' he adds with a smug grin.

'Ahh, you saw it outside,' I say, suddenly self-conscious that he's seen my 1998 plate Honda. It might be old, but it's an amazing car that never lets me down. It's no convertible Porsche though, that's for sure.

'How could I miss it?' He laughs. 'It's the only car for miles.'

I step out from behind the counter and walk Seb towards the door. He stops in his tracks to say something to me, stopping when he notices the mistletoe hanging above us.

'How seriously do you take Christmas tradition?' he asks with an awkward laugh.

'Pretty seriously,' I say cautiously. 'I pretty much live Christmas every day …'

'Hmm,' he replies.

There's an awkward silence between us, but only for a few seconds. I glance around the room awkwardly until I notice Seb's face just inches from mine. He plants a quick peck on my lips, immediately seeming surprised at himself for doing so. Maybe, as cool and as confident as he seems, he doesn't do this sort of thing often. I guarantee this sort of thing happens to me even less.

'OK, well,' he says, a little flustered, but with a smile on his face. 'See you around, Ivy.'

'Bye,' I call after him, running my fingertips over my lips, where Seb's lips touched them even if it was only for a second. As I sit back down behind the counter, I look at my book. For the first time – maybe ever – something happened to me in real life that was fresh out of a romcom, and I can't quite believe it.

He said 'see you around' when he left – it would be great to see him around, but what are the chances I'll ever see him again? He's not about to need another snow globe anytime soon, is he? He's got a posh, southern accent, and we don't have too many men like that in Marram Bay. We have farmers, fishermen – we even have a guy who makes snow globes, but no well-spoken southern men in flashy suits.

Nope, I don't think I'll ever see him again. But if I do, I really hope I'm not dressed as a reindeer.

Dear Reader,

Thank you so much for taking the time to read this book – we hope you enjoyed it! If you did, we'd be so appreciative if you left a review.

Here at HQ Digital we are dedicated to publishing fiction that will keep you turning the pages into the early hours. We publish a variety of genres, from heartwarming romance, to thrilling crime and sweeping historical fiction.

To find out more about our books, enter competitions and discover exclusive content, please join our community of readers by following us at:

@HQDigitalUK

facebook.com/HQDigitalUK

Are you a budding writer? We're also looking for authors to join the HQ Digital family! Please submit your manuscript to:

HQDigital@harpercollins.co.uk.

Hope to hear from you soon!

If you enjoyed *The Time of Our Lives*, then why not try another delightfully uplifting romance from HQ Digital?